MADELINE BAKER

P9-CQT-287

WHISPERS OF LOVE

Michael kissed her slowly, his lips warm, patiently demanding. His hands slid over her flesh, his touch like a soft flame that heated her blood and made her heart sing. And she was touching him in return, all shyness swept away in the magic of the moment. She gloried in his hard-muscled flesh, and in the harsh rasp of his breathing as her untutored hands brought him pleasure. He was beautiful, she thought, the most beautiful creature she had ever seen.

"Nemehotatse," Michael murmured, his breath warm and seductive against her ear.

"Nemehotatse," Elayna repeated. "What does it mean?"

"I'd have taught it to you long ago if you hadn't been so stubborn," Michael replied with a roguish grin. "It means I love you."

MADELINE BAKER

A WHISPER IN THE WIND

LEISURE BOOKS   NEW YORK CITY

To my friends at the
Writer's Club of Whittier
for their creative criticism
and encouragement, and most especially
to my son, Bill, who gave me
the idea in the first place.

A LEISURE BOOK ®

March 1991

Published by

Dorchester Publishing Co., Inc.
276 Fifth Avenue
New York, NY 10001

THE INDIANS

Up from the meadow
Down from the hill
Where the buffalo
Once roamed at will;

The tall grass bends
And gently waves
As if to salute
The long gone braves;

No more the tipi,
Its laughter ceased
Where old men dreamed
And smoked for peace;

For tho' they fought
Till dead or lame
The peace they hoped for
Never came.

The blue coats arrived
With treaties spoken,
With swords and guns
They saw them broken;

Over and over
The traps were sprung
Till from the Indians
All hope was wrung;

Pushed from their land
Hearts full of woe,
The Indian, then,
Had no place to go,

To save the last
From deprivation,
The final shame,
The reservation.

—*Evelyn Campbell*

Part 1

Chapter 1

"Yellow Spotted Wolf is dying. Please come home as soon as you can."

Michael Wolf frowned as he read the telegram a second time, and then a third. His great-grandfather was dying, and he couldn't have picked a worse time to do it.

Michael swore softly as he tossed the crumpled telegram into the wastebasket beside his desk. Death and taxes, he mused ruefully, there was never a convenient time for either one.

Well, he'd have to go. He was all the family the old man had left.

Two hours later he was on his way to the Los Angeles airport. His secretary, Donna Miller, had taken care of his flight reservations, canceled his appointments for the rest of the week,

13

and made sure that a car would be waiting for him when he arrived at the airport in Billings, Montana.

At the airport, he checked his luggage and boarded the plane with the ease of a man accustomed to travel.

Settling back in his seat, he closed his eyes and let out a deep sigh. He hadn't been back to the reservation since his mother died almost ten years ago. He'd left home the day after the funeral and never looked back.

Had it really been ten years ago? He'd only been a kid then, just turned sixteen. He'd hitched a ride to L.A. and after two weeks of living in back alleys and hustling handouts from strangers on the street, he'd found a job busing tables at the Brown Derby restaurant. It hadn't taken him long to realize he needed to finish high school if he ever wanted to amount to anything, so he'd worked days and gone to school nights. It was shortly after he graduated from night school that he met the man who gave him his big break.

Gerald Walsh had been a regular customer at the Derby. He owned one of the biggest Cadillac agencies in Hollywood and was always looking for new blood, people who were unique in one way or another. Walsh had taken one look at Michael's athletic build and swarthy good looks and the wheels had started turning. Wolf was tall, broad-shouldered, and handsome enough to be a movie star. From experience, Walsh knew it was usually the men who paid for the cars, but the women who picked them out. A good-looking salesman, one who had a certain blend of charm and charisma, could help a prospective buyer reach the right decision, and that decision was Cadillac.

Michael grinned as he recalled the sales pitch Gerald Walsh had dished out, dangling the lure of easy money and fast cars before Michael like bait before a hungry fish. It had been the best decision Michael had ever made. Walsh taught him how to dress, how to pick suits that emphasized his broad shoulders and long legs, what colors complemented his dark hair and eyes. He taught Michael all the tricks of the trade and then turned him loose. In less than six months, Michael Wolf was the number-one salesman on the lot. Women were fascinated by his rugged good looks, captivated by his natural charm and lazy smile; the men valued his knowledge of cars, his quick wit, his low-key sales pitch.

Michael had worked hard. He lived in an inexpensive bachelor apartment off Sunset Boulevard, drove a company car, and saved his money. He knew that, by going to work for a white man, he had become what the Cheyenne called a "rotten apple," someone who was red on the outside and white on the inside. But he didn't care. He was out to make a place for himself in the world, and that place would not be on the reservation in Montana.

No one had ever gotten rich living at Lame Deer. Most of the Indians didn't have regular jobs. They just sat back and waited for their welfare checks to arrive on the first of the month. A few of the women did bead work, making jewelry and moccasins and trinkets to be sold to the tourists at the annual powwows. Many of them worked at keeping the Cheyenne culture alive, but there was no money in that, and Michael saw no value in hanging onto the old ways, the old beliefs. Times had changed. The world didn't need great warriors any more; it needed carpenters and plumbers, repairmen and mechanics, office workers and garbage men, doctors and lawyers. And car salesmen.

True, a few of the Indians held down regular jobs, working as teachers' aides at the Indian school at Lame Deer or at the private school in Busby. Some worked in the school cafeteria, serving and preparing meals; some were janitors. But Michael hadn't wanted a life like that. He had wanted out, and Gerald Walsh had been the key.

Michael had been a salesman for Walsh Cadillac for the last eight years, working six days a week, Sundays and holidays if necessary, and when Walsh started looking around for a new Vice President in Charge of Sales, Michael's name had been at the top of the list. He was earning good money now. He lived in a swank two-bedroom apartment in the Hollywood Hills. He drove a new Caddy. He wore expensive, tailor-made suits and hand-tooled leather boots. He drank the best Kentucky bourbon, smoked the most expensive Havana cigars, dated some of the most beautiful women in the city, including an occasional movie star. He was going places, all right. There were already rumors circulating that when Gerald Walsh retired, Michael Wolf would be the new president of the company.

He dozed, his thoughts filled with dreams of power, and when he woke, the plane had landed.

Forty minutes later he slid behind the wheel of a new Lincoln convertible and headed for the reservation.

Memories rode with him as he traveled down the highway, memories of his mother, weeping quietly night after night while his father went to Jim Town to buy the liquor that was forbidden on the reservation. Jim Town was a joke, Michael thought bitterly. It was located only a few feet across the reservation boundary line, making beer and wine and whiskey readily available to the Indians. His father had been on his way home from Jim Town late one Saturday night, dead drunk on the white man's firewater, when he fell headlong into a ravine and broke his neck. Michael's mother had died six months later. The doctor hadn't been able to find anything wrong with her, but Michael knew she had died of shame and a broken heart. And now only Yellow Spotted Wolf remained, an old man with iron gray hair, sharp black eyes, and skin the color of old saddle leather.

Michael grinned as he loosened his tie. Yellow Spotted Wolf had been a formidable warrior in his day. He had fought with Crazy Horse and

Two Moons against Custer at the Little Bighorn. He had been at Standing Rock during the Ghost Dance. He had been one of the first to hear of Sitting Bull's death.

Michael grimaced as he passed the Crow Reservation. The Crow and the Cheyenne were ancient enemies, and it seemed ironic that the white man had chosen to put their agencies side by side. Formerly, the Crow had been scorned by the Cheyenne for their allegiance to the whites, but it had paid off, Michael thought wryly. Of the two reservations, the Crow's was larger, the land more hospitable.

A few miles down the road he passed the Custer battlefield. It was hard to believe that Yellow Spotted Wolf had fought with Crazy Horse at the Greasy Grass; it had all happened so long ago.

Michael goosed the Lincoln up to sixty. Yellow Spotted Wolf was almost ninety-six years old. If he hoped to see the old man alive, he'd better hurry.

The reservation was as he remembered it: flat, colorless, arid. The white man had never been generous where the Indian was concerned, Michael thought bitterly, and felt an old anger stir deep within him as he drove down the heavily rutted road toward his great-grandfather's house. He passed "The Clinic" which was the reservation infirmary, "Our Pump" which was the single gas station, and "The Trading Post" which was a store owned by a white man. Some of the Indians played bingo there on Monday nights. It was one of the few diversions available on the reservation.

Michael let out a long sigh as he parked the convertible beside his great-grandfather's house. Nothing had changed. The house was still the same sun-bleached brown. There were no curtains at the windows, only sheets that had once been blue but were now almost white.

Reluctant to go inside, he stepped out of the car and gazed around. The reservation looked the same as it had the day he left. The dogs still ran in packs; the horses still ran wild. He saw a half-dozen sunflowers growing beside the house next door, together with a few limp tomato plants and a dozen rows of scraggly cornstalks.

He felt a sense of dread as he opened the door to his old home and stepped inside. The house was just as he remembered it. The same sagging blue-green sofa and worn leather chair occupied the same corner in the living room; the same dime-store print hung on the wall. The clock over the fireplace still said five o'clock.

"Grandfather?"

"In here, Michael."

He recognized the voice of old Mrs. Two Bulls and wondered if she'd ever forgiven him for riding his pony through her vegetable garden.

With purposeful strides, he crossed the bare floorboards and went into his great-grandfather's bedroom. It, too, was the same as he remembered it. There was a double bed against the far wall, a three-drawer chest opposite the bed, a faded blue sheet at the window.

Mrs. Two Bulls stood up when Michael entered the room. "It was good of you to come so quickly."

Michael nodded. "How is he?"

"He grows weaker with the passing of each sun," she answered softly. "I think he waits only to see you again before he goes to meet the Creator." She smoothed her apron over her long calico skirt. "You must be hungry after your long journey. I'll go prepare supper."

Michael stared at his great-grandfather, hardly aware that the woman had left the room as memories came flooding back.

"Come, Ho-nehe, let us go fishing."

"Come, Ho-nehe, let us go hunting."

"See, Ho-nehe, this is the mark of the wolf, and this is his brother, the coyote."

"Come, Ho-nehe . . ."

Moving quietly, Michael sat down in the rickety ladderback chair beside the bed. The old man's hair was white now, his cheeks sunken, his hands gnarled with age.

Michael had never loved anyone the way he loved this man. Once, winning the approval of his great-grandfather had been the most important thing in the world.

It had been Yellow Spotted Wolf who had taught Michael to ride, to hunt, to fish. Even now Michael could recall how proud of him the old man had been, how he had basked in his great-grandfather's praise. Yellow Spotted Wolf had been the most important man in Michael's life back then. Michael's father had never had time to go hunting or fishing or to go exploring in the wooded hills. His father had never had time for anything but whiskey. But Yellow Spotted Wolf had nothing but time. He had told Michael wonderful tales of the good old days, the days before the white man came, the days when the People were free. Michael had listened in awe as Yellow Spotted Wolf talked of Crazy Horse and Sitting Bull, of Gall and American Horse, of Two Moons and Dull Knife, of Little Wolf and Tall Bull . . .

"Ho-nehe?"

Michael smiled faintly. No one had called him Wolf in a long time. "I'm here, Grandfather."

"I knew you would come." The old man's voice was low and weak. "Come closer so I can see you."

Michael pulled his chair closer to the bed, a sudden ache welling in his chest as he gazed into his great-grandfather's eyes. Death was there, quietly waiting.

Yellow Spotted Wolf reached for Michael's hand. "I want to go home."

"You are home, Grandfather."

The old man shook his head. "No. Home," he said emphatically.

"To *Mo'ohta-vo'honaaeva*," Michael murmured. "To the Black Hills."

Yellow Spotted Wolf nodded. "Home." The word was a sigh on his lips.

"Yes, Grandfather, when you're better, I'll take you home, I promise."

"Now," the old warrior said. "I do not want to

die here, on the white man's reservation. I do not want to die in this soft bed, or be buried on this land. I want to go home to the land where I was born."

"Perhaps next week, when you're stronger," Michael hedged.

"It must be now," Yellow Spotted Wolf insisted. "Next week will be too late."

Michael swore under his breath. He'd planned to spend a night, maybe two, and then head back to L.A. There wasn't any room in his schedule for a quick trip to the Black Hills. And yet, it was his great grandfather's dying wish. How could he refuse?

"All right, Grandfather," Michael agreed. "We'll leave first thing in the morning."

The old man smiled faintly as he squeezed Michael's hand, then his eyelids fluttered down and he was asleep.

Michael sat there for a long time, wondering what the hell he'd gotten himself into.

Chapter 2

They were on the road early the next morning. Yellow Spotted Wolf had said his goodbyes to Little Wolf and old Two Bulls and the other tribal elders. His cardboard suitcase, packed by a tearful Mrs. Two Bulls, was in the trunk of the convertible.

Michael had remained in the background during his great-grandfather's leave-taking. He knew his presence was unwelcome. He was an outcast, a man who had turned his back on the People.

Yellow Spotted Wolf's farewells had been somber. He knew, as did his friends, that they would never see each other again this side of the Spirit Path. There had been many warm embraces and more than a few quiet tears.

Now, Michael glanced over at Yellow Spotted Wolf who was sitting in the passenger seat beside him. The old man was staring straight ahead, his arms folded over his chest, a gaudy orange and red blanket spread across his lap. The *wohehiv*, or Morning Star, was worked into the design. It was the symbol of the Northern Cheyenne.

The old man grunted softly as they passed a sign advertising the Custer Monument. It was the first sound he'd made since they left Lame Deer.

"Custer, *wagh*," Yellow Spotted Wolf muttered disdainfully. "What did Yellow Hair do to deserve such a memorial? Where are the monuments to the Cheyenne he killed at the Washita? Where are the headstones to honor the People massacred by Chivington at Sand Creek?"

"General Custer was a hero and a great general, Grandfather," Michael said with a shrug. "At least the whites thought so. They like to build monuments to their heroes."

"Where are the monuments for Dull Knife and Little Wolf? For Sitting Bull and Crazy Horse? They were heroes and generals."

"You're forgetting the Two Moons Monument at Busby," Michael remarked, referring to the monument that had been erected back in 1936 to honor the Cheyenne who had been killed at the Little Bighorn.

Yellow Spotted Wolf muttered something unintelligible under his breath, then rested his head against the back of the seat and closed his eyes. *The white man*, he mused bitterly. *Not only has he stolen our land, but my great-grandson as well.*

Michael's thoughts turned to other things as the miles slipped by. He wondered what Melinda had said when Donna called to cancel their date for tomorrow night, and how Walsh was getting along without him, and how the sales meeting scheduled for that morning had gone.

After a while he turned on the radio, and the strains of "Davy Crockett" and "The Yellow Rose of Texas" filled the air.

Yellow Spotted Wolf woke up when they reached Johnson Siding, a small town near the Black Hills. In the old days it had been a train stop for the Black Hills and Western Railroad. It hadn't been much of a town then, and it wasn't much now. There was a decent motel, a restaurant, a country store, a church, and a couple of houses.

"We will need horses," Yellow Spotted Wolf said as Michael pulled into the motel driveway.

Michael frowned. "Horses?"

"You cannot drive up the mountain."

"The mountain?"

"I wish to climb *Mo'ohta'honaaeva* to pray before I go to meet the Creator."

Michael shook his head. This trip was getting more and more complicated all the time.

Two hours later they were mounted on a

couple of rented hacks. The old man's suitcase was lashed behind the saddle of a big gray gelding; supplies and sleeping bags were strapped behind the saddle of Michael's chestnut mare.

Michael knew he'd made a mistake before they'd gone a mile. He hadn't been on the back of a horse in over ten years, and every muscle in his body knew it. He was pretty sure Yellow Spotted Wolf hadn't been on a horse in quite a while, either, but the old man rode easy in the saddle, his frail body moving in perfect rhythm with his mount. Indeed, his great-grandfather seemed to grow stronger with each passing mile.

Perhaps all the old man had needed was some fresh air and a change of scenery, Michael thought optimistically.

Despite a growing numbness in his backside, Michael felt a sense of wonder as they rode across a vast green meadow watered by a shallow winding stream. Tall pines lifted their branches toward a clear azure sky, the Black Hills rose in the distance like an island of granite peaks afloat in a prairie sea. He had never seen such magnificent country in his life, and as they rode deeper into the sacred ground of the Sioux and Cheyenne, he felt as though he had stepped back in time. He had never been a fanciful man, yet he could clearly visualize how it must have been a hundred years ago when thousands of buffalo roamed the plains and the

Cheyenne lived wild and free in the shadow of the Black Hills.

They saw wildlife now and then: an eagle soaring high overhead, a small herd of deer grazing in the tall grass, ground squirrels and chipmunks, a lizard sunning itself on a rock, a bird dusting its feathers.

They rode until dusk and then made camp alongside a shallow stream. Michael prepared a quick meal of canned corned beef, canned potatoes, and canned peaches, but his great-grandfather had no appetite, and after drinking three cups of coffee heavily laced with sugar, Yellow Spotted Wolf crawled into his sleeping bag and was quickly asleep.

Michael poured himself a second cup of coffee, then sat cross-legged beside the dwindling fire and gazed into the distance. The hills drew his eyes. They rose tall and quiet, dark silhouettes against the darker night. A mild breeze sighed out of the north, whispering secrets to the lofty pines, waltzing with the tall grass. Frogs and crickets lifted their voices in songs of good-night; he heard the soft swish of wings as an owl passed overhead in search of prey.

Draining the last drop of coffee from his cup, Michael extinguished the fire and slid into his sleeping bag, but sleep would not come.

Crossing his arms behind his head, he stared up at the night sky. Millions of stars winked down at him, twinkling like tiny Christmas-tree lights strung across a black velvet pine.

An hour passed and the wind freshened, its voice like the sound of rushing water as it moved through the branches of stately ponderosa pines and lacy aspens.

Welcome home, the North Wind seemed to say. *Welcome home*.

Chapter 3

Michael woke to the sun in his face and the cry of a hawk ringing in his ears. Opening his eyes, he gazed up at a clear blue sky. The air was clean and sweet and cool, and he sat up, unaccountably pleased to be in this place with Yellow Spotted Wolf.

Stretching, he glanced over to where his great-grandfather lay sleeping, felt his breath catch in his throat as he stared at Yellow Spotted Wolf. The old man didn't seem to be breathing, and Michael felt a sudden fear that his great-grandfather might have died in the night.

Rising, he hurried to the old man and knelt beside him. "Grandfather? Grandfather!"

Yellow Spotted Wolf's eyes flew open in alarm;

then, seeing Michael, he frowned. "You do not have to shout," he admonished. "I am not yet deaf."

Michael smiled his relief. "I'm sorry, Grandfather. Go back to sleep while I fix breakfast."

"I am not hungry."

"You've gotta eat something."

"You sound just like old Mrs. Two Bulls," Yellow Spotted Wolf complained, grinning.

Michael put the coffee on to heat while he fried up some corned-beef hash. Yellow Spotted Wolf drank several cups of coffee, but ate little. He sat on a rock while Michael washed and dried the dishes and saddled the horses.

Michael could hear his muscles crying out in protest as he climbed into the saddle, but Yellow Spotted Wolf seemed none the worse for yesterday's journey.

As the morning passed, Michael found himself growing eager to reach the hills, to walk where his ancestors had walked. Strange, he thought, the way the towering peaks beckoned him, calling to him in whispered voices of days long past, promising to tell him secrets that were shrouded in the mists of time.

They stopped at noon for coffee and to rest the horses. At Michael's insistence, Yellow Spotted Wolf ate a couple of glazed doughnuts, then climbed back in the saddle. The old man's movements were slower now, and Michael could see the strain in his eyes as he settled into the saddle, see the faint lines of pain etched around his mouth.

"We can stop here for today if you like, Grandfather," Michael suggested.

"No, let us go on."

With a nod, Michael swung aboard his own horse. His great-grandfather had not said the words aloud, but they echoed in Michael's mind: *There is no time to waste.*

They rode steadily. Michael's excitement grew with each passing mile, as did his dread. Death was riding with Yellow Spotted Wolf, and it would not wait much longer.

They'd been riding for about seven hours when dark purple thunderclouds gathered overhead. Thunder echoed from the tall canyon walls and huge drops of rain showered the earth, quickly soaking man and beast.

When Michael drew his horse to a halt, Yellow Spotted Wolf called for him to go on.

"The storm will soon pass," the old man said confidently.

And as soon as it had begun, the rain stopped. The clouds moved past, leaving a bright sun behind. Raindrops sparkled on fresh-washed pine needles, and the grass looked brighter and greener than before.

And then they were at the foot of the Black Hills. Michael gazed up at the gray granite peaks, at the ever-green ponderosa pines and firs and aspens that covered the hills, and felt the wonder and awe that had captured the hearts and souls of the Sioux and Cheyenne and made them fight so hard to hold onto this piece of ground above all others.

Yellow Spotted Wolf sighed heavily as he urged his horse up the hill. The pain that had been his constant companion for the last eight months receded as he breathed in the scent of damp earth and trees. His soul felt light, as though it sensed it would soon be released from the aches and fatigue of mortality.

Higher and higher they climbed, leaving all the cares and worries of the world behind.

In the distance Michael saw a deer and a pair of spotted fawns; further on he spied an antelope grazing on a patch of yellow grass.

They climbed steadily upward, pausing now and then to rest the horses.

At dusk they reached a flat section of ground that lay between two narrow granite spires.

"We will stop here," Yellow Spotted Wolf said.

"You've been here before," Michael guessed.

"*Ai*, yes, a long time ago. I came here, to Eagle Mountain, to seek my vision. I knew then that this was where I would die."

Michael nodded, unable to speak. When Yellow Spotted Wolf died, Michael would have no family left. The thought had never bothered him before. He'd been so busy fighting his way to the top, so engrossed in becoming a white man, he had never given any thought to his family, or to the fact that he would have no family at all once the old man died. He wished suddenly that he had done things differently, that he had spent more time with his great-grandfather. But the old man had always been there . . .

By nightfall they had a small fire going. Yellow

Spotted Wolf crawled into his sleeping bag and closed his eyes, too weary to do anything but sleep.

Michael prepared a quick meal, then discovered he wasn't really hungry. Guilt and remorse did not make for a hearty appetite, and he was plagued with both as he sat there gazing at his great-grandfather. He had left the reservation, left Yellow Spotted Wolf, and never looked back. It occurred to him now, when it was too late, that he should have taken better care of the old man. He should have moved his great-grandfather off the reservation, made his last years more comfortable. At the least, he could have gone to visit him, or written a letter or two.

"It is too late for regrets, Ho-nehe," Yellow Spotted Wolf remarked quietly.

"I thought you were asleep, Grandfather."

The old man shook his head. "What is done is done and cannot be changed. We must each follow the path where our heart leads."

"I failed you."

"No."

"Have you no regrets, Grandfather?"

"Only one, and it has haunted me for eighty years."

Michael frowned. "Will you tell me about it?"

Yellow Spotted Wolf grunted softly. "It was at the Greasy Grass."

"When you fought Custer?"

"*Ai.* I had a younger brother who wanted very much to fight Yellow Hair, but he was not yet old enough to be a warrior. The night before the battle, he told me he was going to follow the warriors into battle, that he was going to count coup on the enemy. I did not believe him. He was only a child of ten summers, always making up stories of the brave deeds he would do, always teasing me. But this time he was not making up stories. He waited until a runner brought word that Yellow Hair had reached the river, and then, in the midst of the excitement and confusion that followed, he caught up his pony and rode after me. He was killed in the first wild rush as the bluecoats crossed the river."

"But you couldn't have known he was serious about following you."

"I should have listened to him," Yellow Spotted Wolf insisted. "At the least, I should have warned our mother to keep an eye on him. He was her youngest child, and her favorite. She grieved for him the rest of her life."

"I'm sorry, Grandfather."

Yellow Spotted Wolf let out a long sigh. "Perhaps it is never too late for regrets, after all. Even when things cannot be changed."

"Perhaps," Michael agreed. He searched for words that would express his regret at not having spent more time with Yellow Spotted Wolf, but such words came hard, and by the time he found them, his great-grandfather was asleep.

The soft low beat of a drum roused Michael from sleep and he opened his eyes, frowning irritably. Turning his head, he saw his great-grandfather kneeling on the ground, a small drum between his knees. Eyes closed, the old man lifted his voice toward the rising sun in what Michael recognized as an ancient morning prayer to the Great Spirit.

Not wanting to intrude on such a private moment, Michael lay still, just listening as the drum and the words spun their magic around him.

Abruptly the drumming stopped and Yellow Spotted Wolf stood up. *"Pave-voonao,* Ho-nehe."

"Good morning, Grandfather," Michael replied. "Are you hungry today?"

The old man nodded. "Yes, very hungry. Fix a big breakfast, one that will sustain me on my journey."

"What journey? I thought you wanted to camp here."

"The journey has already begun," Yellow Spotted Wolf replied. "I will see your great-grandmother and all those who have gone before me before this day is done."

"Grandfather . . ."

Yellow Spotted Wolf lifted his hand. "I am ready to meet my Creator," he said softly. "It is a good day to die."

Michael nodded. Wordlessly he prepared breakfast, which Yellow Spotted Wolf ate with gusto.

"We spoke of regrets yesterday," Yellow Spotted Wolf remarked when he had finished eating. His dark eyes focused on Michael's face. "I have one other regret that haunts me."

"What is it, Grandfather?"

"I have always regretted that you did not seek a medicine dream. A man needs a vision to guide him through life."

Michael started to laugh as he imagined himself crying for a vision, but then he saw that Yellow Spotted Wolf was quite serious. "Did my father seek a vision?"

"No. I think it is one of the reasons he had no purpose in life. He did not know who he was, what he was. He had no direction to follow, no vision to guide him down the path of life. He looked for answers in the white man's firewater."

"What of your medicine dream, Grandfather? Has it helped you in your life?"

Yellow Spotted Wolf nodded solemnly. "Yes, my son. I came here, to this mountain, when I was fourteen summers. I fasted and prayed for four days. I offered tobacco to the four winds, to the earth, who gives life, to the sky where the spirits dwell. I was very tired and very hungry when a yellow wolf with white hail spots on its rump appeared out of the east and walked toward me. As he came closer, I seemed to hear his voice speaking to me, and he said that I would fight in many battles, that I would see many changes in my lifetime, that I would see great chiefs rise and fall. As he spoke, his hair grew long and white and I knew I would live many winters before my spirit went to meet the Creator. Above all, the wolf told me to stay true to the beliefs of the People, to always honor our customs and hold fast to the traditions of our fathers."

Michael stared at Yellow Spotted Wolf. Did the old man really believe a wolf had talked to him? Wasn't it possible it had all been a hallucination brought on by fatigue and hunger?

"You do not believe me," Yellow Spotted Wolf said.

Michael shrugged. "Perhaps it is enough that *you* believe."

"It requires only a little faith and a willing heart," the old man murmured. And then he looked directly into Michael's eyes. "It would please me greatly if you would seek a vision."

"Me?" Michael choked back the laugh that rose in his throat so as not to offend his great-grandfather. "I don't know . . . maybe some day."

Yellow Spotted Wolf nodded, and then he embraced Michael, his bony arms holding his great-grandson close one last time. "Go," he said. "Take a walk. I wish to be alone."

"All right, Grandfather," Michael agreed. "I won't be gone long."

The old man drew himself up to his full height, and his dark eyes were bright and eager. "I will not need much time."

Michael swallowed the lump that rose in his throat. "Grandfather . . ."

Yellow Spotted Wolf nodded, his dark eyes shining with unshed tears as his heart heard the words his great-grandson could not say.

"I won't be long," Michael said again. And

then, fighting tears, he gave his great-grandfather a hug and walked away.

There was a silence in the hills as Michael made his way down a steep slope heavy with timber and brush. No birds sang in the treetops, no wind stirred the branches. There was only the faint hum of winged insects and the muffled sound of his own footsteps.

Fragments of what his great-grandfather had said whispered in the back of his mind: stay true to the People . . . seek a medicine dream . . . a little faith . . . a willing heart . . .

Michael shook the words from his mind. Medicine dreams and visions were things of the past, like the horse-and-buggy and kerosene lamps. No one believed in visions any more. It was just a lot of hocus-pocus.

He swore under his breath. What was he doing walking around in the Black Hills when he should be back in L.A. looking after business? Hell, he'd had enough of playing Indian. It was time to go home . . .

He came to an abrupt halt as he rounded a bend in the trail and came face to face with an old white wolf. Time vanished, the forest seemed to fade away, and he was aware of nothing but the old wolf standing in his path.

Yellow Spotted Wolf has gone home.

The words rang in Michael's ears, as sharp and clear as if they'd been spoken aloud.

The wolf stared at Michael for the space of a heartbeat; then it was gone.

Yellow Spotted Wolf has gone home.

The words rang in Michael's mind as he turned on his heel and ran back to camp.

Yellow Spotted Wolf lay on the Morning Star blanket. His warbonnet was on his head, and a necklace of bear claws circled his neck. There was a war club in his right hand, a turkey feather fan in his left. A single streak of black paint adorned his right cheek. He wore a sleeveless buckskin vest, fringed leggings, a doeskin clout, and a pair of exquisitely beaded moccasins that had been made by Michael's great-grand-mother. His old cardboard suitcase lay a few feet away.

Tears burned Michael's eyes and throat as he gazed at his great-grandfather. The lines of pain were gone from Yellow Spotted Wolf's face and he looked peaceful, almost happy.

Remorse washed over Michael; remorse and guilt and regret. He could have done so much for the old man, and he had done so little. So damn little! He'd even begrudged the old man the last few days because it had taken him away from his business. Well, he could devote all his time to the Walsh Agency now. Yellow Spotted Wolf would never need him again.

Michael Wolf sat down beside his great-grandfather's body and knew, for the first time in his life, what it meant to be alone.

Chapter 4

Michael wrapped *Yellow Spotted Wolf in the* Morning Star blanket, then carried the frail body deep into a stand of heavy timber and placed it in the fork of a tree high off the ground. He hoped that, in this quiet place, his great-grandfather would be allowed to rest peacefully in the land he had loved.

Michael stood beneath the tree for almost an hour, silent tears stinging his eyes and burning his throat. In the old days he would have killed a horse so that Yellow Spotted Wolf's spirit might ride in comfort to the Afterworld.

With a sigh, he turned his back on his great-grandfather's final resting place and returned to their campsite. One of the horses whickered softly as Michael approached, and he was suddenly glad for the horse's company. Scratching the gray's jaw, he gazed out over the vast sunlit prairie spread below. It was a beautiful place, quiet and serene, with only the faint hum of insects and the soft whisper of a slight spring breeze to mar the stillness of the moment.

The sense of being alone in the world was strong within him again. Only now did he realize how much he had relied on the knowledge that Yellow Spotted Wolf was there for him, waiting to welcome him back to the reservation if he ever decided to return.

Blinking back his tears, he saddled the horses and rolled the sleeping bags. He was about to mount his horse when he noticed his great-grandfather's old cardboard valise lying on the ground.

As if guided by some phantom spirit, Michael knelt beside the suitcase and ran his hands over the battered top and sides, and then, releasing a deep sigh of resignation, he lifted the lid.

Nestled inside he found a breechclout of fine black wolfskin, a pair of leggings, heavily fringed along the outer seam, and a pair of moccasins that had belonged to Yellow Spotted Wolf. A small bag of tobacco rested in one corner of the suitcase.

Michael stared at the contents of the suitcase for a long time, and in the back of his mind he could hear the voice of Yellow Spotted Wolf: *A man needs a vision to guide him through life.*

Slowly, hesitantly, Michael removed the wolfskin clout from the suitcase. He examined it carefully, as though he had never seen one before, and then he laid it aside and reached for the leggings. Whom had they belonged to? Even as the question formed in the back of his mind, he knew the leggings had belonged to his father. He ran his hand over the leggings, noting the fine workmanship of his grandmother's hand, the quality of the needlework. The moccasins were of the everyday variety, unadorned with beadwork or quills; the soles were of heavy rawhide for durability.

He found a long-bladed hunting knife encased in a beaded rawhide sheath beneath the moccasins. Sliding the weapon from its sheath, he ran the edge of his thumb along the blade. It was razor sharp, freshly honed.

He did not touch the tobacco pouch.

Time lost its meaning as he sat there gazing at his great-grandfather's legacy, and then, abruptly, he stood up and removed his boots. His shirt came next, then his jeans, and finally his underwear and socks.

For a moment he stood naked, letting the cool spring breeze caress his bare skin. It was a heady feeling, standing naked at the top of the world, and he savored it for a long while, thinking that, unfettered by clothing or convention, he could run like the wind.

The rawhide leggings were cool against his skin, the clout like rough velvet against his bare buttocks. The moccasins fit as if they had been made for him. The knife was a comfortable weight at his side.

But he did not touch the tobacco pouch.

For a fleeting moment he wished he had a mirror. Did he look like a Cheyenne warrior? His skin was the right color, his hair and eyes were black, he was tall and broad-shouldered like the rest of the men in his family, but he knew it took more than heredity to make a warrior. It took a deep, abiding belief in a certain way of life . . . a way of living and thinking and behaving.

It was not for him.

A man needs a vision to guide him through life.

The words rang loud and clear in his ears and he whirled around, his heart pounding like a drum.

But there was no one there and he laughed softly, self-consciously. Had he really expected to find Yellow Spotted Wolf standing behind him?

Michael swore under his breath, feeling a trifle foolish as he stood there in the trappings of a warrior, and more than a little uneasy as his great-grandfather's words echoed in the back of his mind.

"I don't need a vision," he muttered. "What I need is to get back to L.A., the sooner the better."

But he made no move to leave.

He dropped down on his haunches beside the suitcase and watched his hand reach for the small drawstring bag of tobacco. It felt warm in his palm.

Rising, he opened the pouch and took a pinch of tobacco between his thumb and forefinger;

then, almost as if he had done it before, he offered the tobacco to *Heammawihio*, the Creator, the Wise One Above. A second pinch was offered to *Ahktuno'wihio*, the beneficent god who lived underground. Next he made offerings to *Notum*, the god of the North, to *Num'haisto*, the god of the South, to *Ish'i tsis-iss-i-mi'is* and *Ish'i tsis-ta-kit-a'es*, the gods of the East and the West.

"Hear me, *Heammawihio*," he called, his tone flat and disbelieving, "grant me a vision that I may know the path to follow through life."

What would Gerald Walsh think of his star salesman if he could see him now, Michael wondered as he tucked the tobacco pouch into his belt and then raised his hands toward heaven, palms upward.

I feel ridiculous, he thought, and yet, standing there, his arms raised in supplication, he began to feel a oneness with the earth and the sky.

He was not a man given to prayer, yet the words formed on his lips, words as ancient as the blood of the *Tsis'tsistas*, the Cheyenne. They rose toward the vast blue vault of the sky, beseeching a kind Creator to send a vision to one of his red children, to a man who realized, too late, that he had cut out his own heart and soul when he turned his back on the Morning Star people.

"Hear me, *Heammawihio*," he cried in a voice that was now strong and fervent with desire. "I am a poor man in need of your help. Hear me, *Ahktuno-wihio*, he who makes the grass grow and the water flow, who gives life to all the earth, bless me with a vision that my spirit might grow as tall as the mountain on which I stand."

He stood there all that day and into the night, unmindful of the sun's heat or the cold breath of the moon. There was a dull throbbing ache in his arms and shoulders, his mouth was as dry as the dust at his feet, his stomach as empty as his heart.

As the moon climbed high above Eagle Mountain, his legs grew numb and he dropped to his knees, groaning softly. And still he prayed, his need for a vision suddenly stronger than his body's need for food or sleep.

He rose slowly to his feet as the sun gave birth to a new day. His voice was a whisper now, his arms a painful extension of his weary body. He forgot that he had felt foolish only hours before, forgot that he did not believe in visions and dreams. A stubbornness, an inner strength he had not known he possessed, refused to let him give up.

"*Heammawihio*," he cried hoarsely, "grant me a vision that I might fulfill my great-grandfather's dying wish. Show me the way to go. Help me to understand . . ."

Ese-he, the sun, climbed higher in the sky, filling the earth with warmth and light. For Michael swallowing became painful, his tongue felt swollen, his throat ached. Sweat dampened his skin and trickled down his back, his vision blurred, his voice was like a whisper in the wind.

Stoically he ignored the discomforts of the flesh and concentrated on what he hoped to gain. Swaying unsteadily on legs that felt like lead, he gazed up into the sun, his heart crying the words he could no longer speak.

"*Heammawihio*, grant me a vision lest I perish . . ."

Time lost all meaning. Pain and hunger and thirst were forgotten as he stared, unblinking, into the sun, until he was gradually engulfed in a hazy white light that enfolded him like loving arms, soothing his aching limbs, healing the hurt in his heart, fulfilling the void left by the death of Yellow Spotted Wolf.

The light grew brighter, stronger, blinding him to the rest of the world.

You shall have the desires of your heart, the light whispered softly, and Michael Wolf felt himself falling, falling, into the sun . . .

Part 2

Chapter 5

The scent of wildflowers and earth tickled Michael's nostrils and he opened his eyes to discover he was lying face down on the ground. For a moment he could not recall where he was, and then it all came back to him, the hours of fasting and prayer, of hunger and thirst.

He frowned as he sat up. He must have fainted from lack of food and water, and from the heat, he thought with some surprise, and then grinned. Well, so much for a vision. No doubt medicine dreams and visions had gone the way of the buffalo and the warrior.

Rising, he looked around for his clothing. It was time to stop playing Indian and get back to L.A.

Only his clothes weren't where he had left them.

"What the hell," he muttered. Not only were his clothes gone, but so were the horses.

He swore softly, wondering if he had walked in his sleep. This looked like the place where he had spent the night, yet there was no sign that he'd camped there, no ashes where the fire had been.

Bewildered, he walked down the hill toward the stand of timber where he'd left his great-grandfather's body. But he couldn't find the towering pine that had held the old man's remains. He saw trees, but none looked familiar.

"What the hell's going on?" he wondered aloud.

He spent the next hour quartering back and forth on the hillside looking for some sign of his great-grandfather's body, for the horses or his clothing, but there was no sign that anyone had camped there recently.

Michael frowned. The sleeping bags were gone. So were the saddlebags and Yellow Spotted Wolf's battered old suitcase. Even their trash was missing.

Perhaps he'd been robbed while unconscious. It seemed the most logical explanation, and he started down the hill, his footsteps fueled by his anger. He'd had three hundred dollars in his wallet, not to mention his driver's license and his plane ticket home.

He was quietly cursing the thief and dreading the long walk back to Johnson Siding when he rounded a bend in the trail and came face to face with a half-dozen Indians mounted on paint ponies.

It was a toss-up as to who was more surprised, the six warriors, or Michael. For long seconds they stared at each other.

"Hou, tahunsa," one of the warriors said at last.

They were Lakota, Michael thought, and frowned as he tried to recall their language. *"Hou, tahunsa,"* he replied as the words came back to him. "Hello, cousin."

The warrior spoke to him again, but Michael hadn't heard the Lakota language in years and he didn't understand most of what the warrior said.

"My Lakota is not good," Michael said with a shrug. "Do you speak English?"

"Hin," the warrior answered with a nod. "I speak the white man's tongue."

"Good. I lost my horses. Have you seen them?"

The warrior shook his head. "Do you think some *wasicun* stole them?"

"I don't know. Are you camped nearby? Perhaps you could lend me a horse, or give me a ride back to Johnson Siding?"

The warrior frowned. "Johnson Siding?" he repeated. "What means Johnson Siding?"

"Don't you work here, in the park? I thought you might be a ranger of some kind."

"Your words make no sense," the warrior replied. "The Lakota come here every year dur-

ing the Moon of Ripe Berries to celebrate
Wiwanyank Wacipi with their brothers, the
Shyela."

Michael stared at the scars on the warrior's
chest. *Wiwanyank Wacipi?* Was it possible the
Sioux still came here to practice the Sun Dance?
Hadn't it been outlawed by the government
years ago?

"Come," the warrior said, offering Michael
his hand. "I will take you to Tatanka Iyotake.
Perhaps he will understand your words."

Tatanka Iyotake? Speechless, Michael grasped
the warrior's forearm and swung up behind
him. *Sitting Bull*, he thought. *They're going to
take me to see Sitting Bull.*

Michael stared at the vast Indian village
spread across a flat plain thick with buffalo
grass, sage, and spiny cactus. Far off in the
distance he saw Bear Butte rising twelve hundred feet above the plains, studded with spindly
yellow pines and gnarled red cedars. The Indians called it *Paha Mato*. Crazy Horse had seen
his vision there. . . .

Michael closed his eyes and shook his head.
He'd been out in the sun too long, he mused as
he gazed at the village. He was seeing things that
weren't there.

But when he opened his eyes, nothing had
changed. Hundreds of hide tipis were still
spread across the prairie. Countless horses
grazed on the thick grass. Children ran between
the lodges, shouting and laughing. Warriors
paraded through the camp, magnificent in

fringed buckskin leggings and elaborately beaded and quilled shirts and moccasins. Women stood talking together in small groups or sat in the shade tending babes in arms. The smoke from numerous cook-fires spiraled upward.

Michael's mouth watered and his stomach growled loudly as the scent of freshly roasted meat tickled his nostrils.

The warrior glanced over his shoulder and grinned at Michael. "I will take you to my lodge. My woman will have food prepared."

"Le mita pila," Michael replied. "My thanks."

Moments later they were seated in the warrior's lodge eating roasted buffalo hump and boiled vegetables. Michael was ravenous, but he ate slowly so as not to embarrass himself or his host. The meat was blood red on the inside, with a wild gamy taste, but it was not unpleasant.

He tried not to stare as he gazed around the lodge. There had been tipis on the reservation, but they had been used for sweat lodges or counsel lodges. No one lived in them any more. A firepit had been dug in the center of the floor, and there were buffalo robes rolled up in the back of the lodge that Michael assumed were used for bedding. Pots and cooking utensils were stacked near the door, together with a couple of jugs and waterskins. Several large parfleches took up space against one wall, and he guessed they were filled with clothing and other personal items.

When they had finished eating, the warrior lit his pipe and offered it to the earth and the sky and the four directions before handing it to Michael, who took several long puffs before returning it to his host.

"I am Mato Wamatka, of the Lakota," the warrior said.

"I am Michael Wolf, of the Northern Cheyenne."

Mato Wamatka nodded, puzzled by his visitor's peculiar first name. He would have liked to ask how the Cheyenne warrior had received such an unusual name, but to do so would have been considered impolite. A man's name was a personal thing, usually bestowed on a warrior as the result of a vision or a brave deed, or it might be based on an outstanding physical characteristic.

Mato Wamatka tried not to stare at his guest, but there was something vaguely familiar about the man. He glanced at Wolf's short hair curiously. Warriors did not cut their hair except to mourn the loss of a loved one or to express great sorrow or shame.

Mato Wamatka rose smoothly to his feet. He was a simple man, and this new visitor was beyond his comprehension.

"Come," he said, "I will take you to Tatanka Iyotake."

Michael stood up, his stomach in knots as he followed Mato Wamatka out of the lodge and across the village. *This can't be real*, he thought, dazed. *It must be some kind of Lakota powwow, a re-creation of life in the old days.*

He had almost convinced himself he was in

the middle of some kind of tribal get-together where everyone pretended they were living back in 1875 until he saw Sitting Bull. He had seen enough photographs of the Hunkpapa medicine man to recognize the real thing when he saw it.

He closed his eyes. What the hell was going on? He refused to accept the answer that came to mind. It was unthinkable, impossible, ridiculous. But how else to explain the Lakota village where none had been before? How else could he account for his missing clothing and horses, the missing sleeping bags, the trash? How else could he account for the strange white light that had surrounded him, or the man who was standing before him?

He opened his eyes, his gaze searching the face of the Hunkpapa warrior. It really was Sitting Bull, he was sure of it. He thought back to what he knew of the medicine man's life. Sitting Bull had been born in the spring of 1831 on the Grand River. He had gone to war at the age of fourteen and counted coup on the enemy. The counting of coup was the bravest act an Indian could perform. Anyone could kill an enemy from a distance with a well-placed arrow, but to get close enough to strike a living enemy, that was bravery indeed. No warrior could sit in counsel who had not counted coup. At the age of twenty-six, Sitting Bull had been made the leader of the Midnight Strong Hearts. It was one of the highest honors a man could receive. Bravery, fortitude, wisdom, and generosity were the virtues the Lakota held dear, and Sitting Bull exemplified them all. Yellow Spotted Wolf had once told Michael that Tatanka Iyotake believed *Wakan Tanka* had given him the job of protecting the People from the white-eyes.

It was a strange feeling, Michael thought, to be standing beside a man who had died forty years before you were born, to know the full history of another man's life before the man himself had lived it. He wondered what Sitting Bull would say if he told him he had come from the future, that he, Michael Wolf, knew it was foolish for the Indians to oppose the whites, that no matter how many small victories the People might win, they were destined to lose in the end.

Sitting Bull's dark eyes settled on Michael's face as Mato Wamatka explained who Michael was. An eerie feeling crept over Michael as he met the older man's probing gaze; it was almost as though Sitting Bull were reading his mind, gauging the depths of his soul.

"Hau, sunkaku," Sitting Bull said graciously. "Welcome, brother. Mato Wamatka tells me someone has stolen your horses."

"Yes," Michael replied, though he realized now that his horses hadn't been stolen at all. They were waiting for him at the top of Eagle Mountain, right where he had left them. In 1955.

"Come," Sitting Bull said. "Walk with me. We will see if we can find the horses you seek."

"Le mita pila," Michael murmured. He nodded to Mato Wamatka, then followed Sitting Bull toward the river.

Men, women, and children turned to stare at the stranger walking with Sitting Bull. Many of the people smiled at Michael, their faces friendly, their dark eyes filled with curiousity.

"You have come to us from a great distance," Sitting Bull remarked as they walked toward the river where the vast Lakota horse herd grazed. "You have seen things we have not seen."

A chill started at the base of Michael's spine and crept slowly upward. Was the older man clairvoyant?

"You are one of us," Sitting Bull went on, his voice low and hypnotic. "The same heart, the same blood, and yet you are a stranger."

It was as though the sun had suddenly lost its warmth. Michael felt himself shivering under the medicine man's prolonged gaze.

"Who are you, Michael Wolf? Who are your people? Why are you here?"

"I mean you no harm," Michael answered.

Sitting Bull nodded. "There is trouble coming," he remarked. They were standing on the edge of the horse herd now, and Sitting Bull's gaze traveled over the Lakota ponies.

"Trouble?" Michael repeated.

"The Grandfather in Washington wants to buy the *Paha Sapa*, but we will not sell our beloved hills. We will not trade away the land where our ancestors sleep. I sent word to the Grandfather and told him the *Paha Sapa* belong to me. If the whites try to take them, I will fight."

Sitting Bull nodded to himself. "This is my

land," he said again. "I will fight for it, I will die for it, but I will never leave it."

Michael remained silent. Sitting Bull *would* leave this land, he knew, but that was not important now.

He felt a chill pass along his spine as the warrior's dark eyes bored into him.

"I ask you again, Michael Wolf, who are you?" Sitting Bull leaned forward, his voice almost a whisper. "Are you flesh or spirit?"

"A man, like yourself."

"We speak in riddles. Tell me, Wolf, why have you come here?"

Why indeed, Michael thought. And then, out of the blue, he knew why he was there.

"I have come to find my people," he said with conviction. "I have come to find out who and what I am, that I may find my own path through life."

Sitting Bull nodded. "Who are your people?"

Michael did some quick mental arithmetic. Sitting Bull must be in his forties, which would put the year around 1874 or '75. His great-great-grandfather, Mo'ohta-vo'nehe, would have been a man in his prime then, and Yellow Spotted Wolf would have been a teenager.

"I'm looking for the family of Mo'ohta-vo'nehe of the Northern Cheyenne," Michael said, and it was all he could do to keep from laughing out loud. It was all so impossible. He couldn't be here, talking to a man who'd been dead for sixty-five years.

Sitting Bull nodded. The name of Mo'ohta-vo'nehe was well known among the Lakota. "Your people have gone to Tallow River for the summer."

Michael nodded. Tallow River was the Indian name for the South Platte.

"Is my family well?" he asked, hoping to hear some word of Yellow Spotted Wolf.

"Hin, yes." Sitting Bull placed a heavy hand on Michael's shoulder. "Tell me, *tahunsa*, what do you see in the future for our people? What do you see for me? Will I win the war against the white man?"

Michael did not answer right away. He was conscious of the sun on his back, of feeling vulnerable as he stood there before one of the greatest leaders the Lakota Nation had ever produced. But, most of all, he was aware of Sitting Bull's hand resting on his shoulder, of the inescapable feeling that the Hunkpapa medicine man knew exactly who Michael Wolf was and where he had come from. He told himself that was impossible, but the feeling remained.

He drew a deep breath, wondering what his fate would be when he told Sitting Bull the truth. For one brief moment he considered concocting a lie, but he immediately dismissed the idea. Only a fool, or a man without honor, would try to lie to Tatanka Iyotake, and Michael was neither.

But before he could speak, the medicine man lifted a hand to silence him.

"What you have to say matters not," Sitting Bull decided with a wistful smile. "What was meant to be will surely come to pass, and neither of us can change that."

"But knowledge might make a difference," Michael exclaimed. "There are things I should tell you."

"*Wakan Tanka* will tell me what I need to know," Sitting Bull replied, "as he will tell you that which you need to know. You have come here to find yourself, Michael Wolf, but you cannot do that here, among the Lakota. You must go to Tallow River, to your own people. That is where your destiny lies. *Wakan Tanka* will speak to you there."

"You know who I am?"

Sitting Bull nodded. "I know, and it frightens me a little. I think it will be better for you, and for us, if you leave the land of the Lakota and seek the lodges of the *Shyela*, the Cheyenne, as soon as you can travel."

Sitting Bull gazed at Michael for a long moment, and then, without another word, he turned on his heel and walked back toward the village.

Michael grinned ruefully. He had, he mused, just been asked to leave.

Michael gazed into the distance, his expression thoughtful, his mind filling with Sitting Bull's words.

What will be, will be, the medicine man had declared, and Michael could not help but wonder what the future held in store for him. Was he destined to remain here, to become a part of his people's past, or was it just a dream after all?

Chapter 6

He left the Lakota encampment the following morning. His horse, a big calico gelding, had been a parting gift from Sitting Bull.

Leaving the camp behind, Michael shook his head over his conversation with Sitting Bull. Now, away from the camp and the Hunkpapa medicine man, it was hard to believe any of it had been real. It was easier to think it had been some kind of joke, that Sitting Bull had not been Sitting Bull at all, just a remarkable look-alike.

He let out a sigh as he urged his horse toward Johnson Siding. He was going to look pretty silly riding into town wearing nothing but a clout and moccasins, but it couldn't be helped. He wasn't looking forward to telling the man he'd rented the horses from that his animals had been stolen, either, but what the hell. Perhaps the man would take the calico and a hundred dollars and call it even.

Michael shook his head again. Damn, this trip had been nothing but trouble from the beginning . . . well, not entirely, he amended. It had afforded him a chance to spend a little time with Yellow Spotted Wolf before he died. And, despite everything that had happened, he was glad to be here in the Black Hills. The place was beautiful, peaceful, and he knew he never would have taken the time to come here if it hadn't been his great-grandfather's last request.

Putting his worries behind him, Michael let himself enjoy the scenery, the rolling hills, the tall yellow grass, the clear blue sky. He tried to enjoy the ride too, but after a couple hours of plodding along, he decided he much preferred driving a sleek black convertible to riding a horse.

He lifted the calico into a lope, thinking what a good laugh everybody at the agency would have when he told his story back in L.A.

The car was gone when he reached Johnson Siding the following day, and so was the town.

Michael stared at the place where the motel had been. Nothing remained but a patch of sun-bleached ground. The whole town had disappeared as if it had never existed.

He sat there for a long time, staring at nothing while the gradual reality of what had happened hit home. And still he was unwilling to believe it. Urging the calico into a lope, he rode east until he came to the Black Hills Caverns. The cave was there, just as it had been for hundreds of years, but Crystal Cave Park was gone. The reptile gardens had vanished.

Changing direction, he rode north. Wildlife was plentiful as he rode along, and he saw squirrels, birds, rabbits, a black bear off in the distance, an eagle circling high overhead.

The highway was gone, the Black Hills Greyhound Track outside Rapid City was gone. And so was Rapid City.

For a moment he sat unmoving, too stunned to think clearly, and then he reined his horse northwest, toward Deadwood. He grinned ruefully. He knew Deadwood hadn't disappeared.

The discovery of gold in the Black Hills in the summer of 1875 had put Deadwood on the map. The town, built almost entirely of wood, had burned to the ground in 1879 and had been promptly rebuilt. Indians had fought the settlers; floods on Whitewood Creek in Deadwood Gulch had done their share of damage; a blizzard in 1949 had dumped over seventy inches of snow on the town. But it continued to thrive. It was, as historian Watson Parker had once said, a town that would not die.

It was well after midnight the following night when he reached Deadwood. *Civilization*, he thought. *Thank God*.

Loud music and laughter spilled out of a saloon; he saw a pair of men staggering down the center of the dusty street, obviously drunk. There were several horses standing hipshot at the rail in front of Dirty Nellie's Saloon.

A good stiff drink was just what he needed, he mused as he dismounted at the nearest saloon and tossed the calico's reins over the hitchrack. A good stiff drink and something to eat.

Feeling suddenly uneasy, he paused at the swinging doors and peered inside. The tavern was made of wood, with raw plank floors and an open beam ceiling. A long bar took up most of the far wall; several gaming tables competed for space in the narrow room. A half-dozen men, all clad in the rough garb of old-time miners, occupied the saloon. Four of them were engaged in a high-stakes poker game; the other two stood at the bar discussing a shoot-out that had taken place in Saloon #10 the night before.

Saloon #10, Michael thought absently. That was where Wild Bill Hickok had been killed, shot in the back by Jack McCall.

Taking a deep breath, Michael stepped through the swinging doors.

He knew immediately that he'd made a mistake. The bartender hollered, "Indians!" and ducked behind the bar, only to reappear with a rifle in his hands. The miners at the poker table dove for cover, their hands reaching for their guns.

Muttering an oath, Michael turned and raced out of the saloon. Shouts of "Injuns! Injuns!" followed him into the night.

Vaulting onto the calico's back, he galloped

out of town, the miners in hot pursuit, their shouts filling the quiet night.

A cluster of tents rose up out of the darkness, and Michael realized he had ridden into Deadwood Gulch. Miners poured out of the tents at the sound of gunshots, and Michael jerked the gelding's head to the right, hoping to escape into the darkness, when he heard the sharp crack of a rifle, felt a sudden stab of pain in his right shoulder. A second gunshot struck his horse and the animal fell heavily, then lay still.

In seconds, Michael was surrounded by more than a dozen angry miners brandishing rifles and clubs.

"Dirty redskin," one of the men exclaimed, his voice thick with contempt. "What the hell is he doing prowling around here in the middle of the night?"

"I was . . ."

A hard fist caught Michael flush in the mouth. He felt his lower lip split, felt his mouth fill with blood.

"Shut up!" bellowed the man who had hit him. "Shorty, get a rope. We'll hogtie him for now. Come morning, we'll have ourselves a little necktie party."

"No!" Michael shouted. "Listen to me . . ."

He doubled over as one of the miners drove a hard fist into his belly.

"Save your breath, Injun," the man said, sneering. "We ain't interested in nothing you got to say."

A cold knot of fear congealed in the pit of

Michael's stomach as his hands were lashed behind his back. Someone shoved him to the ground, then bound his feet together and secured them to a tree. He heard the miners talking as they returned to their tents, their voices thick with excitement at the prospect of a hanging, come morning.

He choked back the vomit that rose in his throat as he imagined what it would be like to feel the noose around his neck, to feel that first moment of being suspended in the air before the rope brought him up short, either breaking his neck quickly and cleanly or slowly strangling him to death.

The words of the miners lingered in his ears: "dirty redskin . . . damned savage . . . stinkin' gut-eater . . ."

He had never encountered such prejudice in his life. Even in L.A., people had accepted him as an equal once they got to know him. True, there had been some jibes about scalps and war dances, but he had never been subjected to the scorn or out-and-out hatred he had seen reflected in the faces of the miners.

He closed his eyes, willing himself to stay calm. The throbbing in his shoulder made it difficult to think, hunger clawed at his belly. The blood running down his arm was warm and wet, and he began to shiver convulsively as pain and fear took hold of him.

Opening his eyes, he took a deep breath. He had to stay calm, he had to think. These men were hard as hickory, uneducated, ruthless.

They would not listen to any explanations, would not believe his story even if they did listen. Damn! He had to get the hell out of Deadwood before morning. The thought of what his fate would be if he failed overcame the pain in his shoulder, and he began to struggle against the ropes that bound his hands.

Fear of being hanged by a bunch of Indian-hating, blood-hungry whites made him continue to struggle even after his wrists began to bleed. And it was the blood that did the trick, making the rope wet enough and slippery enough to allow him to slip his hands free.

Feeling somewhat light-headed from the blood he had lost from the gunshot wound, he nevertheless managed to untie the rope on his feet. It was an effort to stand up, and once the world stopped reeling, he went in search of a horse.

He found a tall, raw-boned bay tethered to a tree and, after loosing the reins, walked the animal out of the camp. Only when he was well out of earshot did he climb wearily onto the mare's back, and then he slammed his heels into her flanks and headed for the Platte, and Yellow Spotted Wolf.

Yellow Spotted Wolf. He repeated the name in his mind. If he could only reach his great-grandfather, he would be safe. The Cheyenne would give him food and water and shelter.

He rode throughout the night, and the darkness became a part of him, surrounding him, ensnaring him in ebony strands so that the pain in his shoulder seemed to belong to someone else, as did the hunger and thirst that plagued him.

He wrapped his right hand in the mare's flowing black mane and closed his eyes.

Yellow Spotted Wolf. If he could only find Yellow Spotted Wolf before the darkness swallowed him completely . . .

Chapter 7

He woke with a start, and a quiet voice spoke to him, urging him to lie still, assuring him that he was among friends, that everything would be all right. He blinked several times to clear his vision, and he saw two people bending over him. The woman was young, perhaps sixteen or seventeen, with luminous black eyes, straight black brows, dusky skin, and waist-length hair. The man was old. There was iron in his hair and a lifetime of living etched into his weathered features.

"Where am I?" Michael asked.

"Later," the woman said with a smile. "Red-Furred Bear is going to remove the bullet from your shoulder."

Michael shook his head in protest as the aged

medicine man withdrew a long-bladed knife from his belt. Yellow Spotted Wolf had placed great faith in the magical healing powers of the Cheyenne shamans and mystics, but Michael had always been skeptical of such ancient rituals. He'd never needed a doctor before, he mused ruefully, and now, when he was about to go under the knife, literally, for the first time, it would be at the hands of an old medicine man.

The woman seemed to understand Michael's anxiety. Taking his hand in hers, she murmured, *"Hoshuh*, be calm. I have seen Red-Furred Bear heal many wounds, some much worse than yours."

Michael nodded as the old shaman rose to his feet.

Plucking a live coal from the small fire in the center of the lodge, Red-Furred Bear sprinkled it with powdered bitterroot. As the scented smoke filled the air, he held his hands over the smoke, palms down, and then he pressed his palms over the wound in Michael's shoulder.

Michael groaned softly as the old man touched him, purifying the wound.

Lifting his hands, Red-Furred Bear began to sing. Taking up a buffalo-hide rattle filled with small stones, he shook it over the length of Michael's body to drive away any evil spirits that might be within the lodge. After several minutes he stopped singing to pray, and then he began to chant again, shaking the rattle all the while, until he felt the lodge had been purified.

And then he passed his knife through the smoke.

Michael tensed, his gaze riveted on the blade as he imagined the knife slicing through his flesh.

"*Hoshuh*," the girl murmured again. "Be calm."

Michael concentrated on her voice, her face. Her eyes, beautiful and dark, were filled with compassion as she gently squeezed his hand. Her hair was as black as a midnight sky, her lips the color of a dark and dusky rose. Her brows were straight and delicate above almond-shaped eyes, her lashes long and thick.

The touch of her hand was like magic, easing the pain in his shoulder as the medicine man cut the bullet from his flesh and packed the bleeding wound with healing herbs before wrapping it with a strip of clean cloth.

He felt bereft when the girl left his side to walk the medicine man to the door of the lodge and bid him good day.

When she returned, she offered Michael a cup of strong tea. He drank greedily, ignoring the slightly bitter taste, and when he drained the cup, she put it aside, then removed his moccasins and covered him with a lightweight robe.

"Don't go," he murmured as she started to rise.

The woman nodded. Kneeling beside him, she brushed a wisp of hair from his forehead.

"*Naaotsestse*," she said quietly. "Go to sleep."

Chapter 8

He woke slowly. Lying there, his eyes closed, he thought he was at home. Yawning, he contemplated the day ahead: he'd wear the dark blue suit to work . . . he'd have to call Melinda and see if they were still going out that night . . . he'd have to get in touch with Paul Green and tell him his car was ready . . .

The aromatic scents of tobacco and sage and earth filled his nostrils and he opened his eyes. A slice of azure sky was visible through the smokehole of the lodge, and as he watched, a thin column of blue-gray smoke spiraled upward to mingle withhthe air above.

He was not home, he thought wryly.

A voice filtered into the lodge and he recognized it as that of old Red-Furred Bear, the medicine man.

"There was once a *vehoe* who bragged that he was the smartest white man in all the world, the shrewdest trader, the sneakiest thief. No one ever got the best of him in a deal. But one day another *vehoe* told him he was mistaken. 'I know someone who can outcheat you any time,' the second *vehoe* said. 'That's not possible,' insisted the first *vehoe*. 'Who is this person? Bring him to me.'

" 'His name is Coyote,' the second *vehoe* said. 'He can best you in any deal you can think of . . .' "

Michael grinned as he listened to Red-Furred Bear continue the story of how Coyote cheated the *vehoe* out of his horse and clothes.

The Indians loved to tell stories of Coyote, the trickster, of *Unktehi* the water monster, of *Iktome*, the spider man. *Mih'n* was an underwater monster shaped like a large lizard. *Mih'n* had two large horns and was partly covered with hair. *Ahke* was another underwater monster. *Hi'stowunini'hotua* was a small, humpless buffalo with sharp-pointed horns and a short snout. Mothers told their children that *Hi'stowunini-'hotua* ate little children who would not go to bed.

From outside came the sound of childish laughter as Red-Furred Bear finished the story of Coyote. The children began to beg for another, and after a few minutes the aged shaman agreed and began to tell the tale of how Coyote brought death into the world.

Michael started to get up, but a sharp pang in his shoulder changed his mind and he fell back on the robes, his teeth clenched against the pain.

He squinted as the door flap opened, admitting a bright shaft of sunlight, and then the woman was kneeling beside him, a bowl of *wojapi* in her hands.

She smiled cheerfully when she saw he was awake. *"Ne-haeana-he?"* she asked. "Are you hungry?"

Michael nodded. He was hungry enough to eat a horse, hair, hide, and hooves.

He started to protest as she lifted the spoon to his mouth, but then he shrugged. What the hell, it was nice to be pampered by a beautiful woman.

The berry soup was sweet and good, and he ate it all, then accepted a drink of cool water. It was the water that was his undoing.

"I need to . . ." He cleared his throat under her inquiring gaze. "I need to go outside."

Comprehension brought a quick flush to her cheeks. "Come," she said, not quite meeting his eyes as she offered him her hand, "I will help you."

Outside, the sun was hot and bright. The camp was humming with activity as women stirred kettles of venison stew, or nursed their children, or sat in the shade, sewing and talking.

Men walked about the camp, chatting with friends. Others could be seen fashioning new weapons or repairing old ones. A half-dozen warriors were gambling outside the chief's lodge. There were children and dogs everywhere; in the distance, the vast Indian pony herd grazed on the lush buffalo grass.

The woman led him away from the village and into a stand of timber.

"Thanks," he murmured. "I think I can manage the rest alone."

She nodded and walked away, and Michael found himself wondering what she thought of him. So far, the burden of his care seemed to have fallen on her shoulders. Did she mind?

He felt his spirits rise when he heard the woman call to him a few minutes later, inquiring if he was ready to return to the lodge.

Michael walked slowly, pretending his wound pained him more than it did, and the woman quickly slipped her arm around his waist, as he had hoped she would. The top of her head barely reached his shoulder. Her hair, as black as pitch, fell in twin braids down her back. Her tunic was ankle-length, shapeless.

When they reached the lodge, Red-Furred Bear was waiting for them. He nodded gravely as the woman invited him into the tipi, then he waited politely for Michael to take a seat before he removed the poultice from his shoulder and carefully examined the wound.

"*Epevomoxtaeoxz,*" Red-Furred Bear murmured, nodding. "It is better." Pleased with his handiwork, he bound the wound in a fresh poultice. *"Ne'sta'va'hose-voomatse,"* he said in parting. "I will see you again."

"You should rest now," the woman suggested.

"I'd rather sit outside."

"Very well." She picked up a robe and carried it outside where she spread it in the shade of a tree.

"I must go and help my mother," she said after making certain he was comfortable. "I will bring you something to eat when I return."

"Will you tell me your name before you go?" Michael asked.

"I am called Winter Song," she replied with a shy smile.

"I am called Wolf."

Michael spent a quiet hour sitting in the shade, somewhat bemused by what he saw. Nearby, an aged warrior was making arrows. Any warrior worth the name could make an arrow, but this man was a true artisan. He used red willow branches for the shafts, making sure they were the proper length, the correct weight. Michael had learned from Yellow Spotted Wolf that an arrow too light in the shaft would not fly straight; one that was too heavy would not carry far enough to be of much use. The old warrior used the feathers of a red-tailed hawk for fletching. Three feathers, Michael noted, never more, never less.

Across the way he saw a woman scraping the flesh from a deer hide, using the leg bone of a buffalo to remove the last bits of meat and skin.

It was hard work to turn a green hide into a piece of soft, workable cloth. Stripping the meat away was only the first step. Next, a mixture of brains, liver, and melted fat would be worked into the hide. When that was done, the skin would be soaked in water for several days, then the excess liquid would be stripped out with a long stone blade and the hide would be stretched to dry. Lastly, the hide would be pounded with a rock until it was soft and pliable.

Gazing into the distance, Michael saw two young boys racing their ponies along the riverbank. Nearby a handful of warriors were gambling. Across the way two young girls were taking turns brushing each other's hair. In the next lodge a woman was making a cradleboard.

Michael let out a long sigh. Everything was just as Yellow Spotted Wolf had said it had been in the shining times before the white man came. It was incredible. It was impossible. But it was true. He had prayed for a vision, had begged the Great Spirit for understanding, and he had been sent back in time to discover the past for himself.

And so, he mused, *I'm here. But for how long? A week? A month? A year? The rest of my life?*

He glanced around the village and thought of what it would be like to give up all the creature comforts he had so taken for granted: the expensive suits and luxury automobiles, the nights on the town, the beautiful, sweet-smelling women he had dated. It might be fun to stay here for a week or two, but what if he was here to stay? Could he adapt to the kind of life his great-grandfather had known? Living in a hide lodge, wearing a clout and moccasins, eating rough food . . . such things were all right for a lark, but forever?

He closed his eyes and thought of home. His apartment was large, comfortable, totally masculine. Every girl he had ever taken there had hinted that it needed a woman's touch, but he liked it as it was, a blending of earth tones, predominantly greens and browns.

He thought of the things he had taken for granted: radio, television, a daily newspaper to keep him informed on world events, running water, flush toilets, air conditioning in the summer and heat in the winter, fast cars, cold beer, fine wine, a good steak.

And his job. He liked what he did for a living, perhaps because he was damn good at it. His job . . . he'd told his secretary he'd be gone a couple of days, and now he'd been gone over a week. What would she think when he didn't call in and no one answered at his place? What would his boss think? No doubt Walsh would be angry at first, and then he'd begin to worry.

And what about Melinda? What would she think when he didn't call? They weren't engaged, or even going steady, but he dated her more often than anyone else, and he knew Melinda expected him to propose within the year.

Melinda. He liked the sound of her name, the

way she always looked up at him as if he were a cross between Valentino and Cary Grant. She was a tall, willowy girl, with shoulder-length blonde hair and peaceful blue eyes.

Melinda. He knew part of the reason she was so enamored of him was because of his Cheyenne blood. His ancestry fascinated her, and she often teasingly referred to him as her handsome savage, especially when they were alone in his apartment, curled up on the rug in front of the fireplace. There was no derision in her voice when she called him a hot-blooded heathen, only a kind of curious excitement, stirred, perhaps, by the distant memory that, in another time and place, he would have been forbidden to her.

He chuckled softly, wondering what Melinda would think of him if she could see him clad in fringed buckskin leggings and moccasins instead of a sharp three-piece suit and hundred-dollar boots. Would she still find him fascinating? He knew instinctively that she would be repelled, and the thought made him angry.

At dusk he made his way into the timber, walking deep into the shadowy forest until he could no longer hear the sounds of the village. There, alone, he lifted his arms toward heaven. He had prayed himself into this mess, he mused with a wry grin, perhaps he could pray himself out.

Head thrown back, eyes closed, he prayed to *Heammawihio*, asking the Great Spirit to send him back where he belonged.

He prayed fervently, heedless of the cool wind that blew down out of the north, unmindful of the growing ache in his wounded shoulder.

The moon rose high in the sky, and still he prayed, but no vision appeared to him, no spoken words broke the stillness of the night. Instead, a gentle peace dropped over him, like the touch of loving arms, and a quiet voice whispered in the back of his mind, assuring him that he was where he was meant to be.

With a low groan, he lowered his arms and sank down on the ground.

And again he heard that faint inner voice.

You are where you were meant to be.

Chapter 9

That evening after dinner Michael asked Winter Song if Mo'ohta-vo'nehe was a member of the tribe.

The girl's mouth dropped open and she clapped her hand over it as her eyes widened. "Yellow Spotted Wolf!" she exclaimed. "That is who you remind me of. Are you related? You look much like him."

"He is my . . . my cousin."

Winter Song jumped to her feet. "I will get him for you," she said, and ran out of the lodge.

She returned minutes later, followed by four Indians. Michael recognized Yellow Spotted Wolf immediately. They did, indeed, look very much alike. At sixteen, Yellow Spotted Wolf was tall and broad-shouldered. He wore his long black hair in two thin braids in front and loose down his back. A single white eagle feather adorned his hair, a necklace of shells and turquoise circled his throat, a wide copper band hugged his right bicep.

"I am Mo'ohta-vo'nehe," said the tall warrior standing beside Yellow Spotted Wolf. "Winter Song tells me that you and I are related."

"We are distant relatives," Michael said. "I have come a long way to find you."

Mo'ohta-vo'nehe lifted one thick black brow. "How are we related? Who are your people?"

"It is difficult to explain," Michael replied, wishing he dared tell them the truth. "My name is Wolf, and I am related to your family by blood. More than that I cannot tell you."

Mo'ohta-vo'nehe pondered that for a moment. He had no doubt that the man called Wolf was related to him. The resemblance between the stranger and Yellow Spotted Wolf was too remarkable to be coincidence.

"If what you say is true, what do you want of me?" Mo'ohta-vo'nehe asked.

"I need shelter until I can build a lodge of my own. I was raised a long way from here, and it is my desire to return to my people, to learn their ways."

"You are welcome here, Wolf," Mo'ohta-vo'nehe decided. "You will stay with us as long as you wish." He nodded to the woman standing on his right. "This is my wife, Hemene, and these are my sons, Yellow Spotted Wolf and Badger.''

Michael nodded at each one in turn, his heart pounding like a war drum as he gazed at Yellow Spotted Wolf. This was his great-grandfather, the man he had loved and respected. And buried less than a week ago. He longed to throw his arms around the young man, to pour out who he was and where he had come from, but the time was not right. Perhaps later, when his family knew him better, when they trusted him, perhaps then he would tell them who he was.

"Come," Mo'ohta-vo'nehe said. "Let us go to our lodge. We have much to discuss.''

Michael thanked Winter Song and her family for their hospitality, then followed Mo'ohta-vo'nehe to his lodge, his excitement mounting with each step.

Mo'ohta-vo'nehe's lodge was large and comfortable. Willow backrests were placed on either side of the firepit, sleeping robes were situated at the back of the lodge.

Mo'ohta-vo'nehe sat down and indicated that Michael should sit on his left, the place of honor in a Cheyenne household.

Michael obligingly sat down, remembering that it was not considered good etiquette to pass between the owner of the lodge and the fire. Well-bred people passed behind a lodge's occupants.

Hemene took up a moccasin and began to decorate it with porcupine quills. Badger sat on his sleeping robe, his dark eyes alight with curiosity for their guest. Yellow Spotted Wolf sat across from his father, his hands resting on his knees.

Mo'ohta-vo'nehe took up his pipe. For a moment he held it reverently, and then he pointed the pipestem to the sky, to the ground, and to the four directions, saying, "Spirit Above, smoke. Earth, smoke. Four directions of the earth, smoke."

Smoking meant more to the Indians than it did to the white man. Among the Cheyenne, it was an important ceremony. The pipe, when passed, always went with the sun, from right to left. It was considered unlucky to touch anything with the pipestem while smoking. The ashes were not scattered after smoking, but were kept in a little pile near the edge of the fire, as befitting the sacred act of smoking.

On the reservation, Michael had known old men who would not smoke unless they were alone. There was to be no noise within the lodge, no dishes knocked together. Some men would not smoke if there was a woman in the lodge.

When the pipe had been passed, Mo'ohta-vo'nehe politely questioned Michael about his past, and Michael told him as much as he could, saying that he had been taken from his people at an early age and raised by a white family, and that when his white family died, he left their home to return to his own people, to learn the ways of his ancestors.

Mo'ohta-vo'nehe accepted his story, and Michael breathed a sigh of relief.

Later that night, lying beneath a soft buffalo robe, he gazed into the darkness and thought about who he was, and where he was. These Indians were nothing like the Indians on the reservation. These were not tame Indians. These men were warriors, fighters. They wore eagle feathers in their hair, necklaces made of bear claws at their throats, beaded armbands, and shirts decorated with the hair of their enemies. They carried stolen U.S. Army rifles and scalping knives.

The Cheyenne. They were his people, known to be the finest horsemen on the Plains, fearless in battle, ruthless to their enemies. And he was here, in their midst, one of them, and yet a stranger.

But he was here. Incredible as it seemed, he was here.

A thrill of excitement brought a smile to his face. He was here, and while he was here, he would learn to be a warrior. He would learn to ride like the wind, to hunt the buffalo, to fight and to kill. And, yes, to take a scalp. He would join one of the warrior societies if they would have him, the *Wohkseh'hetoniu*, perhaps, or the *Mota'mita'niu*. He would make a name for himself, a name Yellow Spotted Wolf would be proud of. And perhaps he would court Winter Song.

He closed his eyes and summoned her image to mind: smooth dusky skin, hair as black as ebony, eyes as dark as onyx, and a smile to warm a man's soul. Winter Song.

Yes, he thought with a wide grin, living in the past held many interesting possibilities.

Chapter 10

*T*he days that followed were filled with discovery and excitement.

He had prayed for a vision, hoping for some blinding burst of knowledge that would better help him understand his heritage, some miracle that would enable him to fulfill his great-grandfather's dying wish. And instead of a vision, he had been plunged into the past. Rather like asking for a glass of milk and being given the whole cow instead.

Be careful what you ask for, lest you get it.

But for now, he would change nothing. He embraced the Cheyenne life-style, eager to learn. And he gained a new appreciation for the Indian people. But best of all were the hours he spent with his great-grandfather.

Each day Michael vowed to tell Yellow Spotted Wolf who he was, but somehow he could never find the words. It was hard to listen to his great-grandfather talk about the future, about how good life would be when the whites were defeated and the land belonged to the People again.

"What if you could see into the future?" Michael asked Yellow Spotted Wolf one night.

Yellow Spotted Wolf shook his head. "I do not want to know what turns my path in life will take. I want to discover what lies ahead one step at a time, as *Maheo* intended. If there is happiness waiting, I will be glad, and if sorrow comes, I will mourn."

"But what if you could know for certain what life held in store for you?" Michael argued. "What if you could know how long you would live, the girl you would marry?"

Yellow Spotted Wolf grunted softly. "I know what lies before me," he said confidently. "I have received a vision from the Great Spirit and He has told me the path to follow. Life is not life without change, but I have been told that long life awaits me if I hold tight to the ways of the people."

"But . . ."

Yellow Spotted Wolf silenced him with a gesture. "To know the future is to rob it of life. There would be no honor in battle, no risk, if I knew I could not be killed. There would be no excitement in courtship, no anticipation of acceptance or fear of rejection, if I knew who my mate would be. It is enough to know that the Great Spirit has promised me long life. I do not want to know how long."

Michael nodded. Yellow Spotted Wolf was right, he mused, and wished that the knowledge of what the future held for his people did not weight so heavily on his mind.

He had been in the Cheyenne camp a little over a week when some of the warriors began preparing to go in search of the buffalo. Mo'ohta-vo'nehe was in charge, so naturally Michael went along.

They left early in the morning, the medicine man's blessing on the hunt, the warriors, and their horses still ringing in their ears. Michael carried a bow made of mulberry wood. A quiver containing a half-dozen arrows was slung over his left shoulder. The quiver was made of panther skin, the tail still attached. It was, he thought, a thing of beauty. No one had asked him if he knew how to use a bow; he was a Cheyenne, after all. It was assumed that he was a warrior, that he was familiar with weapons.

Mounted on the big bay he had stolen from Deadwood Gulch, he rode alongside Yellow Spotted Wolf, wondering what he'd do if he actually had to use the bow. Yellow Spotted Wolf had taught him to string a bow, how to hold an arrow, how to sight down the shaft. But Michael had been a boy then, and his bow had been more of a toy than a real weapon.

They rode all that morning, and as the hours passed, Michael felt himself growing more at ease on horseback. The bay had a smooth walk and a soft, responsive mouth. But then Mo'ohtavo'nehe urged his horse into a trot, and Michael knew his horsemanship needed a lot of improvement before he could ride as well as his companions.

It was nearing noon when they spied a small herd of buffalo. Once, the herds had covered hundreds of miles. Yellow Spotted Wolf had told of a time when the huge animals covered the earth like a great shaggy brown blanket, when it had taken a warrior three days to ride around the Northern herd. But those days were gone. The whites had been slaughtering the buffalo for years, taking the hides and sometimes the tongues, and leaving thousands of tons of meat to rot in the sun. It was the loss of the buffalo as much as anything else that had forced the majority of the Indians onto reservations. The Indians depended on the buffalo for their very life; they could not survive without them.

He put the thought from his mind as he watched the warriors move into position. They moved like drifting shadows, making no sound to spook the herd. There was a soft sibilant twang of bowstrings, the muted swish of feathered shafts, the solid smack of arrows penetrating tough shaggy hides.

The bodies of some ten to fifteen of the huge, curly-haired animals littered the ground before the herd took flight.

It was amazing, Michael thought. One minute the buffalo were grazing peacefully, unconcerned by the sight of their fellows dropping to the ground all around them, and the next the herd was on the move. Heads lowered, tails lifted, the buffalo thundered across the plains, their cloven hooves stirring great clouds of yellow dust, their squeals and snorts filling the air.

He had never seen or heard anything like it. Like a runaway freight train, the herd raced away, the sound of their passing lingering in the air long after they were out of sight.

"We should have brought the women," Mo'ohta-vo'nehe remarked as Michael rode up beside him.

Dismounting, Michael examined Mo'ohta-vo'nehe's first kill, a huge old buffalo bull.

"His hide will make a fine shield," Mo'ohta-vo'nehe remarked.

Michael grinned in reply, then felt the vomit rise in his throat as Mo'ohta-vo'nehe slit the buffalo's throat and lapped up a handful of steaming red blood.

The warriors laughed and called back and forth as they dined on fresh hearts and livers and sucked the marrow from the bones.

Michael shook his head as Yellow Spotted Wolf offered him a chunk of bloody buffalo heart.

The men worked hard for the next couple of hours. They skinned the buffalo, quartered the meat, and packed it in the hides, which were then placed on hastily made travois for the trip back to camp.

"You did not join in the hunt," Yellow Spotted Wolf remarked as they rode back to the village.

"It has been many years since I used a bow," Michael said. "I did not want to shame Mo'ohta-vo'nehe with my ignorance."

"I will teach you," Yellow Spotted Wolf offered.

Michael nodded, aware of the close bond that was being forged between them. He wondered if Yellow Spotted Wolf felt it too.

A shout went up as the hunters returned to the village. Women swarmed around the travois, their mouths watering as they began to divide the meat. There would be a feast that night, with singing and dancing as the People expressed their joy and gratitude to *Heammawihio*.

Michael spent the rest of the day sitting in the shade, his gaze forever straying to where Winter Song and her mother were working side by side, scraping the hair from one of the buffalo hides that Winter Song's father had brought home. The scent of roasting buffalo meat filled the air, as did the squeals and growls of the camp dogs as they fought over bones and scraps.

As dusk fell, the women fed their little ones and put them to bed, and then the men gathered in a circle, sitting on the ground or on blankets.

Before the feast began, a little from each kettle was offered to the spirits, the food being held up to the sky and then placed on the ground near the edge of the fire.

Michael's mouth watered as the women began to serve up platters of steaks and ribs, wild vegetables and freshly picked berries. It was, he decided, the best meal he'd ever had, or perhaps it only seemed so because of Winter Song. He smiled at her as she served him a slice of succulent tenderloin, felt his heart beat fast when she smiled back at him, her dark eyes warm with affection and promise.

Later, after everyone had eaten their fill, the drumming began. The warriors who had participated in the hunt danced first, telling how they had tracked the buffalo, boasting of their daring as they stalked the herd, bragging about their kills.

The dancers were magnificent, Michael thought as he watched them. Paint streaked their faces, feathers adorned their long black hair, sweat glistened on their bodies as they danced around the fire. They were free men, free in a way that white men were never free. The Cheyenne owned little, and so they had no need for big houses or fancy apartments. They had no need for money, so they didn't have to worry about jobs or making ends meet. They had no debts, no mortgages, no loan payments. Their religion was an integral part of their daily life, so they had no need for churches or temples. Their god was found in the mountains, in the grasses, in the rushing rivers and sun-kissed trees. They were not bound by the rules and restrictions of civilization, only by the ancient traditions of their fathers.

He watched as they danced and sang, the sights and sounds alien and yet familiar. The beat of the drum was the beat of his own heart, the soft guttural sounds of his childhood tongue were like sweet music. The smell of smoke and pine and aromatic sage surrounded him like welcoming arms. But it was Winter Song who held his attention.

How beautiful she was! Her hair was as black as the night, her skin the color of the earth, her eyes as dark and fathomless as the sky. She wore a doeskin tunic the color of fresh cream, the texture of velvet. Soft moccasins beaded in red and yellow hugged her feet. A shell necklace circled her throat.

Someday, he vowed, she would be his.

He was becoming a warrior. Little by little, he was becoming a warrior. He sat with the men in the evening, listening to their tales of courage and bravery, hearing the names of chiefs he had read about in history books, caught up in battles that had been fought a hundred years before he had been born. He ate what the warriors ate—succulent tenderloin, roast buffalo hump, venison, elk, wild fruits and vegetables, jerky and pemmican, stews and broths and thick soups flavored with onions and sage and turnips. He dressed as they dressed, wearing only a clout and moccasins when it was warm, fringed leggings and a heavy buckskin shirt when it was cool. He played their games, slept in a hide lodge, smoked *na'koo'neeheso*, a mixture of dried leaves and bark.

And he courted a Cheyenne maiden. To this

end, he acquired a flute from a medicine man known for his power in affairs of the heart. It was a thing of beauty, his flute, made for the music of love. Its shape was that of a long-necked bird with an open beak, and he often played it outside Winter Song's lodge in the dark of the night.

His chances to see her alone were rare. Often he rose early in the morning so he could meet her at the river when she went to draw water. But those moments were brief and the chance of discovery great.

Courting a white girl had been much easier, Michael mused. Alone, in the dark cocoon of a parked car, anything could happen, and often did. But he was rarely alone with Winter Song, for the Cheyenne held the chastity of their women in high regard. He thought often of coaxing her away from the village, but leaving the camp was risky. Alone in the tall grass there was always danger. You could be gored by a buffalo, attacked by a grizzly, killed by a band of marauding Pawnee or Crow, or captured by the *mila hanska*, the Long Knives.

But late at night he could let his emotions soar in the plaintive notes of his flute. Sitting in the dark outside Winter Song's lodge, he let the soft, crying notes of the flute speak to her of the feelings in his heart, of his longing, of his loneliness.

Of course, he was not the only man courting Winter Song. She was a woman of rare beauty, a woman from a good family, one with pleasing manners. Many of the young warriors, and a few of the older ones, sought her hand, but her most persistent suitors were Michael and Two Ponies. Some nights there were as many as six or seven men gathered outside her lodge, each waiting for a chance to speak with Winter Song. There was much speculation in the camp as to whom she would eventually choose for her husband. Most of the people favored Two Ponies, for he had been courting her for almost two years, but a few of the more discerning women in the tribe shook their heads, declaring that Two Ponies had lost the race the day Wolf took up residence in the village.

When he was not courting Winter Song, Michael was practicing the skills necessary to be a warrior. He spent one whole day learning the proper way to take a scalp. Though scalps were not held in high regard by the Cheyenne, the taking of a scalp was something a warrior needed to know. Often scalps were used as emblems of victory, and it was a good thing to carry an enemy's scalp back to camp to rejoice and dance over, although any part of an enemy's body would serve just as well. Scalps were often used as trim for war clothing or fringe on shirts and leggings, or to tie to a horse's bridle when going to war. Usually a scalp was only a little larger than a silver dollar, though on occasion the whole skin of the head was taken.

"Now you know how," Yellow Spotted Wolf said after describing the procedure. "When you take your first scalp, you will receive instruction from my father on how the scalp should be handled."

"What do you mean, handled?"

"Scalps must be stretched over a hoop, but before any work is done, my father will light his pipe and offer it to the earth and the sky, then the stem will be held toward the scalp and he will offer a prayer for further good fortune.

"Next, the scalp will be placed on a buffalo chip, flesh side up. You must take a piece of charcoal from the fire and rub it over both sides of your knife, from the hilt to the point, then you must hold the knife over the scalp and say, 'May we again conquer our enemies.' Then, using the point of your knife, you will cross-cut the scalp from north to south, then east to west, always beginning at the edge of the skin away from yourself. Once the scalp is properly prepared and secured to the hoop, it will be attached to a willow pole, unless you wish to use it for decoration."

"Seems like a lot of trouble for a piece of hair," Michael remarked.

Yellow Spotted Wolf shrugged. "It is the way of our people. Did those who raised you not teach you how to lift a scalp and how to preserve it?"

"No, they didn't do a lot of scalping where I come from."

Yellow Spotted Wolf grunted softly. "If you find the taking of a scalp distasteful, it need not be done. It is the counting of coup that denotes bravery and courage, not the taking of a scalp.

Any man who goes into battle carrying only a hatchet or a war club is considered brave indeed, for these weapons require hand-to-hand combat and cannot be used from a distance. A lance is more creditable than a bow. Bravest of all is to carry only a coup stick. Our people count coup on an enemy only three times."

"Sounds like a good way to commit suicide," Michael muttered.

"A brave man does not consider suicide, but a man who has been long sick, or one who has had great misfortune and wishes to die often declares that he is going to give his body to the enemy."

"You're kidding."

"Some years ago, Sun Path declared he would do just such a thing. He had been ill for many months and had given up all hope of recovery. His father agreed and, after giving his son his strongest medicine and a fine horse, sent Sun Path off with a war party, armed only with a small hatchet.

"After they reached the land of the Pawnee, they encountered two warriors returning from a hunt. Both of the Pawnee had guns. Our people charged the Pawnee. Sun Path, who was riding his father's best war horse, quickly overtook one of the Pawnee warriors, who turned and tried to shoot him, but the gun misfired and Sun Path killed him with his hatchet and took his scalp. The other Pawnee was also killed.

"Sun Path had completed his vow and he returned to our people, a hero."

Michael frowned. "I thought he went out to die."

"He did. But he did not die, and his sickness left him."

"Because he took a scalp?"

Yellow Spotted Wolf shrugged. "Who can say?"

"I think you made that story up."

"There is his lodge," Yellow Spotted Wolf said, gesturing at a tall tipi painted with suns and moons and bright blue stars.

"Okay," Michael said, "I believe you."

Yellow Spotted Wolf grinned. "The taking of a scalp is important, but more important is being able to ride, to be one with your horse."

"I can ride."

Yellow Spotted Wolf snorted. "You ride like an old woman. I have a fine gray stallion, but he has not yet been broken to ride. If you can tame him, he is yours."

"And if I can't?"

"I have an old mare my girl cousins ride."

"All right, where's this horse?"

Michael was soon sorry he had agreed to try to break the stallion in question. The horse bucked like a rodeo bronc, quickly unseating Michael.

Word soon spread that Wolf was trying to break Yellow Spotted Wolf's big gray stallion, and a score of men and women gathered to watch the fun.

Michael swore softly when he saw Two Ponies and Winter Song in the front of the crowd. He could not give up now. No matter how many times he was thrown, he could not give up. There was more at stake now than a horse.

But riding a bareback pony was like sitting on a piece of waxed paper, and no matter how hard he wrapped his legs around the gray's middle, the horse threw him with ease. Michael knew there were places on his body that would be black and blue and sore in the morning, but he mounted the stallion again and again, determined not to let Two Ponies see him defeated, determined to look good in Winter Song's eyes.

Gradually he managed to stay on the horse's back for longer and longer periods of time. He learned to match his movements to that of the horse, and he began to realize that it wasn't brute strength that kept him on the animal's back, but the ability to move in rhythm with the horse, to anticipate its next move, to roll with the punches, so to speak.

And finally, after what seemed like hours, the stallion stood quiet and Michael was still on its back. Both were sweating profusely and breathing hard.

Michael smiled faintly. He didn't know if he'd broken the horse to ride or just worn it out, but at the moment it didn't matter. He had won.

He saw the admiration in Winter Song's eyes, the envy and thinly veiled loathing in the hard stare of Two Ponies, and he knew he had won a great victory.

And he owed it all to Yellow Spotted Wolf.

There was a courtship dance that night, given by the *Wohkseh'hetaniu*, or Fox Soldiers, one of the warrior societies. There were several such groups, among them the *Mim'oweyuhkis*, or Elk Soldiers; the *Hota'mita'niu*, or Dog Soldiers, and the *Mahohe'was*, or Red Shields, who were also called the Bull Soldiers. The Kit Soldiers claimed superiority over all other bands; both Mo'ohta-vo'nehe and Yellow Spotted Wolf belonged to this society.

Michael did not hesitate when Winter Song chose him to be her partner in the first dance. Nor did he miss the look of resentment on the face of Two Ponies as he took his place across from Winter Song. Two Ponies was a tall warrior, with broad shoulders and muscular arms. Many of the maidens desired him, but he had eyes only for Winter Song, and everyone in the village knew it.

Michael felt a slight twinge of guilt, knowing that Two Ponies had been sure of winning Winter Song's hand in marriage before he, Michael, had entered the picture. But his guilt was quickly swept away when Winter Song's gaze met his. Face to face, they moved to the right and then to the left. The steps were simple and uncomplicated, and though they never touched during the dance, he was ever aware of the young woman across from him. Once she smiled at him and he felt the warmth of it touch his soul.

Some time passed before he had a chance to dance with her again, and when the dance was over, he spoke to her quickly and quietly, urging her to meet him in the shadows, and then he left the dance lodge, wondering if he had been too bold.

He walked into the darkness beyond the first lodge, certain she would never follow him.

And then he heard the sound of her footsteps.

He felt the blood pound in his brain as she drew close to him. She was trembling like a rabbit caught in a trap as she slowly lifted her gaze to his, and he knew that she had never gone walking into the shadows with any other man. But she had come to him. The thought filled him with exhilaration, and a sudden, unwelcome sense of responsibility.

"Do you want to go back?" he asked.

Winter Song shook her head. "No."

"Is it wrong for us to meet like this?"

A shy smile curved her lips. "No. Young people often sneak away to be alone."

"But . . ."

"It is best not to get caught."

Michael chuckled, amused by her answer and her honesty.

Taa'e-ese'he, the night sun, washed her hair in silver, and Michael thought he had never seen anything more lovely than Winter Song standing in the moonlight.

Murmuring her name, he drew her into his arms and held her close. Her hair was like black silk beneath his cheek.

After a long moment he tilted her face upward and kissed her, gently. She had never been kissed before; he knew it instantly, and it pleased him beyond words. She would be his, only his.

Winter Song gazed up at him, her eyes filled with wonder and surprise as she placed her fingertips to her lips.

"Did that not please you?"

"It pleased me very much," she replied, and standing on tiptoe, she pressed her lips to his.

She was, Michael mused, a quick study. Her kiss was sweet and inexperienced and left him yearning for more, much more.

It would be so easy to press her to the ground and make love to her. So easy . . . he let his hand slide down her back, along her thigh. He paused as he felt the protective rope. It was something all proper and decent Cheyenne women wore, a thin rope that passed around the wearer's waist and was knotted in front, then passed down and between her thighs, each end of the rope wrapping around the thigh and down to her knee.

All men, both young and old, respected the rope.

And so did Michael.

"Come along," he said, taking her by the hand. "We'd better go back to camp before one of us gets in trouble."

Chapter 11

It was surprising how easily he adapted to the Cheyenne way of life.

Songs he had been taught as a child came back to him, old stories he had heard from Yellow Spotted Wolf, games he had all but forgotten.

He practiced with his bow, wanting Yellow Spotted Wolf to be proud of him. He used a hide for a target; a buffalo hide at first, then the hide of an elk, then a small deer, and finally a rabbit.

Yellow Spotted Wolf taught him how to track a deer, an elk, a bear, how to find water on the plains, which plants were good for food, which were poisonous. Despite his youth, Yellow Spotted Wolf had acquired a great deal of knowledge and he shared it willingly. If he wondered at his cousin's ignorance in such basic skills, he never mentioned it.

For Michael, it wasn't so much learning as remembering the lessons that a much older Yellow Spotted Wolf had taught him at the reservation so long ago.

When he wasn't hunting or tracking or practicing with his bow, Michael was stalking Winter Song. He waited for her at the river, hoping to catch her alone so they might share a few words. Sometimes he followed when she went to gather wood, pleased when she smiled in his direction. And at night, he continued to let his flute sing to her of his love.

A Cheyenne warrior was expected to court the maiden of his choice from one to five years. After he felt certain of her consent, he applied to her parents or older brother for approval, usually sending an old friend or his mother to ask for the girl's hand in marriage. With the messenger he sent a number of horses, as many as he could afford to give. The messenger tied the horses in front of the father's lodge and then went inside and said, "A young man wishes to take your daughter to wife."

After naming the young man, the messenger left the lodge without waiting for a reply.

But Michael could not wait five years, and after waiting five months, he went to Yellow Spotted Wolf for advice.

The young warrior shook his head. "Winter Song's parents will never approve the marriage. You must be patient. Prove yourself in battle.

Count coup on our enemy. Offer her parents a part of your next kill. They must know you can protect their daughter, that you can provide for her."

"I can't wait," Michael insisted. "Two Ponies will not wait. You have seen the way he looks at her."

Yellow Spotted Wolf nodded. "The father of Winter Song has long approved the match between Two Ponies and his daughter. Two Ponies is a fine warrior, a brave man in battle, a hunter of great knowledge and skill. This is what you must become."

"Then show me how."

Yellow Spotted Wolf grinned. "First, we must prove you can provide meat for Black Knife's daughter. Tomorrow we will go hunting."

They left at dawn, just the two of them, armed with bows and arrows. Michael rode behind Yellow Spotted Wolf, admiring the easy way his great-grandfather sat his horse, the proud lift of Yellow Spotted Wolf's head. He was already a warrior, a man who was well respected by the elders of the tribe. He had proved his bravery in battle, he had counted coup on the Pawnee and taken a Crow scalp. He had captured ponies from their enemies, and ridden to war against the *vehoe*. All who knew Yellow Spotted Wolf expected that, one day, he would be a great leader among his people.

But it would never happen, Michael thought with regret, and shook the bleak images of the future from his mind. Today was not a day for sad thoughts about what would be. Today was a day for rejoicing. He smiled as he recalled how his day had begun.

As was the custom, he had left his lodge early and offered a morning prayer to *Heammawihio* before going to the river to bathe. The water was icy and he wished fleetingly for a warm bath, but he scrubbed himself vigorously and returned to the lodge. It was amazing how quickly he had become accustomed to praying each morning, he who had never put much faith in prayer. But it was a good way to start the day, filling him with a sense of peace, of unity and belonging. Usually, Hemene had breakfast waiting for him when he returned to the lodge, but he had gone without on this day, for he had risen before dawn to meet Yellow Spotted Wolf.

Michael grinned as his stomach growled loudly. Perhaps being hungry would give added purpose to the hunt.

They had reached a well-traveled game trail now and Yellow Spotted Wolf dismounted, motioning for Michael to do likewise. Side by side, they knelt behind a clump of brush, bows ready.

Michael took a deep breath, drawing in the cool, crisp scent of early morning. The grass was damp beneath his moccasined feet, the air cool where it whispered across his cheeks. A bird twittered in one of the trees, a rabbit scurried across the trail and then, seeing the two warriors, quickly disappeared into a hole, its tail flashing white before it ducked out of sight.

And then the deer came, their dark noses

testing the breeze as they made their way toward the stream. Four does, a buck, two yearlings, and three spotted fawns.

Like two men pulled by the same string, Michael and Yellow Spotted Wolf loosed their arrows and one of the does and a yearling fawn sprang into the air and then fell to the ground. The rest of the herd turned and fled.

Yellow Spotted Wolf stood up and examined the kill. "Why did you chose the yearling?"

"It was hurt."

Yellow Spotted Wolf nodded his approval. "Well done," he declared. "Winter Song's father will be impressed with a good clean kill, and with the prospect of fresh meat."

It was early afternoon when they returned to the camp. Michael's gaze quickly sought Winter Song's lodge and there, to his dismay, he saw six ponies tethered near the entrance.

He knew immediately that Two Ponies had sent someone to ask for Winter Song's hand in marriage. The warrior had purposely picked a day when Michael was out of the village. The horses were all prime stock, young and in good health.

"She has not yet said yes," Yellow Spotted Wolf remarked.

Michael nodded. If the proposal had been accepted, Black Knife would have sent Winter Song and at least seven horses to the lodge of Two Ponies.

"I have eight fine horses," Yellow Spotted Wolf mused. "They are yours."

Michael smiled broadly. *"Ne'a'ese!"* he said fervently. "Thank you!"

"I will be your go-between," Yellow Spotted Wolf offered. "We will place the deer we killed this morning on the backs of two of the horses. Surely, if Black Knife will consider you at all, he will accept such a generous offer, for it is greater than that of Two Ponies."

"When?" Michael asked. "Should you do it now?"

"Yes," Yellow Spotted Wolf answered gravely. "We dare not wait any longer."

Michael went to Mo'ohta'vo'nehe's lodge, where he paced restlessly back and forth. Once, he peered out and saw that the eight horses had been tied across from the offering of Two Ponies, and even as he watched, Yellow Spotted Wolf emerged from Black Knife's lodge.

"There is nothing to do now but wait," Yellow Spotted Wolf remarked as he entered the lodge a few moments later.

Mo'ohta-vo'nehe and Hemene exchanged a-mused grins as Michael began to pace back and forth again. It was the way of youth, the waiting, the anxiety. Often, a girl held her answer until the last minute, knowing that her suitor would be anxiously awaiting a reply.

As darkness fell, Michael heaved a heavy sigh of exasperation. Winter Song would have to make her decision soon. According to custom, the horses might not stand outside her lodge for more than one night. The horses must be accepted or sent back. If the horses were accepted, the marriage would take place within the week.

He scowled bleakly. What chance did he have to win her hand in such a short time? Two Ponies had been courting her for years. And what would he do if she decided to marry Two Ponies? How could he stay in the village, see her every day, and know she would never be his?

He halted in mid-stride at the sound of hoofbeats approaching the lodge. His heart seemed to stop, and then raced in wild excitement as Hemene welcomed Winter Song into the lodge.

The next few minutes seemed to pass in a blur as Mo'ohta-vo'nehe and Hemene offered Winter Song a seat and something to eat, and then they discussed the wedding, when it should be, and decided it would be in two days.

Two days, Michael thought, elated. In two days she would be his.

Chapter 12

Michael reined his horse toward home. He had gone riding along the river, needing time to be alone, time to think.

Tomorrow was his wedding day, and he supposed he had a bad case of premarital jitters. He had never seriously contemplated marriage before and he wondered if he was ready for it now. He thought briefly of Melinda, the only woman he'd ever been serious about, and wondered what she was doing and if she ever thought of him any more. He wondered who had taken over his job at Walsh Cadillac, and what the new cars looked like, but somehow those things didn't really matter now. His life in L.A. and the people he had known there all seemed like a distant dream. This was his reality now, the endless plains, the distant mountains, the close bond he shared with Yellow Spotted Wolf, the mystery that was Winter Song . . .

Winter Song. She was so beautiful, so fragile. He could not believe his good fortune in winning her hand. Even now he was hard-pressed to believe she would be his, afraid she would disappear in the mists of time.

He felt a sudden chill, as if the sun had gone cold. Filled with a sudden anxiety, he urged his horse into a lope.

Too late, the wind seemed to say. *Too late*.

He reined his horse to a walk as he reached a sharp bend in the river. He was almost home.

Rounding the bend, he saw three women struggling with three men. At first he thought the couples were wrestling in good fun, but then he heard the frightened cries of the women, noticed the roached scalplocks of the men.

Pawnee!

Raising his lance overhead, Michael raced across the river. Fear clawed at his heart, fear that he was indeed too late, and that he didn't have the courage to fight, to take a life.

By the time he reached the opposite shore, two of the women had managed to free themselves from the enemy and were running back to the village. The third had collapsed. She lay still, one arm above her head. A thin trickle of blood oozed from the corner of her mouth. Her eyes were dark and lifeless.

It was Winter Song.

He gazed at her broken body for what seemed

an eternity and as he did so, he felt the last vestiges of civilization break and fall away.

Reining his horse in a tight rearing turn, he charged the three retreating warriors, killing the first with a well-aimed thrust of his lance.

The other two warriors vaulted onto their horses and galloped for home with Michael in pursuit.

She was dead.

The thought pounded in his brain, relentlessly repeating itself. He glanced at the blood dripping from the tip of his lance and knew he would not rest until the other two lay dead at his feet. He would take their scalps and dip his hands in their blood . . .

The land dropped and he lost sight of his prey. With a wild cry he urged his horse onward, and only when he started down the brush-covered slope did he realize he'd ridden into a trap.

The Pawnee on his left fired at him point-blank, and Michael felt the heat of the bullet sear his flesh as it tore into his right side. He reeled backward, his hand grabbing for his horse's mane, and as he did so, the second Pawnee warrior struck him across the back of the head with the butt of his rifle.

Bright lights flashed before Michael's eyes and he kicked his horse into a lope, the instinct for survival stronger than the agony in his bullet-torn flesh. He could hear the Pawnee yelling as they chased him and he knew certain death awaited him if he surrendered to the darkness that hovered all around him.

A narrow ravine loomed ahead and Michael jammed his heels into his mount's sides, felt the horse's hindquarters bunch as the animal prepared to make the jump.

A gunshot echoed in the stillness and Michael felt his horse shudder convulsively before it collapsed.

Time slowed to a crawl as the horse's momentum carried it over the edge of the ravine. A harsh cry of pain and fear exploded from Michael's lips as he tumbled head over heels down the rocky slope. He landed hard, the breath driven from his body as he hit the floor of the ravine.

Sound drifted down to him—the voices of the Pawnee as they debated whether he was dead or not, and whether his scalp was worth the long climb down the ravine . . . the distant notes of a bugle . . . the sound of many horses running hard . . . gunshots . . .

He frowned as he tried to make sense of it all, but before he could sort it out, blackness closed around him and he felt himself falling, spiraling down, down, into nothingness . . .

Part 3

Chapter 13

Elayna O'Brien swallowed the vomit rising in her throat as her father cut through the bone of the young soldier's left leg, severing it just below the knee. It was so sad, Elayna mused, so very sad. And so hard to watch, to know that Kelly North would be crippled for the rest of his life.

She mopped the sweat from her father's brow, quickly handed him the instruments and sutures needed to complete the operation, and all the while her heart ached for Kelly North, and for the pain and anger and frustration that awaited him when he regained consciousness.

Robert O'Brien sighed as he removed his surgical mask and gloves and stepped away from the bloody operating table.

"It'll be touch and go for a while," O'Brien remarked, "but I think he'll make it."

Elayne nodded as she gazed at Private North's pale face. "But will he want to?"

Her father shrugged. "I saved his life. The rest is up to him."

Elayna was still thinking of Kelly North when she left the infirmary an hour later. Kelly was a likable young man, energetic and athletic. What would he do now?

She felt a renewed hatred for the Indians, who were forever on the prowl, attacking innocent settlers, massacring whole families, burning homesteads. Kelly North would still have two good legs if it weren't for a band of marauding Cheyenne who had attacked a peaceful Army supply train the day before.

She brushed a stray wisp of hair from her forehead as she thought of all the fine young men she had known who had been killed, the agony the wounded had suffered, the tears that had been shed by grieving families.

And yet, for all the danger of life in the West, she loved it. The glowing sunsets, the peaceful dawns, the vast rolling plains, the sense of wonder and awe that engulfed her whenever she looked at the distant mountains.

She sighed as her thoughts returned to Kelly North and the grim surgery she had witnessed. She'd never planned to be a nurse, but it seemed she was becoming one just the same. Her mother had always assisted at the hospital, and when she passed away, it had seemed natural for

Elayna to take her mother's place. Her initial squeamishness at the sight of blood and broken bones had soon passed, and in a short time she was helping her father stitch knife wounds, treat burns and snake bites, set broken bones, remove bullets and arrowheads from torn flesh. But watching as a man's leg was amputated was a new experience and one she hoped never to have again.

She was crossing the parade ground when she saw Lieutenant Lance Smythe walking toward her. He was a tall, handsome young man, with hair as yellow as an Iowa cornfield and eyes as blue as the sky overhead.

Elayna smiled a welcome as he closed the distance between them. She expected to marry Lance before the next year was out. Lance was the kind of man every woman dreamed of: dependable, loyal, honest, unfailingly kind, and if she sometimes wished he were more exciting, more unpredictable, well, she would learn to live with it, for his virtues far outweighed such questionable lacks.

"Bad time in surgery?" Lance asked as he fell into step beside her.

Elayna nodded. "Father had to amputate Kelly's leg just below the knee."

Lance swore softly. "Poor kid. I wonder what he'll do now. The Army was his whole life."

Elayna shook her head. "I don't know. Does he have any family?"

"A sister, I think. Down south someplace. Georgia, maybe, or South Carolina."

Lance took Elayna's hand and gave it a squeeze. She was a kind-hearted young woman and he loved her for that as much as for the beauty of her face and form. He placed a quick kiss on the top of her head. Her hair was a deep dark red, soft and thick, always tempting his touch. Her eyes were dark brown, like a handful of freshly turned earth, filled now with compassion for young North.

"Try not to think of Kelly for a while," Lance said. "He's young. He'll get by."

"How?" Elayna demanded. "His life is ruined, and all because of those damned savages! I hate them! Why don't they leave us alone? The West is big enough for all of us."

Lance grinned, amused by her temper and the unladylike profanity that occasionally slipped into her speech when she was angry.

"Why don't they leave us alone?" Elayna asked again. "We're not hurting them."

"I've no love for the Indians, Elayna, you know that. But this time they do have a legitimate grievance. We're trespassing on land our government promised them under treaty, and we'll continue to trespass so long as it's profitable."

"Profitable!" Elayna exclaimed. "All the gold and grazing land in the territory won't help Kelly get his leg back, or compensate him for its loss.

"Damned savages," she murmured. "I hope I never see another Indian again."

Chapter 14

*H*e *was lost in a land of gray shadows. Rough* hands took hold of him. He knew somehow that they were the enemy and he tried to fight them, but his arms and legs refused to do his bidding and he felt himself being lifted, carried.

The pain was more than he could bear, and he reached out for the welcome darkness that hovered all around him, melting into the blackness until he was lost in oblivion . . .

"A vision," Yellow Spotted Wolf said, his aged voice filled with conviction. *"A man needs a vision to guide him through life . . ."*

"What was meant to be, will be," Sitting Bull declared. *"You cannot change the future . . ."*

He swam through the darkness, and other voices reached his ears.

"Stupid savage, looks like he rode into that ravine on purpose . . ."

". . . Sioux, maybe, or Cheyenne . . ."

". . . bad hurt. Probably won't make it to the fort . . ."

White voices. He surrendered to the darkness again, letting the blackness enfold him like loving arms, protecting him from hurt and harm . . .

He was walking through a field of white flowers. The sky was white, the earth was white, and he was alone. And then he saw a woman walking toward him, her arms outstretched.

A white woman with dark red hair and earth-brown eyes. And a familiar voice whispered in the back of his mind.

She is waiting, the voice said. *Waiting for you.*

Chapter 15

Elayna O'Brien was breathing heavily when she awoke. A fine layer of perspiration dampened her forehead, her hands felt cold. Her mouth was dry.

She'd had it again, the same dream that had haunted her sleep for the last four nights.

Rising, she lit the candle on the table beside her bed, then went to stand at the window, looking out.

The night was dark and quiet. A pale yellow moon hung low in an indigo sky, lazily playing hide and seek with a handful of wispy, silver-tipped clouds.

Opening the window, she drew in a deep breath. The dream was always the same. A man came to her, bleeding and unconscious. A tall man, with dark hair and tawny skin. A forbidden man.

Elayna let out a long sigh. Her mother had been blessed with "the sight," or cursed, depending on how one viewed the gift. Mary Kathleen O'Brien had passed a portion of her gift to her daughter. Mary Kathleen had welcomed her talent for seeing into the future; her daughter did not.

She had not told anyone about her dream, not her father, not Lance, not even her best friend, Nancy Avery. She wished suddenly that her mother were still alive. Mary Kathleen would know what to make of the dream, if it signified a specific person or event or was merely a recurring dream of no importance at all.

Elayna shivered. She never saw the face of the man who invaded her dreams, yet she knew she would recognize him, and that he would change her life forever.

So much for a dream of no importance, she thought ruefully.

Shaking the phantom from her mind, she closed the window, blew out the candle, and climbed into bed, drawing the covers up to her chin.

It was just a dream. Nothing more.

"Just a dream," she murmured as she closed her eyes.

The notes of a bugle calling reveille made her frown and she flopped over on her stomach and pulled the covers over her head.

"No," she thought petulantly. "Not yet."

She heard her father's bedroom door open, heard his footsteps in the hall. He would be wanting breakfast soon, she thought, and wished someone else would go into the cold kitchen and light the fire and start the coffee.

Rising, she threw off her long white nightgown, washed quickly in the water she had drawn the night before, then dressed in the navy blue skirt and short-sleeved shirtwaist she wore when she helped her father in the camp infirmary.

But there were no patients in the infirmary today, and after sick call she would have the whole day to do with as she pleased. She might lay out a pattern for a new dress, she mused, or spend a quiet hour browsing through the latest mail order catalog, or catch up on the mending she had been neglecting for the past two weeks.

Humming softly, she made her bed, then went into the small sunlit kitchen to prepare breakfast.

She had just mixed the batter for flapjacks when there was a hurried knock at the back door and Private Anthony Jamison rushed into the room.

"Good morning, Tony," Elayna said, smiling at the young man. "Would you like some coffee?"

"No, thank you, Miss O'Brien. Your father sent me. Said for you to get over to the hospital right away."

"What's wrong?"

Jamison shrugged. "Lieutenant Smythe's patrol rode in a few minutes ago. Got a wounded Injun with 'em. He looks about dead, but you know your father. He's determined to save him.''

A cold chill passed down Elayna's spine as she removed her apron and tossed it over the back of a chair.

"Help yourself to coffee, Tony," she said, and hurried out the door.

A few minutes later she donned a clean white apron and slipped a net over her long red hair before stepping into the back room where her father performed surgery. There was a man on the operating table, a long lean man with straight black hair and dark skin.

A forbidden man. An Indian.

A quick mental image of young Kelly North lying on the same table flashed through Elayna's mind, and her stomach churned as she recalled the horror of watching her father amputate Kelly's leg below the knee, her hatred for all Indians growing stronger and deeper with each cut of the saw.

The Indian was unconscious. A sheet covered him from just below his waist to his knees. There was dried blood matted in his hair and across his chest, numerous lacerations on his arms and legs, and a wound that she quickly recognized as a bullet hole in his right side.

"He'll need stitches," her father said as he probed the wound in the back of the man's head. "He's got a deep gash here. When I get it closed up, we'll dig the slug out of his side."

Elayna nodded. Quickly, efficiently, she gathered the instruments her father would need, then began to wash the blood from the patient's wounds while her father washed his hands and slipped on a clean surgical gown.

"What happened to him?" Elayna asked as she began to disinfect the cuts on the man's right leg.

"I don't know. Lance's patrol found him lying unconscious in a ravine. Most of the men wanted to leave him there to die, but Lance thought the Indian might be able to give us some information on Sitting Bull's whereabouts."

Elayna nodded, her gaze on the man's face. It was a strong face, a handsome face, familiar somehow.

"What are his chances?" she asked, not certain she wanted the Indian to survive.

Robert O'Brien shook his head as he began to swab the man's right side with carbolic acid. "Not good. He's lost a lot of blood."

Elayna nodded, her heart thudding in her breast as her father began to stitch the man's wounds: twelve in the back of his head, twenty-eight in his side.

When her father was finished, Elayna wrapped a loose bandage around the Indian's head, another around his lean torso; then she covered him with a lightweight gray wool blanket and placed a pillow beneath his head.

"Well, we've done all we can," her father said as he washed the blood from his hands. "Let's go have breakfast."

* * *

Elayna sat at the wounded man's side, unable to take her eyes from his face. She was certain now. This was the man who had haunted her dreams and troubled her waking moments for almost a week. Though she had never seen his face in her dreams, she had recognized him instantly. Recognized him and been afraid.

Indian.

Earlier in the day they had moved him out of the operating room to a cot in the infirmary. During sick call, several of the men had made caustic remarks about having a "damned redskin" in the place.

"We're supposed to be killing the bastards," one of the old-timers had complained. "Not makin' 'em better."

Elayna had silently concurred, but her father had ordered the men to keep their opinions to themselves.

The post commander, Major Cathcart, had looked in on the wounded man shortly after noon, declaring that the Indian would have to be moved to the guardhouse as soon as possible. Until then, the major had insisted on cuffing the Indian's left leg to the cot's iron frame.

It was a decision that pleased Elayna. She would nurse him, but she did not want to have to worry about him getting out of bed and coming after her. She knew what Indians did to white women. She had seen the results more than once.

The man stirred restlessly on the bed, tossing the covers aside, mumbling incoherently. His fever was mounting, and she dipped a clean cloth into the basin of cool water in her lap and began sponging his face and chest, his arms and legs.

His eyelids fluttered open as the cool water touched his skin, and Elayna quickly dissolved one of her father's medicinal powders in a glass of water and held it to his lips. He drained the glass, and then his eyes closed and he was asleep.

An hour passed, and Elayna continued to sponge the man's face and torso. He muttered words occasionally, words she did not understand.

Once he wept softly, and she heard him murmur, "Grandfather, I'm sorry," over and over again.

She had never considered the fact that Indians had families, that they were capable of feeling sorrow or regret. It made him seem less savage, more human, and she hardened her heart, refusing to feel sorry for him. He was still an Indian. Nothing could change that.

At dusk she went home to prepare her father's dinner, and when she returned to the infirmary, the Indian's fever was worse. Removing the blanket that covered him, she replaced it with several large towels soaked in cool water. She tried not to notice his nakedness, but he was beautifully proportioned and she could not help but admire the lean length of him, the broad shoulders and well-muscled torso, his flat belly and muscular thighs.

Abruptly she drew her gaze away, her cheeks flaming. He was an Indian, and she was admiring him as if he were a work of art.

Each time he awoke she offered him water to drink, and then she offered him some broth she had made.

Her father stopped by once and prescribed some strong medicine to combat the fever, but he didn't sound hopeful.

"I'm afraid the major will have to find another source of information," Robert O'Brien remarked as he checked the patient's pulse and temperature. "I don't think this one's going to make it."

Chapter 16

Michael woke slowly, aware of nothing but the pain in his head and side, and a powerful thirst. It was an effort to open his eyes, and when he did so, his vision was blurred.

For a long moment he stared up at the white-washed ceiling, trying to remember what had happened, but his mind was a blank. And then, slowly, it all came back to him.

Winter Song was dead.

The pain of her death was worse than the pain in his body, and he wished suddenly that he had died too.

He closed his eyes and his mind filled with her image: beautiful black hair, expressive ebony eyes, a warm smile. Her laughter had filled him with joy, the promise in her eyes had made him invincible. He had wooed her and won her, and now she was lost to him forever.

"*Maheo*, hear me," he murmured. "If you really exist, send me home where I belong."

Home. If only he could go back to L.A. and forget the sight of her broken body lying on the sand, her eyes staring sightlessly at the sky, the blood on her chin, so red against the deathly pallor of her skin.

He had been content to be here, with her, but now she was gone and all the joy of life had died with her. What difference did it make who he was if she wasn't there?

He retreated into the darkness, withdrawing from the pain and the memory of her death.

He felt as though a long time had passed when he opened his eyes again. His first thought was of Winter Song and he vowed to avenge her death as soon as he recovered his strength. No Pawnee would be safe from his wrath until her blood had been avenged tenfold.

But first he had to return to the Cheyenne.

Slowly he turned his head to the left, wondering where he was and how he'd gotten there. A row of narrow cots took up most of the floor space along the wall. There were several large windows, closed against the night.

Turning his head to the right, he saw a woman sitting in a straight-backed chair beside his bed. She was asleep, her hands folded in her lap, her head resting against the back of the chair. She had a delicate nose, a generous mouth, and fine unblemished skin. Her hair was a rich dark red, and the color tripped a memory somewhere in the recesses of his mind.

He had seen her before, he thought. But where?

He tried to sit up, but a stabbing pain in his right side changed his mind and he swore softly. The past was a damned dangerous place, he mused bitterly. He'd been a part of it only a short time, and he'd already been wounded more times than he cared to count.

He shifted his weight on the bed, seeking a more comfortable position, and made two startling discoveries: he was stark naked under the sheet, and his left ankle was securely shackled to the cot's iron frame.

A crude oath escaped his lips as he rattled the chain on his ankle. Obviously he was a prisoner. But whose? And why?

He closed his eyes, trying to recall exactly what had happened after the Pawnee had attacked him, but his mind was a blank.

Voices whispered in the back of his mind. *What will be, will be . . . You are where you were meant to be. . . . She is waiting for you.*

A white woman.

With dark red hair.

He opened his eyes to find the woman awake and staring at him. He recognized her now. The woman whose image he had seen.

She is waiting, a voice had said. *Waiting for you*. What did it mean?

The woman rose gracefully to her feet and came toward him, her movements cautious. Bending, she placed her hand on his brow.

"You're going to be fine," she said, speaking each word slowly and distinctly, and then she frowned. "Do you speak English?"

"Of course," Michael replied, amused by her question.

"Well, good," she said. She smiled uncertainly as she took a step back from the bed, out of his reach. "How are you feeling?"

"I've been better," he muttered. "Where the hell am I? How'd I get here? Who are you?"

Elayna O'Brien frowned. She'd been out West for ten years now and had seen a number of Indians, both friendly and hostile. None of them had talked quite like this one. He sounded more like a white man than a savage.

"You've got a concussion," she informed him. "And a bullet wound in your side. My father says you're lucky to be alive. As for where you are, you're at Camp Robinson. One of the scouting patrols brought you in."

"How long have I been here?"

"Three days."

"Three days!" he exclaimed. "Damn!"

The woman leaned forward and he saw that her eyes were a clear brown, as dark as a handful of freshly churned earth.

"You didn't tell me who you are," he reminded her.

"My name's Elayna O'Brien. My father's the doctor here. He saved your life." She cocked her head to one side, studying him openly. "Who are you? Where did you learn to speak our language so well?"

"I'm Michael Wolf. I learned English in . . ." He broke off in mid-sentence. He had been about to tell her he had learned English in school, but this was 1875 or thereabouts and Indians didn't go to school. "I learned English from my father. I don't know who taught him."

"Isn't Michael an odd name for an Indian?"

Michael shrugged. "My mother liked it."

Elayna was about to ask who his mother was when the door opened and her father entered the room.

"How is he?" Robert O'Brien asked as he crossed the room.

"He seems fine," Elayna replied. "I was just about to take his temperature."

O'Brien grunted softly as he placed a hand on his patient's brow, then checked his pulse and listened to his heartbeat. "His fever's gone, heart and pulse are normal."

Elayna nodded, her feelings ambivalent.

"We'll have to get Crowfoot in here tomorrow. I'd like to ask our patient a few questions."

"He speaks English, father."

"He does?" O'Brien said, his surprise obvious as he looked at Michael. "You speak our language?"

Michael nodded.

"Well, good," O'Brien said. "Do you remember how you got here?"

"No."

"Do you know your name?"

"*Ho-nehe*," Michael replied. "Wolf."

"Well, Wolf, you've had a rather bad bump on the head, but, barring any unforeseen complications, I think you'll be all right. Try and get some sleep now, and I'll look in on you tomorrow."

Michael nodded, but sleep was the farthest thing from his mind. He watched the woman extinguish the lamp, listened to her footsteps fade away as she followed her father out of the room.

She is waiting, the voice had said, *waiting for you*.

He remained awake a long time, wondering what it meant, wondering if Winter Song had been killed so that he would chase the Pawnee and end up here, with the red-haired woman. Slowly he shook his head. Such a thing was unthinkable.

With a sigh, he closed his eyes, and when sleep finally came, he dreamed of blood. Pawnee blood.

Chapter 17

Elayna tossed and turned all night long, unable to drive the Indian from her mind. Michael Wolf. What an odd name for an Indian. He was tall and dark and handsome. Every woman's dream, she thought, and yet her dream had become a nightmare, and the nightmare had become reality.

She had dreamed of a tall, dark-skinned man who would change her life, and now he was here and his presence frightened her. And the fact that she was attracted to him frightened her still more.

She made up her mind to avoid the infirmary while Michael Wolf was there. She would plead a headache or a sore throat until he had been moved to the guardhouse where he belonged.

Wolf . . . he reminded her of a winter-starved lobo, long and lean, always on the scent of blood.

The comparison sent a chill down her spine and she pushed it away, then snuggled deeper into her blankets.

She was at the infirmary immediately after breakfast, a tray in one hand, a roll of bandages in the other. She had thought to find him asleep, but he was awake and sitting up, the pillow propped behind his back. The sheet was bunched across his hips, the linen very white against his sun-bronzed flesh. The sight of him caused her stomach to flutter and her heart to quicken. *From fear*, she told herself as she placed the tray across his lap and lifted the cover, revealing a plate filled with bacon and eggs and fried potatoes.

"I hope you're hungry," she said curtly.

Michael nodded, a wry smile twitching at the corner of his mouth. She was afraid of him. The scent of fear rose from her, unmistakable for what it was.

"Smells good," Michael remarked, wondering what she had to fear from him.

"Thank you." She took a step away from the bed, conscious of his eyes watching her every move.

"I've got to change your bandage," she said, her words tumbling out in a rush. "I'll come back when you're done eating."

He frowned as she rushed out of the room. Damn, what the hell was she afraid of?

She was a good cook, he thought as he swallowed the last of the bacon and eggs, but his mind was not on food. He was a prisoner, and he did not like it. For the first time in his life, he was unable to come and go as he pleased. Growing up on the reservation, he had answered to no one except Yellow Spotted Wolf. His mother had given him free rein to come and go as he pleased, sensing, perhaps, that he would rebel against any show of authority. His father hadn't cared what Michael did so long as he stayed out of the way. In Los Angeles, he'd had all the freedom he needed. True, he had been bound to certain conventions. He'd had to learn to be punctual, to do what was expected, to submit to some degree of authority, but the knowledge that he could leave it all behind at any time and return to the reservation had made those few restrictions easier to bear.

He swore softly. He did not like being shackled, did not like knowing his fate rested in the hands of strangers.

The enemy.

He had never thought of the *vehoe*, the white man, as his enemy before. But he was somewhere in the past now, and the whites and the Indians were at war. Friendly Indians were being caged on reservations; hostiles were being shot, or imprisoned in faraway places where they sickened and died.

A tide of useless anger swept through him and he jerked against the chain that imprisoned him, muttering a foul oath as he did so.

It was then that Elayna returned. "What is it?" she asked. "Is something wrong?"

"You're damn right there's something wrong! I don't like being chained up like a damn dog! How long do they plan to keep me here?"

Elayna bit down on her lower lip, the first stirrings of sympathy rising in her breast. "I don't know. Another day or two, I think. And then . . ."

"And then?"

"They're going to move you to the guard-house."

Michael's eyes narrowed ominously. "The guardhouse? Why? I haven't done anything."

"Major Cathcart thinks you were part of a scouting party sent here by Sitting Bull to spy on us. He wants to question you."

Michael's jaw went rigid. Locked up. He had never realized until now that he harbored a fear of being confined. He thought of Yellow Spotted Wolf. His great-grandfather had hated small places, dark rooms, high walls. He had never closed his bedroom door because he did not like the feeling of being shut in. The old man had often said that the Cheyenne were meant to live wild and free. Not like the *vehoe* who fenced his land and hid himself inside his house, but like the eagle who soared high in the heavens, unfettered by walls or clocks or the chains of civilization.

"What happens after this major questions me?"

"I don't know," Elayna replied, not meeting

his eyes. "Perhaps they'll let you go."

"And perhaps they won't."

There seemed nothing more to say. Wordlessly Elayna took the tray and placed it on the bedside table, then gently removed the bandages from Michael's head and side. The gash in his scalp was healing beautifully, as was the nasty wound in his side. Her father was a wonderful doctor, she thought proudly. His knowledge and skill and dedication had saved the Indian's life.

She wrapped a fresh bandage around the wound in his side, but did not replace the one on his head. The wound was not as severe as the one in his side and no longer needed protection. Her father was a great believer in leaving certain wounds open to the air, to breathe, he said.

She rolled the bloody bandages into a neat ball and placed them on the tray. "I'll be back later with your lunch," she said. "Do you need to . . . to relieve yourself before I go?"

Michael nodded curtly, a fit of helpless rage rising within him as she offered him a bedpan.

He was not going to be a very good patient now that he was feeling better, Elayna mused as she left the infirmary. Most of the men made jokes when she offered them a bedpan. Some of the jests were crude, some reflected the patient's embarrassment. But Wolf was the first man who had ever been angry. But then, perhaps he had a good deal to be angry about.

The Indian filled her mind as she did her chores at home. Who was he, and why was he here? Why had she been warned of his coming? Did he mean her harm?

No matter how many times she put him out of her thoughts, his image returned to haunt her. It irritated her that she found him attractive, that his hair was thick and black and straight, that his eyes were as dark as pitch, that his skin was like smooth copper, that his shoulders were broad and his arms corded with muscle. She had seen other Indians. She had thought them ugly, disgusting in their buckskins and feathers, barbaric in their paint. But this man . . . he looked at her and her stomach quivered and her heart pounded. And it wasn't fear, she admitted now. It was something much worse.

He was lying flat on his back, one arm thrown across his eyes, when she entered the infirmary with his lunch. She walked quietly toward him, not wanting to wake him if he was asleep. Her father was fond of saying that rest was the best healer of all.

She studied his profile, wondering what there was about Michael Wolf that intrigued her so. She could feel herself reaching out to him, wanting to help him, to comfort him.

She was turning to leave when his voice called out to her. "Don't go. I'm awake."

"I've brought your lunch."

"I'm not hungry."

"I'll see you at dinner then."

Michael sat up, dreading the long hours ahead, the boredom, the anxiety of not knowing what the future held for him.

"Can't you stay a little while?" he asked.

His tone was brusque, but Elayna caught the underlying note of despair and her heart went out to him. Right or wrong, he deserved some company.

"I'll stay," she said, "if you'll eat."

"That's bribery."

"I know," she admitted with a smile, "but sometimes it works."

Michael grinned as he reached for the tray. She'd made fried chicken for lunch, and his mouth watered as he uncovered the plate, surprised to find that he was hungry after all.

Elayna pulled a newspaper from her apron pocket and sat down on the cot beside his. She read while he ate, and he marveled at how much better he felt just having her there.

He glanced at the front page and the date seemed to leap out at him. *August 29, 1875*.

Michael grunted softly. "1875," he muttered. "I'll be damned."

Elayna put the newspaper aside. "Is something wrong?"

"Nothing you can fix," Michael remarked. "*Heammawihio* must be having a good laugh at my expense."

"Heamma . . . who?"

"*Heammawihio*. The Great Spirit of the Cheyenne."

"I didn't think Indians believed in God."

"They believe in many gods. My people believe everything has its own spirit, its own soul, that everything is alive."

"Everything? You mean like rocks and trees?"

Michael nodded. "And water, and grass. Everything." A wry smile touched his lips. "The Indians won't drink water that sits overnight because they believe it's dead."

"That's silly."

Michael shrugged. "Maybe."

"I've never thought of Indians as being religious. Are you? Religious, I mean."

"More than I used to be." He shifted his weight on the cot and the chain around his ankle rattled, reminding him that he was a prisoner here. Impulsively he reached out and took Elayna's hand in his.

Elayna tried to jerk her hand free, a hundred nameless fears aroused by his touch.

"I've got to get out of here," Michael said urgently. "Now. Before it's too late." His eyes searched hers. "Will you help me?"

"How?" Her hand was lost in his. His skin was warm and firm and brown. Very brown. So different from her own.

"How? I don't know. Cut off my foot, steal the keys to these irons. Dammit, I don't know how!"

The intensity in his voice and the sudden wildness in his eyes frightened her, and she jerked her hand from his and stood up.

"I can't," she said, backing away from him. "I'm sorry, I just can't."

Despite her nightly vows to stay away from the infirmary as long as the Indian was there, she found numerous excuses to visit the hospital in the next three days. When the orderly came down with a cold, she took over his chores: changing the linen on Wolf's bed, sweeping the floor, opening the windows in the morning and closing them at night. She decided the linen closet needed a good cleaning out, and the next day she shook out all the blankets on the empty beds.

She handled each task with cool efficiency, pretending to be totally oblivious to Michael Wolf's presence, even though she could feel his eyes watching her every move. They rarely spoke other than to exchange empty pleasantries.

There was a wariness about him now that he was feeling better. His eyes were sharp and alert, his senses keen. She could feel the tension in him whenever her father or one of the soldiers entered the room. In truth, he often reminded her of the animal for which he was named. Even when he was asleep, she had the feeling he was aware of everything happening around him.

She began preparing him more elaborate meals, thinking that eating was probably the only pleasure he had. She didn't know why she was suddenly so concerned with his welfare, only that she was. Perhaps it was because her sense of fair play was outraged that a man, even an Indian, should be held prisoner at the whim of another. Perhaps it was because she was drawn to Michael Wolf in spite of herself. Whatever the reason, she began heaping his plate with food, bringing him snacks between lunch and dinner: chocolate cake and cold apple cider, sugar cookies and lemonade, spice cake and coffee.

Elayna was lingering in the infirmary, aware of Wolf's steady gaze on her back, when her father entered the room, followed by four burly soldiers armed with Winchester rifles.

"What's going on?" Elayna asked, staring at the four armed men.

"Nothing," her father replied. "The Indian's well enough to be moved, that's all. They're here to take him to the guardhouse until Major Cathcart gets around to questioning him."

Elayna nodded, her gaze moving toward Michael. He was sitting very still, hardly breathing, and she could sense the tension building in him, see it in his tightly clenched hands.

Robert O'Brien was also aware of the prisoner's apprehension. He could feel the barely suppressed anger radiating from the Indian. "Go home, Elayna," he said curtly. "Now."

She sent a quick, sympathetic glance in Michael Wolf's direction, then hurried from the room. He would not like being locked up, and she wondered if he would go peacefully or if he'd put up a fight in spite of the odds against him. Somehow she thought he was too smart to argue with four rifle-toting troopers.

Michael eyed the soldiers warily as they surrounded the bed, their rifles aimed at his chest. One of the men handed the doctor a key, and O'Brien unlocked the iron cuff that shackled Michael's leg to the frame of the cot.

"Get up," the soldier at Michael's right ordered brusquely. "And don't try anything funny. We got orders to shoot to kill if you try to make a run for it."

The man was lying, Michael thought. Cathcart couldn't question a corpse. They might shoot him later, but not now. Still, he wasn't about to put his theory to the test. All four troopers looked capable of shooting him in the back, and enjoying it.

Slowly he swung his legs over the side of the cot and stood up. He hadn't been on his feet in over a week and the room swayed beneath him. He reached out to steady himself and felt a rifle barrel nudge his spine.

"Take it easy, Calhoun," Robert O'Brien snapped. "He's not going anywhere."

"Damn right," Calhoun retorted with an easy grin.

One of the troopers handed Michael his clout and leggings and he dressed under the amused gaze of the troopers, a muscle working in his jaw as he listened to their crude taunts and jibes.

When he was dressed, Calhoun prodded him in the back again. "Move it, Injun," the trooper ordered impatiently. "We ain't got all day."

There was nothing to do but obey. Feeling somewhat light-headed, he started for the door, conscious of the four armed men behind him, of their jeering laughter about gut-eaters. But it was the derogatory comments about his mother that stirred his anger, and he clenched his hands into tight fists, beginning to understand why his people had hated the *vehoe*. The soldiers' remarks were crude, childish, but they cut like a knife.

Stepping out of the infirmary, he saw a sign that said CAMP ROBINSON. The name hadn't registered before, but now it jarred his memory. Camp Robinson. Crazy Horse had died here.

He knew a moment of panic as they shoved him into one of the small, iron-barred cells and shackled his right leg to a length of chain that was bolted to the far wall.

Crazy Horse had died here. The sight of these iron bars had sent him into a frenzy that ended in death.

Michael sank down on the floor, his back braced against the wall. He stared at the iron bars, the same iron bars that Crazy Horse had viewed with horror and revulsion.

With a sigh, he closed his eyes and focused on the last days of the Oglala war chief in an effort to forget his own troubles.

It had been after the battle at the Little Bighorn. Sitting Bull and his people had fled to Canada to escape the soldiers, but Crazy Horse would not leave the land he loved. Tired of fighting, he had decided to accept the Grandfather's offer of food and clothing and shelter and he had come to Camp Robinson to make his peace with the white man. But then they had taken him toward the guardhouse to await Colonel Bradley's pleasure. The sight of the iron bars had driven Crazy Horse into a frenzy and he had drawn a knife, fighting to be free of the white man's treachery. They had promised him peace if he surrendered, but it was a lie, as all the words of the white man were lies. The rumors he had heard were true. They were going to take him away from his people, away from the *Paha Sapa*, from all that he loved.

Knife flashing, Crazy Horse turned to fight. It was then that Little Big Man grabbed him from behind, holding his arms. Crazy Horse struggled to be free and finally, with a tremendous jerk, he broke Little Big Man's grip, and Little Big Man staggered back with blood running down his shoulder. And now other Indians grabbed at Crazy Horse. The officer of the day was screaming, "Stop him! Don't let him escape! Kill the bastard!"

Two guards ran forward, their bayonets driving toward Crazy Horse. The first guard lunged forward and missed, his bayonet stabbing the guardhouse door, but the second guard had better aim. He stabbed the Oglala war chief twice, and the blood on his bayonet glistened like crimson teardrops in the harsh yellow lamplight.

And then the quiet voice of Crazy Horse had pierced the sudden stillness that followed the blooding: "Let me go, my friends," he pleaded softly. "You have hurt me enough."

And so it was that *Tashunka Witko*, the greatest of all the Lakota fighting chiefs, had died at the age of thirty-three, just before midnight, September 5, 1877.

Michael Wolf let out a long sigh. Crazy Horse

had been killed in 1877, but this was 1875 and Crazy Horse still lived. Somewhere out in the vast rolling hills the Oglala chief was still making war against the whites, still shouting his war cry: *"Hoka hey*! It is a good day to die!"

The thought brought a smile to Michael's face. If he could get out of here, he might yet meet the man who had been his lifelong hero.

Chapter 18

He woke at the sound of Elayna's voice. She was arguing with the guard on duty, insisting she had been sent by her father to check on the prisoner's condition.

Michael grinned. No one had been sent to look in on him since he'd been locked up four days ago. It was obvious, at least to him, that Elayna O'Brien was lying through her teeth, but her righteous indignation fooled the young corporal on duty and he unlocked the door to Michael's cell and let Elayna in after cautioning her to be careful.

Elayna shivered as she entered the narrow, iron-barred room. She had never been inside the guardhouse before. The bars and the gloom were depressing, and she wondered again what had prompted her to come here. She had no business in this place. What would she do if her father should stop by to check on the prisoner? What possible excuse could she give for being in a place where she had no right to be? Worse, what would she do if Major Cathcart showed up? Just thinking about the possible repercussions made her mouth go dry.

She felt Michael watching her and felt her cheeks flame. What excuse could she give *him* for being here?

"How are you feeling?" she asked.

"The truth?"

"The truth."

He tugged on the heavy chain that secured his right leg to an iron ring in the wall. "I'm scared." It was a fact he would have admitted to no one else.

Elayna nodded sympathetically. He had every right to be frightened. Major Cathcart despised Indians. All Indians. Few of his red-skinned prisoners were ever released unharmed. She had lost count of the number of warriors who had been killed "trying to escape." But they were just Indians, after all, and no one ever complained.

"What are you doing here?" Michael asked.

"I . . . I came to examine your side."

She was lying, but he didn't care. In the last four days he'd seen no one but the man who brought him his meals.

"Does it hurt?" Elayna asked.

"No."

Her hand was shaking as she removed the bandage from his side. She examined the wound carefully, pleased that there was no sign of infection.

"You're afraid of me, aren't you?" Michael remarked as she replaced the bandage. "Why?"

"I don't know what you're talking about. Why should I be afraid of you?"

"You tell me."

"You'll laugh."

"I could use a good laugh."

"I knew you were coming, that you'd be brought here, hurt and bleeding."

Michael frowned. "How the hell could you know that?"

"I dreamed about you. Every night for almost a week." She saw the amusement in his eyes and she lifted her chin defiantly. "It's true."

"I believe you."

"You do?"

"I believe in dreams. And visions."

His words should have made her feel better; instead, they only served to frighten her the more. There was an odd look in his eyes, a faraway expression on his face, as if his spirit had left his body to wander elsewhere.

"Hey! You finished in there?"

Elayna stood up as the guard appeared outside the cell door.

"Yes, thank you, corporal," she said, flashing him a winning smile.

She glanced at Michael, who was still staring into the distance, and then she followed the guard out of the cell.

Lieutenant Lance Smythe was waiting for her when she reached home.

Lance smiled as Elayna reached the porch. "I was just about to leave," he remarked. "I stopped by the infirmary, but your father said you'd left for home. Where've you been?"

"I was checking on one of the wounded."

Lance frowned. "Has someone been hurt?"

"The Indian," Elayna explained, trying to keep her voice casual.

"The Indian? Shouldn't your father be looking after him? I mean, it's not fittin' for a lady like you to be fussing over a damned savage."

"I don't think of him as a savage," Elayna replied without thinking.

"Oh?"

"I mean, he seems quite civilized."

Lance frowned. "Civilized?"

"I just mean he speaks very good English, that's all."

"You've been talking to him!" Lance exclaimed, horrified. "For heaven's sake, Elayna, the man's a savage, probably a killer. You stay the hell away from him, you hear me? And if he needs medical attention, you let your father dish it out. Is that clear?"

Elayna glared up at the lieutenant, angered and stunned by his outburst. It was the first time he had dared raise his voice to her, the first time he had cussed in her presence. The first time he had tried to order her around like she was one of his troopers. Well, it was time he learned she had a mind of her own!

"I'll do as I please, Lieutenant Smythe," she replied, her voice as cool as a frosty morning. "And I'll thank you to keep a civil tongue in your head, as well. Furthermore, you are not my father, or my husband, and I don't have to answer to you. Is *that* clear?"

Lance Smythe chuckled softly, amused by her sudden fit of temper. She was damned attractive when her Irish was up.

His obvious amusement at her expense infuriated Elayna all the more. Thrusting out her chin, she planted her fists on her hips and glowered at him.

"You'd best wipe that smirk off your face right now, mister, if you ever expect to call on me again," she suggested, her voice several degrees cooler than before.

"I'm sorry," Lance apologized. "But if we had a hundred more like you, we'd have these savages rounded up in no time at all."

His sincere apology and ready smile melted her anger and she smiled up at him, her good mood restored. The Indian was nothing to her, after all, certainly not worth arguing with Lance about.

"I'm sorry too," she said. "Come in, and I'll make some lemonade."

There was a party at the major's house that night. Elayna did not want to go, but an invitation to the major's house was like a command from the king, and his subjects attended, willing or not.

She wore a modest gown of light blue velvet trimmed with yards and yards of lace dyed the same color. The bodice was fitted, the waist tucked, the skirt full, the sleeves tapered and long. She wore her hair piled high atop her head, set with two jeweled combs that had belonged to her mother. Her only other adornment was a slender gold chain at her neck.

She sat between her father and Lance at dinner. As usual, the talk turned to Indians—where they might be hiding out, when they were most likely to attack next, how long it would take to completely subdue them. Most of the men felt it was only a matter of time before the hostiles were rounded up.

"The Injuns can't live without the buffalo," remarked Captain Lewis, "and the buffalo are just about gone."

Major Cathcart grunted, and Elayna was repulsed by the hatred in his close-set gray eyes. He did not want to round up the Indians. He wanted them exterminated. And, she reminded herself, so did she. Didn't she? Unbidden, she thought of Michael Wolf.

"Here now, enough about Indians," Gertrude Cathcart said, smiling, and deftly turned the subject to something more pleasant.

They played whist after dinner. It was a lively card game, one the major's wife was addicted to. Usually Elayna loved the game, but tonight she could not concentrate on her cards and when Lance was partnered with Carolyn Whitfield, Elayna slipped out the back door.

She walked aimlessly for ten minutes and then, as though drawn by invisible cords, made her way across the parade ground toward the guardhouse. The building was dark and quiet as she made her way to the back.

Michael Wolf frowned, certain his imagination was playing tricks on him. But no, he could see her clearly in the moonlight. Elayna O'Brien.

Grasping the bars, he leaned forward. "What the hell are you doing out there?" he called in a loud whisper.

"I was at a party at the major's house," Elayna answered, peering up at the window. "I got bored and decided to take a walk." It had been a mistake to come here. She knew that now, when it was too late.

"And do you always take a stroll around the jail when you get bored?"

"No," Elayna admitted, stifling a giggle. "This is the first time." She felt the pull of his eyes, the unmistakable attraction between them. Did he feel it too? "Are you all right?"

"Bored," Michael replied, his voice tinged with bitterness.

Elayna toyed with the chain at her throat. Why had she come here? She had nothing to say to this man, nothing at all. He was a stranger, the enemy. Why was she standing out here, risking discovery, when Lance was waiting for her back at the major's house?

Frustrated and confused by emotions she dared not examine too closely, she bid Wolf a hasty good night and hurried away, vowing she would never see him again.

Michael watched her out of sight. The sound of her voice and the faint lingering fragrance of her perfume kept him awake far into the night.

Chapter 19

*M*ajor *Jonathan Cathcart glared at the Indian* leaning negligently against the cell wall. He had been questioning the redskin for over an hour and all he'd learned so far was the bastard's name and tribe.

Michael bit back a grin of satisfaction as an angry flush spread over the officer's clean-shaven face. The major was about out of patience, and Michael wondered how much longer he could defy Cathcart's authority before the man's temper exploded.

"Where are your people?" Cathcart demanded. "What are they planning? Where's Sitting Bull?"

"I don't know," Michael replied, his own

anger rising. "And if I did, I sure as hell wouldn't tell you!"

Jonathan Cathcart frowned. The prisoner looked like an Indian, he was dressed like an Indian, he even smelled like a damned redskin, but he didn't talk like one. Not by a damned sight!

Cathcart took a step forward. "Who are you? And I don't mean your name. Who the hell are you?"

Michael pushed away from the wall. Head high, shoulders back, he faced the major. "For the last time, my name's Wolf and I'm a Cheyenne warrior."

"Like hell! Who sent you here? What were you supposed to find out?"

"No one sent me," Michael said, curbing his anger. "I got into a fight with a couple of Pawnee. One of them had a rifle and got off a clean shot." He pressed a hand to his side, remembering the white-hot pain that had seared his flesh. "I came to a ravine and one of the Indians shot my horse out from under me and we went over the side."

Michael paused as he tried to recall what had happened next. "I could hear the Pawnee trying to decide if my scalp was worth the climb down when one of your patrols rode up. I guess I passed out, because I don't remember what happened after that. When I came to, I was here."

Major Cathcart grunted. "You don't talk like any Indian I've ever known."

Michael shrugged. "I've spent a lot of time around whites."

"Where?"

Michael stirred uneasily. Where indeed? "In California," he replied at last. "I was raised by nuns."

Cathcart laughed out loud. "A Cheyenne Indian raised by nuns in California! Do you really expect me to believe that?"

Michael shrugged again. "Believe what you want."

"You're an insolent bastard," Cathcart remarked. "Perhaps we can beat the truth out of you. What do you think, Saunders?"

The sergeant standing at the major's elbow grinned, revealing a row of crooked yellow teeth. "I guess it's worth a try."

Robert O'Brien slammed the door behind him as he stepped into the guardhouse. "You will *not* beat that prisoner, Major Cathcart," he said curtly. "This man is still under my care, and he is not yet fully recovered from his wounds. If you dare lay a hand on him, I'll go straight to General Crook."

"You dare to threaten me?"

"You're damn right, sir. This man hasn't been charged with any crime that I'm aware of. In my opinion, you have no reason to hold him, much less flog him."

"Damn you, O'Brien," the major hissed. "You've been a thorn in my side since the day you arrived."

"Yes, sir!" the doctor agreed. "Now, if you'll

excuse me, I'm here to examine my patient."

Face mottled with rage, the major stalked out of the cell.

Elayna chuckled softly as her father related the incident over dinner that night. How she would have loved to have been there, to have seen the look on the major's face when her father challenged his authority.

"I'm afraid that Indian's in for a rough time," O'Brien mused as he helped himself to another serving of chicken and dumplings. "You know Cathcart. He won't rest until he gets what he wants."

"Do you really think he'll beat Michael?"

O'Brien raised a bushy black brow. "Michael, is it? I thought his name was Wolf."

"It is. Michael Wolf."

"Strange name for a full-blooded Cheyenne."

Elayna lowered her gaze to her plate, unable to meet her father's questioning stare.

"Elayna. Elayna, look at me. You're not becoming . . ." O'Brien cleared his throat. "You're not becoming infatuated with this Indian, are you?"

"Of course not."

O'Brien propped his elbow on the table and rested his chin in the palm of his hand. His daughter had always had a soft heart. As a child, she was always bringing home strays, nursing sick dogs and cats, hand-raising a litter of kittens when the mother was killed. She could not abide seeing another in pain, be it man or beast, could not abide cruelty or injustice. Despite her oft-professed hatred for Indians, he was afraid her sympathy for the prisoner would overrule her good sense.

"Perhaps it's time you went back East for a while," O'Brien suggested. "You could stay with your Aunt Mary. Visit your cousins. Do some shopping, buy some new clothes. I think it would do you a world of good to get away from here for a while."

"You're not very subtle, are you, Papa?"

"I guess not. But I still think it's a good idea."

"Whatever you say, Papa," Elayna agreed. It was useless to argue with her father once he'd made up his mind, and she didn't try. But she had no intention of leaving the fort while Michael Wolf was in the guardhouse.

It was a little after nine o'clock that night when Michael heard footsteps approaching his cell. He felt the short hairs prickle along the back of his neck, felt his stomach knot as Major Cathcart, Sergeant Saunders, and a rather portly trooper stopped outside the door. Saunders was grinning as he toyed with the heavy rawhide quirt in his right hand.

The trooper unlocked the cell door, then drew his sidearm and aimed it at Michael. Cathcart also drew his weapon, a sinister smile twisting his lips as Saunders entered the cell and removed the chain from Michael's ankle.

"See that crossbar?" Saunders said, jerking his thumb toward the ceiling. "Reach for it."

Michael stared at the heavy quirt in Saunders'

hand. Was it a bluff? Were they hoping fear would loosen his tongue, or did Cathcart really intend to let the sergeant beat the hell out of him? Damn! The mere idea made him break out in a cold sweat.

For a moment he thought of knocking Saunders aside and making a break for the open door and freedom even though he knew he'd never make it out of the cell alive.

He glanced at Cathcart. The major was watching him intently, his forefinger curled around the trigger of his pistol.

A beating or a bullet in the back, Michael thought. Not much of a choice. Muttering an oath, he reached for the crossbar above his head. He could feel Cathcart's disappointment as Saunders lashed his hands to the bar. The major had wanted him to make a run for it, hoping for an excuse to gun him down. And Saunders and the other trooper would be there to testify in the major's behalf. Yes, they would say, the Indian tried to escape and the major had to shoot him.

Michael's hands curled around the crossbar. The iron bar was hard and cold, like the fear knotting in his stomach, and he wondered how many times Cathcart had done this. How many warriors had tried to run rather than take a beating? How many Indians had died here, in this ugly little cell?

He could feel his heart pounding wildly as Saunders walked back and forth in front of him, idly slapping the quirt against the palm of his hand. It was a wicked-looking thing, about two feet long, made of rawhide and leather. It reminded Michael of a miniature cat-o'-nine-tails.

Saunders walked behind Michael, slowly, deliberately, and Michael felt his mouth go dry as he waited for the first blow.

"Where's Sitting Bull?" the major asked. "Why did he send you here?"

"Nobody sent me here," Michael replied tersely, and it occurred to him suddenly that Cathcart didn't give a damn about Sitting Bull. Asking for the Hunkpapa's whereabouts was just a ploy, an excuse to mete out a beating to another Indian.

Cathcart let out a sigh of anticipation. "Sergeant."

Michael's hands tightened around the crossbar. *Heammawihio, help me.*

The first blow came and it was almost a relief. The waiting, at least, was over.

"Why were you sent here?" Cathcart demanded. "What were you supposed to find out?"

"Nothing."

Saunders laid the quirt across Michael's back again, and then again. Michael gasped once and then clenched his teeth, refusing to cry out as the narrow strips of knotted leather bit into his back, splitting the skin.

"We can do this all night if you like," Cathcart remarked. "Or we can quit now. It's up to you."

"Fine," Michael replied sarcastically. "Let's quit."

Cathcart swore under his breath as he

grabbed the quirt from Saunders hand and brought it down across Michael's back. Michael began to shiver spasmodically as the quirt fell again and again, each blow seeming harder and longer than the last. Heat suffused him, a bright red haze born of pain and humiliation. He closed his eyes, felt the strength go out of his legs, and he wondered which was worse, the agony of the flesh or the slow destruction of his pride.

It took him a few minutes to realize the beating had stopped. Opening his eyes, he glanced warily over his shoulder.

The cell door was closed.

He was alone.

Vehemently, yet silently, he cursed Major Jonathan Cathcart, and then, in the same breath, he cursed his own stupid pride. He should have made up a lie about Sitting Bull's whereabouts, he thought ruefully. Cathcart might have spared him a beating, though Michael knew the major intended to kill him sooner or later. He shuddered convulsively as he felt the blood trickling down his back, felt the wetness of it, the heat of it.

But the pain was not as strong as the insidious tentacles of fear that were slowly coiling around his insides. He was going to die here. He had seen his fate in the major's hard gray eyes.

His head dropped forward and he closed his eyes again, trying to relax, trying to separate himself from the pain that ebbed and flowed with each labored breath.

"Heammawihio, help me," he murmured.

The minutes ticked by, but he was unaware of the passage of time. His thoughts turned inward. Was this why he had been transported through time and space, he mused bleakly, to be humiliated by some strutting braggart who thought Indians were less than human, to die slowly, an inch at a time?

He tried to concentrate, to focus all his energy on home in the slim hope that the Great Spirit might take pity on him and send him back where he belonged, but the pain in his back made it impossible to think of anything else.

Time, he thought. Time had become his enemy.

He drifted in and out of consciousness, barely aware of his surroundings. When he was awake, a cocoon of pain engulfed him, as bright and red as the blood that coated his back.

Saunders came and cut him down and he fell heavily, grunting softly as he hit the floor. A fresh wave of agony jolted through him as Saunders dumped a pail of salted water over his back.

"Best get some sleep," Saunders suggested with a malevolent grin. "The major'll be wanting to question you again tomorrow night."

Tomorrow . . .

Heammawihio, have mercy . . .

"Poor bastard," Lance was saying. "Cathcart spent the better part of an hour trying to get that redskin to talk."

"Is he . . . is he dead, then?" Elayna asked.

"Not yet."

They were sitting on the porch step. Lance put his arm around Elayna's shoulders, but she was hardly aware of his touch. She was picturing Michael Wolf, bound and helpless, while Major Cathcart questioned him. And whipped him. She had seen one of the Indians after Cathcart had questioned him. The man's back had been cut to ribbons before he had been shot while "trying to escape."

Would that be Michael Wolf's fate?

She told herself she didn't care. Michael Wolf was an Indian, perhaps the very Indian responsible for what had befallen Kelly North. Poor Kelly. He had left the Army a broken and bitter man.

Elayna was still sitting on the porch step an hour later. Lance had gone back to the barracks, but she had been too restless to go inside, too distraught to sleep.

She saw her father leave the hospital and head toward the guardhouse. Impulsively she stood up and followed him.

Chapter 20

Voices. The sound of a key in the lock. A bright light. And then a new awareness of pain as someone probed his torn flesh.

"Relax."

Michael recognized Robert O'Brien's voice and took a deep breath, relieved that it was only the doctor and not Cathcart come to torment him again.

He looked past O'Brien and saw that the cell door was ajar and that the guard was standing inside the cell, a bored expression on his face.

Escape. Michael felt the adrenalin flow through his veins as he weighed the chance of getting past the doctor, overpowering the guard, grabbing his gun, and getting away.

Not good, he admitted. And yet this might be his only chance. The guard would no doubt replace the shackle on his leg once the sawbones had finished tending his back. And tomorrow Cathcart would return with more questions . . .

O'Brien had just finished bandaging Michael's back when a woman's footsteps sounded in the hallway. O'Brien and the guard both turned toward the sound.

O'Brien stood up, frowning. "Elayna, what are you doing here?"

Michael rolled to his feet. With the doctor's attention distracted, this was the best chance he'd get. Ignoring the pain in his back, he drove his elbow deep into O'Brien's belly, slammed his fist into the guard's jaw as he whirled around.

"What are you doing?" Elayna shrieked as Michael jerked the guard's service revolver from his holster, stepped out of the cell, and slammed the door.

She stared at Michael, her eyes wide, as the barrel of the gun swung in her direction.

"We're leaving," he said curtly. "Let's go."

"Leave her here, you bastard!"

"Shut up, doc," Michael said quietly. He gave Elayna a little push with his free hand. "Move it."

"No."

"I'm in no mood to argue," Michael snapped. "You'd best do as you're told."

He did not threaten her father's life. He didn't

176

have to. She saw the warning in his eyes and wondered how she'd ever felt sorry for him. He was nothing but a savage after all.

"Damn you!" Robert O'Brien roared. "Leave my daughter alone!"

"Shut up, doc, or I'll kill her here and now."

Fear rose in Elayna's throat, choking her, as Michael shoved her toward the door. She moved stiffly, aware of the gun aimed at her back, praying that another guard had arrived. But the room was empty.

"Wait."

She stopped abruptly, waited, trembling, while Michael lifted an overcoat from a hook on the wall. He winced as he put it on, and she smiled, pleased by his pain. He found a bottle of whiskey in one of the desk drawers and slipped it into the pocket of his coat. He took a late model Winchester rifle from the wall rack and emptied a box of ammunition into the other pocket of his coat.

"Let's go," he ordered brusquely, and Elayna opened the door and stepped outside.

"Don't try anything," Michael warned. "I've got nothing to lose."

She nodded, understanding completely.

Michael stood unmoving in the shadow of the guardhouse, pondering his next move. He needed a horse. Two horses, he amended. He perused the nearby buildings, smiled faintly when he saw two saddled horses hitched to the rack outside the subtler's store. *Maheo* was with him.

"Start walking," he told Elayna. "Nice and slow."

Side by side, they crossed the ground toward the horses. Michael kept the rifle out of sight in the folds of his coat, all his senses on edge as they neared the store. All it would take was one cry from Elayna, he thought bleakly, one shout for help, and it would be all over.

He slid a glance in Elayna's direction. Her face was pale, her movements wooden. Did she really believe he'd kill her? The thought made him angry, yet he knew he'd never get out of the camp alive unless she *did* believe it.

"Mount up."

He slid the revolver in his pocket and took hold of both sets of reins while she climbed into the saddle, afraid she might try to make a run for it.

It was an effort to pull himself into the saddle, and then they were riding in the shadows toward the rear of the camp.

He had no answer when the sentry challenged him, and only a quick blow to the side of the soldier's head kept the man from sounding an alarm. And then they were riding away from the camp, two dark silhouettes that blended into the night.

She was cold and hungry and tired. And scared. She glanced at Michael Wolf's back and wondered how he managed to stay in the saddle. Surely his back was a constant throbbing ache. Surely he would have to stop soon, to rest the horses if for no other reason.

But he did not stop.

On and on they rode through the dark night, moving like phantoms across the face of the land. She was shivering now, the cold air seeping through her clothing, chilling her to the bone. She gazed enviously at the heavy overcoat he wore. No doubt he was as warm as toast.

She saw his head drop, saw him sway in the saddle before he jerked upright, and she smiled knowingly. He was hurt. He had lost some blood, perhaps a lot. He couldn't stay awake forever. Sooner or later sleep would claim him, and when it did, she would take the horses and ride for home.

It was dawn when he finally stopped. In the faint gray light, she saw that his skin was drawn and pale, his expression haggard.

"Get down." His voice was flat.

She had been on the verge of exhaustion, but now she felt suddenly wide awake and alert as she slid from the saddle. He looked dead on his feet. Soon he would be asleep and she would make her escape.

"Sit down."

She did so warily, her eyes never leaving his face.

With a sigh, he dropped down on his haunches. Taking hold of her skirt, he tossed it into her lap, then reached for the hem of her petticoat.

"What do you think you're doing?" Elayna exclaimed, slapping his hand away.

"I'm going to tie you up so I can get some

179

sleep," he explained, reaching for her petticoat again.

"No, you're not!" she shrieked, and bounded to her feet, pushing against his chest with both hands as she did so.

Knocked off balance, he fell, landing on his back, hard. Elayna heard his pain-filled curse as she ran for her horse. She screamed as his hand closed over her arm.

"Damn you!" he rasped, his eyes dark with pain as he halted her flight.

She whirled around, striking his back with her free hand while she tried to free her arm from his grasp.

"Let me go!" She kicked out at him as he imprisoned both her hands in his.

"You little hellcat. I ought to skin you alive."

"Try it!" Fear gave her courage, and she lunged forward, her teeth closing on his right wrist.

He was tired and hurting and out of patience. Without thinking, without meaning it, he released her left hand and slapped her.

Elayna stopped fighting immediately, her brown eyes wide with fright, her cheek already turning red from his blow. She didn't resist when he pushed her, gently, to the ground, nor did she offer any resistance when he tore the ruffle from her petticoat and used it to tie her hands and feet.

On the point of exhaustion, Michael removed his overcoat and spread it over Elayna, and then, his right hand fisted around the revolver he had removed from the pocket of the coat, he dropped to the ground, asleep.

She woke slowly, her body aching from lying on the ground.

Michael lay a short distance away, his back toward her. Dried blood stained the bandage swathed around his middle. She knew she had caused his wounds to bleed anew when she'd struck him the night before. Ordinarily she would have felt regret at causing another human being pain, but now, remembering how he had slapped her, she felt only satisfaction.

Sitting up, she worked her hands back and forth, trying to loosen her bonds, but the knots held and she hurled silent curses at Michael Wolf's back, hating him for his rough treatment, for taking her away from her father, and Lance.

Lance. Her mood brightened with the realization that Lance would be looking for her by now. They'd hang Michael Wolf for kidnapping her, and she'd be there to watch when it happened!

Michael groaned softly as he woke up. The long ride, followed by sleeping on the cold ground, had left him stiff and sore in every muscle. His back throbbed without letup.

He sat up slowly, grimacing with the effort. The thought of spending the day in the saddle filled him with dread, but there was no help for it. The Army was probably already in pursuit. If he wanted to stay ahead of them, it was time to move.

Gritting his teeth, he stood up. Elayna was eying him warily and he let out a heavy sigh. He had almost forgotten about her.

He untied her feet, but one look into her defiant eyes convinced him to leave her hands bound. The look she gave him was cold enough to freeze all the fires of Hades.

Shrugging into the overcoat, he walked the horses to where Elayna stood waiting, her back ramrod straight, her head high. Damn, she was a feisty one, he thought ruefully.

"I feel like hell," he said, "and I'm in no mood for any of your little tantrums, so I'm warning you here and now, if you try biting me or kicking me while I boost you into the saddle, you'll find yourself walking."

Elayna took his warning to heart and meekly accepted his help as he lifted her into the saddle.

"I'm hungry," she said petulantly.

"So am I," he retorted, and reined his horse west, toward home.

"They'll be after you, you know," Elayna called after him. "Lance will hunt you down and then you'll hang!"

Michael nodded wearily. "No doubt you'll have a seat in the front row."

"I'll spring the trap if they'll let me," she replied, and then shuddered at the mere idea.

He was made of stone, Elayna thought bitterly. An inhuman, unfeeling monster. It was hot, so hot. Sweat poured down her face and back, collecting between her breasts, making her clothes stick to her skin. She was hungry and thirsty, her thighs felt raw, her backside was numb from so many hours in the saddle.

And still he did not stop.

She stared at his back. He had removed the overcoat and she studied the blood-stained bandages wrapped around his middle, wondering how he had reacted to the beating he had received. Had he screamed in pain? Had he finally told Major Cathcart what he wanted to know?

She cocked her head to one side. No, she decided, he would not have cried out. And he would not have betrayed his people, of that she was certain.

She tried to imagine what the pain had been like, and then she realized that the humiliation would have been worse than the pain of the whip.

And then she wondered why she cared.

Hours passed, and still he did not stop.

Tears of impotent rage and self-pity stung her eyes. Did he intend to ride forever, until they both died of thirst?

He reined his horse to a halt so abruptly she almost toppled out of the saddle as her own mount stopped beside his.

She stared at him blankly as he lifted the rifle to his shoulder and fired. Only then did she see the deer that had been flushed from its cover by their approach. Her mouth began to water at the thought of food.

Dismounting, Michael draped the deer carcass over his mount's withers, then swung into the saddle and put his horse into a trot.

Elayna was about to beg him to stop, at least for a few minutes, when he reined his horse to a halt in the shade of a sparse stand of timber. She gazed with longing at the shallow stream that seemed to appear out of nowhere.

Climbing eagerly from the saddle, she ran toward the stream and buried her face in the cool water.

"Drink it slow," Michael warned, dropping down beside her. "No sense having it all come back up."

Water, Elayna thought; when had anything ever tasted so good! She splashed her face and plunged her arms into the stream, cooling her heated flesh, and then she drank again.

Rising, Michael began to rummage around in the saddlebags tied behind his saddle. He grinned as he withdrew a skinning knife and a mess kit.

"*Ne-a'ese, Maheo,*" he murmured as he discovered a box of matches as well. The gods were still smiling on him.

A search of the second set of saddlebags yielded a bag of tobacco, a pipe, and a set of hobbles, as well as another box of matches.

He left Elayna splashing in the water while he built a fire, then sliced a couple of thick steaks from the deer carcass. While the meat cooked, he cut several thin strips of meat from the haunch to be cooked now and eaten later, on the trail.

Sometime later Elayna left the stream, drawn to the fire, the scent of roasting meat making her mouth water.

She sat across from Michael, her hands folded in her lap. She studied his profile as he turned the steaks, trying to find fault with his fine straight nose, the high cheekbones, the thick dark lashes that shaded his eyes. She wished he was ugly. It would be so much easier to hate him if he was ugly.

"Who's Lance?" He spoke to her without looking up.

Elayna grinned. So, he was worried, was he? Well, good. "He's a lieutenant at the fort," she said brightly, "and he's probably right behind us."

"Probably," Michael muttered. "Is he sweet on you?"

"Maybe."

"And are you sweet on him?"

"That's none of your business!"

Michael grunted softly, surprised to find he was jealous of a pale-faced lieutenant.

Elayna ate ravenously, not caring that the venison was rare, or that she had to share a knife and fork with Michael Wolf. The meat was tender and succulent, but she would gladly have eaten it raw, she thought, for she'd never been so hungry in her life.

She had eaten her fill and was ready for a long nap when Michael pulled her to her feet.

"Let's go."

"So soon?" she wailed.

He did not bother with a reply, merely lifted her into the saddle. He had extinguished the fire. The cooked venison was wrapped in a square of hide; the rest had been left for the scavengers. Ordinarily he would have burned it or buried it in an effort to cover his trail, but he knew the Army had an Indian scout who would have no trouble following their tracks. No trouble at all.

Elayna's spirits perked up as she gazed at the countryside. The plains stretched endlessly westward, thick with grass. Stands of timber stood like wooded islands in a grassy sea, and she began to understand why the Indians were fighting so hard to keep their land. Who could blame them for refusing to surrender, to leave the beauty of the plains for the misery of the reservation?

They rode until dusk, then stopped in the lee of a tall rocky spire. She was too weary to put up any fight when Michael lifted her to the ground; she only stood there, shoulders slumped, awaiting his commands.

He unsaddled the horses, rubbed them down with a handful of dry grass, hobbled her horse, knowing the other one would not wander far from its companion.

That done, he spread the saddle blankets on the ground and motioned for Elayna to sit down. She did so without question, grateful to be sitting on something that wasn't moving beneath her. She watched as Michael quickly and efficiently built a fire, accepted a strip of cold meat with a curt nod.

He had filled the deer's bladder with water. At first she refused to drink from anything so disgusting, but finally her thirst won out. Closing her eyes, she took a long drink.

When she opened her eyes again, he was watching her, his dark eyes unfathomable. She felt a sudden tremor in the pit of her stomach, a quick heat in her veins. Would he take her now that his other hungers had been satisfied?

Michael saw the fear surface in Elayna's eyes as he reached out to brush a wisp of hair from her face. Even now, with her hair mussed, her clothing covered with trail dust, and her cheeks stained with perspiration, she was lovely. She lifted her bound hands as if to ward him off, and he caught both her hands in one of his.

She froze at his touch, her eyes showing white, like a rabbit caught in the clutches of a . . . Michael grinned . . . in the clutches of a wolf.

He felt the need rise hot and quick within him, aroused by her scent and her nearness. Was it possible he had always wanted her, that he'd been blind to it all this time because of his grief at Winter Song's death?

Winter Song . . . she had been young and beautiful, and he had been drawn to her from the moment they met. He knew now that part of Winter Song's attraction had been the fact that she was Indian, as he was. The same blood, the same heritage. He had been fascinated by her naiveté, charmed by her smile. Now, he realized that what he'd felt for her had been a first, sweet love, one that might be followed by a fiercer passion.

His gaze lingered on Elayna's face. She was trembling now. He saw the shine of tears in her eyes, read the silent plea on her lips, but he could not resist touching her again. His fingers brushed her cheek, and he marveled at the softness of her skin. He lifted a lock of her hair and pressed it to his lips, inhaling the faint fragrance of lilacs that lingered in the soft strands despite their grueling ride.

He wanted her. But not like this. He wanted her warm and willing and eager, not helpless and frightened.

"Go to sleep," he said gently, and left her there, wide-eyed and trembling.

There was a new awareness between them now, a raw and primal tension that hummed and sparked like static electricity.

He wanted her.

The thought was never far from her mind. Each look, each accidental touch, was an unspoken declaration of his desire. He had untied her hands, confident she would not make a run for it. And the idea never seriously occurred to her. She could not survive out here in the wilderness alone and they both knew it. She was at his mercy now, dependent on him for food and water and protection.

He drew his horse to a halt on a flat-topped

ridge at noon. His hand brushed hers as he offered her a slice of cold venison, and she felt her nerve endings tingle at his nearness. She had never been so aware of a man before, or so attuned to another human being. Time and again her gaze wandered in his direction, her eyes pleased with what they saw. He had removed his overcoat, and she could not help admiring the play of muscles in his shoulders and arms as he checked the rigging on his saddle and tightened the cinch.

The bandage was very white against his skin, and even as she watched, he removed it, exposing a broad expanse of bronzed flesh crisscrossed with half-healed scars left by the whip.

Michael turned then, his face going hard when he saw the expression of horror on her face.

"Not very pretty, I guess," he muttered, and his voice was cold and bitter.

"There will only be a few scars," Elayna assured him, "and they'll fade in time."

"Time," Michael repeated. If he went back to his own time, would the scars disappear, or were they a part of him now, an ever-present reminder of his journey into the past?

They were riding westward again when it began to rain. One minute the sky was clear and blue, the next great dark clouds had gathered overhead.

They were both soaked to the skin by the time they found shelter under a large outcropping of

189

rock. They sat close together, not quite touching, the overcoat spread over their shoulders. Elayna stared at the rain, acutely aware of the man sitting beside her, of the narrow space between them, of the heat radiating from his thigh where it almost brushed her leg.

"It shouldn't last long," Michael remarked. "It's only a summer shower."

Elayna nodded. She had always loved the rain. She liked to sit wrapped in a warm blanket by the window and watch the lightning, listen to the thunder, the soft splash of the raindrops against the windowpane. She did not, she realized, care as much for the rain when she was drenched to the skin.

Michael gazed into the distance, trying to ignore the woman beside him. Her dress clung to her, the damp cloth clearly outlining every curve. Her hair fell down her back, unbound, like a dark waterfall. Her cheeks were red where the wind had kissed them, her lips moist from the rain, her eyes luminous. Her scent tickled his nostrils, unmistakably feminine.

She was shivering. And so was he. There was only one way to get warm, but he doubted she'd care for it.

Surprisingly, she didn't resist when he put his arm around her and drew her body against his.

"I'm so cold," she murmured. "So cold."

His right arm was around her shoulders and now he placed his left arm around her waist, hugging her to him. Their faces were only a breath apart, and as he gazed into her eyes he saw the fear, and the waiting.

He lowered his head to hers, his lips feather-light as he kissed her, drinking in her sweetness, savoring the taste of her. Her eyelids fluttered down and a long shuddering sigh escaped her lips, her breath mingling with his.

His arms drew her closer as he kissed her again, more deeply this time. She was trembling, but it had nothing to do with the cold, for she was no longer aware of the rain or the wind, only his lips on hers, his hand moving under her hair, stroking the sensitive skin of her neck. His tongue laved her lower lip, then slid to caress the side of her neck, the lobe of her ear, releasing a thousand quivering butterflies to dance in her belly and make her heart pound erratically.

She sighed as his lips returned to hers, his tongue sliding into her mouth to explore the depths within. It was only when his hand cupped her breast that sanity returned. Her eyes flew open and she twisted out of his arms, her shame and embarrassment clearly etched on her face.

A muscle worked in Michael's jaw as he fought the urge to finish what he had started. He had been long without a woman. Too long.

He drew his gaze from Elayna's face and stared out at the rain-swept plains. The storm had passed and a rainbow stretched across the sky. Raindrops glistened in the tall yellow grass and adorned the leaves of the trees.

He stood abruptly, knowing he had to put some distance between himself and Elayna before he did something they'd both regret.

"Let's go," he said curtly. Swinging onto his horse's back, he moved out at a brisk trot, not even looking back to make sure Elayna was following.

Chapter 21

The search party left at first light. Robert O'Brien watched them out of sight, his expression troubled. Lance was a good officer. Crowfoot was the best tracker the Army had. If anyone could find Elayna, they would. He tried not to think of his daughter at the mercy of a damned redskin. He had seen what Indians did to white women, the torture, the mutilation.

He shook the grisly images from his mind. Lance and Crowfoot would find her. With any luck, she'd be back by tomorrow night, scared but unhurt.

And yet he could not shake off the niggling fear that he'd seen his daughter for the last time. The Indian had a nine-hour head start. And even

Crowfoot might have trouble trailing an Indian who didn't want to be found.

The patrol returned to the fort five days later, saddle-weary and empty-handed.

O'Brien was in Cathcart's office when Lance made his report. The patrol had followed the Indian's tracks out of the fort, Lance said. They had followed the trail easily at first, had located the place where Elayna and the Indian had stopped to rest. And then it rained.

Lance made a gesture of helplessness. "The trail was completely washed out. Even Crowfoot couldn't pick it up again."

O'Brien nodded, his expression bleak. Where was she now? Dead? Lying out on the plains, prey to scavengers? Or was she a prisoner in some Cheyenne camp, being passed from one buck to another?

Better she should be dead than the plaything of some Cheyenne warrior, he thought miserably, and cursed the day he had saved Michael Wolf's life.

Chapter 22

Michael and Elayna reached the Cheyenne camp on the South Platte late in the afternoon. Elayna could not stifle the tremor of apprehension that rose within her as she gazed at the numerous Indian lodges spread beside the shallow river. She stared at the men and women going about their business as she followed Michael into the camp. These were godless savages, cruel and barbaric. They killed soldiers and tortured settlers, scalped women and children, destroyed homes and lives. She was a white woman, an enemy. What if they demanded her death? Would Michael protect her, or would her scalp adorn his lodge?

The Indians paused in their labors as Michael

and Elayna rode into the heart of the village. Young children ran to their mothers, pointing and talking excitedly as they stared at the white woman, fascinated by her red hair and fair skin.

Elayna swallowed hard as a tall warrior rode into camp, a long blond scalp fluttering from the tip of his lance. Her mouth was suddenly dry, her palms damp, as she looked at the people around her. She turned toward Michael, saw him smiling at a tall, handsome young man.

"We have missed you," Yellow Spotted Wolf said, grasping Michael's forearm in a gesture of welcome. He stared at Elayna. "Who is the woman?"

"A captive," Michael replied, dismounting.

Yellow Spotted Wolf grunted softly. His cousin had good taste in women.

"Perhaps you will want a lodge of your own now," Yellow Spotted Wolf suggested, still eying the woman.

"Perhaps."

"I will speak to my mother about it."

Yellow Spotted Wolf was about to say more when Two Ponies pushed his way between Yellow Spotted Wolf and Michael.

"She who should have been my wife is dead," Two Ponies said gruffly.

A cold fist wrapped itself around Michael's heart at the mention of Winter Song. "I know."

"She has been avenged."

"She will not be avenged until I dip my hands in the blood of the Pawnee," Michael declared fervently. "And I will do it."

Two Ponies glared at Michael, and then his gaze swung in Elayna's direction. "Who is this white woman?"

"She is mine," Michael replied tersely. "That is all you need to know."

Two Ponies nodded curtly, then turned on his heel and walked away, his head high and proud.

"He will never forgive you for winning the heart of she who is dead," Yellow Spotted Wolf remarked.

"I know."

"You have been gone from us a long time," Yellow Spotted Wolf said, changing the subject. "Will you tell me what kept you away?"

"Later," Michael promised.

Yellow Spotted Wolf looked at Elayna and smiled a knowing smile. "Come, my mother has food waiting."

"Get down," Michael told Elayna, "and follow me."

Elayna did as she was told, keenly aware of the many curious eyes that followed her every move. She was an outsider, the enemy. A prisoner. What would Michael do with her now? Humiliate her? Torture her?

Other, more degrading, more intimate alternatives rose in her mind and she pushed them away. She would worry about such things when they were alone.

With great trepidation, she followed Michael into a large hide-covered tipi.

The mother of Yellow Spotted Wolf welcomed Michael warmly and immediately offered him something to eat. Michael accepted, and in a short time Hemene served them bowls of roast hump meat, wild berries, and strong black tea.

Elayna sat in the rear of the lodge, filled with resentment because she was being ignored, relegated to the back of the lodge as if she were a child or a servant.

She did not care for the food. It tasted wild and gamy, the tea needed sugar, the berries were tart. Worst of all was the fact that she could not understand the conversation, though she was certain Michael was telling his family, if indeed they were his family, what had happened to him at Camp Robinson and how he had managed to escape. Occasionally one of the Indians glanced in Elayna's direction and grunted something unintelligible.

She was seeing Michael Wolf in a new light, too. Before, she had fooled herself into believing that he was a civilized man. He spoke her language. He seemed intelligent. But he looked wholly Indian now. He spoke his native language fluently, his skin was as dark as that of the others, his hair as black if not as long. He scooped the meat from the bowl with a knife, wiped his mouth on his arm, dried his hands on the sides of his leggings. It took no wild stretches of imagination to visualize him in paint and feathers, wildly gyrating around a campfire, with a war club in one hand and a scalp in the other . . . a long red scalp. Her scalp.

Yellow Spotted Wolf was as good as his word,

and when he told his mother that Wolf wanted a lodge of his own now that he had a woman, she immediately told Mo'ohta-vo'nehe that they needed a number of hides for the new dwelling. Mo'ohta-vo'nehe set out the very next day to trade horses and furs for the required skins, and Hemene called on her friends and relatives for help with the sewing.

The women started on the new lodge early the following morning. Elayna, bone weary after a restless night spent in the unfamiliar confines of a hide lodge, sat in the shade and watched as the Indian women worked on the new lodge. It took twenty-one buffalo hides, thinned and tanned, to make the cover. The process of cutting and sewing and fitting the pieces together took most of the day.

"Don't you want to help?"

She looked up to find Michael standing beside her. "No."

He shrugged. "It'll be your home. I just thought you might want to help."

"I don't want to live in a house made of skins," she retorted. "Nor do I want to be here with you. I want to go home, to my father."

Michael shook his head. "You're going to stay here. With me."

"Why?"

Why, indeed? His eyes swept her face and figure and he felt a sharp stab of desire, and in the back of his mind he heard a voice whispering, *She is waiting, waiting for you*. What did it mean? He told himself he was only keeping her here because he wanted an answer to the riddle, but that wasn't the reason at all. He wanted her, and that was why she was here, why he wouldn't let her go.

"Why?" she asked again, but there was no need for him to reply; she had seen the answer in his eyes.

The lodge was completed by nightfall. It was then that Soaring Eagle, the bravest man in the village, stepped forward and counted coup on the lodge. When that was done, he ducked inside, followed by several other outstanding warriors, including Mo'ohta-vo'nehe and Yellow Spotted Wolf.

Elayna stared at Michael in disbelief when he explained what was going on. Counting coup on a lodge, indeed! It was the silliest thing she had ever heard of.

"The women have completed a hard task," Michael told her. "By counting coup on the lodge, Soaring Eagle is recognizing what they have accomplished."

Hemene smiled at Elayna as she offered her an odd-looking bundle, then, bidding Michael and Elayna good night, she ushered everyone out of the lodge.

"It's a tanning kit," Michael said as Elayna examined the strange-looking items. "The scraper is used to remove meat and fat from the inside surface of a hide, the flesher is used to pare down the hide until it's the right thickness. That one's a drawblade. It's used to shave the hair from the outside of a hide, and that's a softening rope. It's drawn over the hide until it's soft and pliable."

"I don't want it."

A muscle twitched in Michael's jaw. "Those tools belonged to Mo'ohta-vo'nehe's mother," he said, hoping he could make Elayna see what an honor it was for her to have them. "A woman's sewing kit is buried with her, but her tanning kit is passed on to her daughter or daughter-in-law. Hemene has the one that belonged to her own mother, so she has given you her mother-in-law's. It's a fine gift."

"I don't care. I don't want it."

She dropped the tools on the floor, her gaze falling on the cooking utensils that Michael's family had provided, spoons made of buffalo horn, bowls made of wood, pots made of clay. Two beds made of buffalo robes were spread in the back of the lodge. Everything was foreign to her, reminding her again that she was among an alien people, alone with a man who was a stranger. A man whose eyes were hot when he looked at her.

It was suddenly quiet save for the crackling of the flames. Michael stared at Elayna's back. Her hair was as red as the glowing coals, and he felt a sudden heat in his loins as he gazed at her, wanting her.

Her gingham dress was covered with trail dust, the lace collar limp. The hem was torn where she'd caught it on a bush, her shoes were scuffed and caked with mud. He wondered if she felt as out of place as she looked.

He should not have brought her here. He was of the People, a Cheyenne, and sometimes even he felt like an outsider. How much worse would it be for her? What right did he have to keep her here, away from everything she knew and loved?

And still he wanted her. Regardless of right or wrong, regardless of whispered voices in the back of his mind, he wanted her. And she wanted him. Whether she admitted it or not, it was true. And he meant to have her, would not rest until she was his. A wry grin twisted his lips. Perhaps he was more of a savage than he cared to admit.

Elayna stood staring at the wall of the lodge, her arms wrapped around her waist. She could feel Michael's eyes on her back. Unbidden, came the memory of his kisses and her unexpected reaction. She had enjoyed his kisses, enjoyed the pleasure his touch aroused. She had drawn away, not because she was afraid of him, but because she had been afraid of her own desires, her own turbulent emotions. She was a white woman and he was an Indian. It was wrong for her to want him, and even worse because she hated him. It didn't make sense, she thought, to want to be held by a man she despised, a man who had slapped her. A man who had kidnapped her at gunpoint and threatened her life.

She turned, unable to resist the pull of his eyes, and found herself trapped in the hard web of his gaze. She stood frozen, unable to move, as he crossed the lodge toward her. For a moment he just stood there, staring down at her, and then, unable to resist the powerful urgings of his heart, he kissed her. Desire hotter and brighter than the rays of the sun exploded in his veins as his tongue plundered the silky depths of her mouth. He did not close the narrow space between them, did not take her in his arms. Only their mouths touched, and he thought that if she pulled away, he would let her go. But she did not pull away. Her eyelids fluttered down and she swayed against him, surrendering to the yearning she had been denying for too long.

His right arm went around her waist, drawing her length against him, letting her feel the heat of his desire. She moaned softly, and for one fleeting moment, sanity returned to him. He had to let her go. She did not belong here, in his world. He had no right to involve her in his life, no right at all, and nothing to offer her . . .

Only his love. He was here, and she was here, and he wanted her in his life more than he'd ever wanted anything.

He bent to kiss her, his hands playing over her back and buttocks as she pressed against him, the womanly warmth of her igniting the fires of passion. He kissed her until she was breathless, soft and pliant in his embrace. Gently he carried her down to the floor and undressed her, his own breathing becoming rapid as he gazed at her. She was a study in alabaster perfection, from her full, rosy-tipped breasts and narrow waist to her long, coltish legs and shapely calves.

He whispered her name as he drew her close, burying his face in the heavy silken mass of her hair.

Elayna tugged at his leggings, wanting to see him, all of him, and blushing furiously because of it. Michael sucked in a deep breath as he removed his clout, leggings, and moccasins, then stretched out beside her. For a moment they stared at each other, Michael's gaze bold and admiring as he let his gaze wander over her smooth ivory flesh, Elayna's gaze shy and curious as she marveled at the hard-muscled beauty of Michael's face and form.

And then he was caressing her, arousing her, until there was no room in her thoughts for anything but the wonder of his touch, the pleasure of his kisses, the magic of his hands. He was whispering to her, words she did not understand. Later she would wonder what he had said, and why he spoke to her in his native tongue, but for now nothing mattered but the touch of his hands and his kisses, kisses that filled her with breathless elation. Her own hands were never still. They moved over his back and shoulders and arms, marveling at the smooth silk of his skin, at the muscles that bunched beneath her questing fingertips. His eyes were as black as the sky on a dark night, his lips firm and demanding as he savored every inch of her face and neck, his tongue like a darting finger of flame, igniting new fires wherever it touched.

Only when she cried his name did he take her,

fulfilling her, satisfying every longing, every desire, as their bodies melded together, heat to heat.

His voice, muffled against her neck, followed her to sleep. "I love you," he murmured. "God help me, I love you."

Chapter 23

She woke to the sound of drums. For a moment she couldn't remember where she was, and then, as the memory of the night before surfaced, she was flooded with shame. She had behaved abominably, surrendering herself to a man she didn't love, didn't even like!

She sat up, the ecstasy she had known forgotten in the cold light of day. She felt used, dirty. Her skin seemed tainted with his touch, her thighs were stained with blood. The sign of her lost virtue. It should have been a gift, lovingly given, to her husband.

She glanced around the lodge. Where was he? She refused to acknowledge the possibility that she might be missing him, that she wanted to feel his arms around her, reassuring her.

She frowned, remembering his passionate vow of love, spoken as she fell asleep. Had she dreamed it? *I love you*, he had said. *God help me, I love you.*

Had he meant it? And how did she feel about him, really?

Before she had time to examine her feelings, he was there. He wore only a clout, and her eyes were drawn to the broad bare expanse of his chest and long, muscular legs. Speechless, she sat staring at him, her sleeping robe clutched to her breast to hide her nakedness.

"I'm going down to the river to bathe," Michael said. "Will you join me?"

It was in her mind to refuse. Being alone with him was the last thing she wanted just now. But the thought of being clean again outweighed her reluctance to accompany him.

"I'd like that," she said. "Just give me a minute to get dressed."

They found a secluded place upriver, separating so they could each have privacy.

Elayna stood on the sandy bank for several minutes, reluctant to undress in the open with Michael so near. But the prospect of a bath overcame her modesty and she undressed and stepped into the cool water, clutching the hard chunk of yellow soap Michael had given her.

Michael washed quickly, not wanting to leave Elayna alone too long, the memory of Winter Song's death still fresh in his mind.

On silent feet he made his way toward where Elayna was scrubbing herself. Seeing that she was still washing, he stood behind a tree, allowing her to bathe in private.

He didn't mean to spy on her, but he couldn't keep his gaze from straying in her direction, couldn't help but marvel anew at the beauty of her, the perfect symmetry of face and figure. Her hair, freshly washed, gleamed a dark red, like an autumn leaf washed by the rain. Her skin was smooth and unblemished, clothed in sparkling drops of sun-kissed water.

Elayna was humming softly when she left the river, her mood much improved now that she was clean again.

Standing on the bank, she lifted her arms toward the sun, letting its heavenly warmth dry her skin and hair. She wondered how her father was getting along, and if Lance was still searching for her. The rain would have washed out her tracks, but surely he would not turn back. Not so soon.

Kneeling beside the river, she washed her dress and petticoat and chemise, and then her stockings. She wished fleetingly for a change of clothes, for a hairbrush, a towel to wrap herself in.

She whirled around, her hands covering her breasts, at the sound of footsteps.

It was Michael.

"Ready to go?" he asked.

"Hardly," Elayna retorted. "Go away."

"It's not safe for you to be out here alone."

"I don't mind."

"I do."

Sensing her distress at being naked in front of him, he turned around, her image imprinted on his brain. She was beautiful, so beautiful. It took every ounce of will power he possessed to keep his hands from reaching for her.

Elayna breathed a sigh of relief, glad to be out from under his watchful eye, then stood there, staring at his back. The scabs were a dark crusty brown now, and she wondered if his back still hurt. He had a beautiful back, she thought absently. It was a shame to scar such a work of art.

She shook her head, disgusted with the trend of her thoughts. He was nothing but a savage, a kidnapper, a despoiler of virgins. She refused to acknowledge that she had wanted his lovemaking. He was an Indian. No decent white woman would want such a man. He had taken her from her home and brought her here, to live with a bunch of heathens. He had destroyed her life. She would never forgive him. Never.

She pulled on her damp clothes, took up her shoes and stockings, and began to run downriver, away from the village, away from Michael.

She heard him call after her, heard the sound of his footsteps as he pursued her, and she was overcome with panic. She had to get away. She could not stay here. She could not live with these awful people. Or with him.

She ran faster, running wildly, blindly. She gasped as she cut her foot on a sharp stone, but still she ran, fear adding wings to her feet.

His footsteps were louder now, closer. He was going to catch her. And even then she felt his hand close around her arm. She tried to shake him off, but his grip was like iron as he pulled her to a halt. Caught off balance, she fell, dragging him with her.

Her struggles were futile and she found herself flat on her back, her hands imprisoned in his, while he straddled her hips. They were both breathing heavily. And both were angry.

"Why the hell did you run?" Michael demanded.

"To get away from you. I want to go home."

"By yourself?" One black brow arched in amusement. "You think you could find your way home?"

"Yes," she said defiantly.

He chuckled softly. "Liar."

"I don't care. Let me go!"

"No."

She glared at him, trying to hate him, but his hands were warm where they held hers, his weight reminding her of the night past. It would be so much easier to hate him if he was ugly or mean, she thought helplessly, or if his touch didn't excite her so.

She saw the desire rise in his eyes and she turned her head away, afraid he would see that she, too, was remembering the night they had shared. Remembering and wanting him again, like some cheap harlot.

Michael grinned, his mood suddenly light. She would come around, he mused. She could deny it all she liked, insist she hated him, but there was an attraction between them that could not be ignored.

"Let's go back to camp," he said, rising. "I'm hungry."

"No."

Michael shook his head. "Cheyenne women are obedient wives," he said, reaching for her hand, and then he frowned. "What happened to your foot?"

"I cut it on a rock." She pushed his hand away. "Leave me alone. I'll fix it."

"I'll do it," he said, his voice leaving no doubt in her mind. Lifting her into his arms, he carried her down to the river and washed the blood from her foot, his hands gentle and concerned. Tearing a strip from her petticoat, he wrapped it around her foot and tied off the ends.

"I won't have any petticoat left if you keep ripping it into pieces," Elayna complained.

"You'd be more comfortable in a tunic," Michael said. "I'm sure Hemene has an extra one."

"I'm not a savage and I don't intend to dress like one," Elayna retorted. "Put me down."

"I'll carry you back to camp. You shouldn't put any weight on your foot."

"I'm fine."

"I said I'll carry you back to camp," Michael repeated firmly. "Am I going to have to argue with you about everything we do?"

"Probably."

He laughed softly. She felt good in his arms.

Her cheeks were flushed, her hair a riot of damp red curls, her mouth pouting and inviting. He gazed deep into her eyes, wondering how loudly she'd protest if he kissed her. Would she scream and holler if he laid her down in the soft grass and made love to her, or would she admit she wanted him as he wanted her?

He was looking for a place when a dozen shrieking boys came running toward them, their mock war cries filling the air.

Elayna grinned with relief. She had seen the look in Michael's eyes and known what it meant. But they were too near the camp now. She looked up at him, her expression triumphant.

But Michael only looked at her and shrugged. "There's always tonight," he murmured. "Or today, after breakfast."

Chapter 24

To Michael's chagrin, Elayna refused to accept the Cheyenne life-style.

He didn't ask anything of her the day she cut her foot, but the following morning when he returned from the river, he mentioned he was hungry.

"So eat," she retorted with a shrug.

"I will, just as soon as you fix it."

"I'm not hungry," she lied.

"I am."

"So eat!" she hollered. "Who's stopping you?"

"Perhaps I should explain the way things work here," Michael said. "You will do the cooking and the other domestic chores. You will prepare food when I'm hungry, bring me my pipe when I wish to smoke, and be polite to my guests, especially my family."

"Will I?"

"You will," Michael assured her. "You will fix my meals or you won't eat. You'll do as you're told, or you'll find yourself looking for another place to live. You may not think much of me or my lodge, but it's the only shelter you're likely to find, unless you want to play the whore for the single warriors in exchange for food and a place to sleep."

He regretted the words as soon as they were out of his mouth. Elayna recoiled as if he'd slapped her, her eyes mirroring horror and disbelief at the images his words brought to mind.

Before she could form a reply, he stalked out of the lodge.

Elayna stared after Michael for several minutes and then, frustrated beyond words, she stamped her foot. It was a childish display of temper, but it made her feel better.

The day stretched before her. She nosed around the lodge, but there wasn't much to see and nothing to eat but a strip of dried venison. She looked at it with distaste, but it was better than nothing.

When had time passed so slowly? She wondered what Michael was doing, and if he'd really meant the dreadful things he'd said. She wondered why he wouldn't let her go, and if she really wanted to leave him. She could have loved him, she thought, if they'd met in another time and place, but there was no hope for them now. Their people were at war, their ways as far apart as the moon from the sun.

She let out a long sigh. She'd never been so bored in her life. If only she had a book to read, or something to occupy her hands.

Lifting the lodge flap, she peered outside. The camp was bustling with activity—women cooking, men gambling, children playing in the sun. They all looked busy and happy, she thought, and a wave of self-pity washed over her. Everybody had something to do, someone to talk to. Everybody but her.

She was in bed, feigning sleep, when Michael finally returned to the lodge.

She tried not to watch as he undressed, but she couldn't seem to draw her gaze away, nor could she deny the powerful attraction she felt for him, even now when she was trying so hard to hate him.

She was still awake long after Michael had gone to sleep, more miserable than she'd ever been in her life.

A week passed, and they formed a truce of sorts. Elayna cooked and kept the lodge tidy, and Michael kept them supplied with meat, rabbits and deer and an occasional turkey.

They slept apart, denying the attraction between them, but Elayna heard every breath Michael took, knew when he rolled over, knew when he was watching her, his dark eyes alight with desire. And then, as if things weren't bad enough, she began to dream about him, about his hands caressing her, his voice whispering her name. There was nothing to keep them apart in her dreams, no barriers, either real or imagined. In her dreams, Michael was a man, neither red nor white, and she was a woman, neither white nor red, and they made love boldly, passionately, satisfying the longing that plagued them both.

The constant frustration of being his prisoner combined with her troubled dreams made an explosion inevitable. It came on a cool cloudy evening.

"I'm sick of venison," Elayna snapped as Michael dropped a deer haunch at her feet. But the abundance of venison was the last thing on her mind. She felt trapped, caught between her yearning to go home and her forbidden desire for Michael.

"If you don't like it, don't eat it," Michael retorted, unable to draw his gaze from her pouting pink lips, or the angry swell of her breasts.

"I want to go home."

"No."

"I'm lonely."

"It's your own fault. The women have tried to be friendly, but you refuse to go with them when they go for wood or water." With that he turned and stalked from the lodge.

Elayna's expression turned sullen. The women *had* tried to include her in their outings, though none of them spoke more than a word or two of English. Still, she would have liked to be a part of their group, but for one thing: she was afraid they'd laugh at her because she was ignorant of their ways and customs, afraid they'd ridicule her if she made a mistake. Better they should think her aloof than a fool. She felt so out of place here, so apart. Perhaps if Michael would spend more time with her, explain the customs of his people, but he rarely spoke to her.

When they had first arrived, he told her they were at the South Platte. The river was running low this time of year. Sand bars and islands rose in the midst of the shallow muddy water. Sandhill cranes were plentiful here. Michael had told her the Indians believed the birds possessed strong protective powers. Their feathers were often used on war shields. Some warriors believed that if they imitated the cry of the sandhill crane during a battle, they would not be hit by an enemy arrow. She wondered if one of the bird's feathers would protect her from Michael.

She stepped outside and glanced around the village. The Indian lodges stood in a great circle. The entrance of each lodge faced the rising sun. Most were decorated with moons or stars, with comets and bright yellow suns. The tops were blackened from the smoke of countless fires. On warm days the sides were rolled up so air could circulate through the lodge; in the winter grass was stuffed between the lodge cover and the inner liner for added protection from the cold and the wind.

The daily routine rarely changed. In the morning the women prepared breakfast while the men and young boys went to the river to bathe. It was a ritual observed both summer and winter by Cheyenne males, for they believed that bathing washed away sickness.

After breakfast, the men went hunting while the women gathered wood and water, cleaned the lodge, and looked after the children. The younger ones stayed close to their mothers while the older ones went to the river or into the tall grass near the camp. Many of the older boys spent long hours practicing with the bow and arrow, while the older girls learned to sew and quill.

Her gaze swept the camp, but there was no sign of Michael. Nearby she saw the old warrior who was the camp crier. He made his rounds on horseback each morning, always starting at the opening of the camp circle, which faced east, riding south, then west, then north. His announcements varied from day to day. This morning he had announced that the Dog Soldiers were having a dance, and that Red-Furred Bear had lost his turkey-tail fan.

Seeing some of the young men getting ready for the dance, she watched, amused, as they labored over their appearance, painstakingly plucking hairs from their faces, applying paint, braiding their long black hair. Sometimes they dressed in their finery in the middle of the day and rode through the camp so the people, especially the young, unmarried women, could admire them.

Then she saw Michael. He was walking with Yellow Spotted Wolf, and she noticed again how alike they were. The two men stopped to talk to Red-Furred Bear, and the sound of Michael's laughter reached her ears.

And then he was looking at her, and the distance between them seemed to disappear. She felt the tension hum between them as his eyes met hers, felt her heart flutter as his gaze lingered on her lips, then slid over her breasts and hips. And then, with a grimace, he looked away.

She felt a keen sense of disappointment. He had been avoiding her, and she had no one to blame but herself. She tried to tell herself she didn't care, that he was nothing to her but a godless savage, a ruthless man who had kidnapped her and carried her into the wilderness to live with a bunch of heathens, a man who had forced her to submit to his lust, but she knew it was a lie.

Michael had been kind to her. He had made love to her gently, tenderly, and she knew in her heart that he would have stopped if she had but said the word. He had tried to make her feel at home, had offered to teach her his language, but she had rebuffed him at every turn, often pretending to be unaware of his presence. But there was no way to ignore Michael Wolf. The lodge offered no privacy, and he seemed to have no qualms about dressing or undressing in front of her, nor could she seem to keep her gaze from straying in his direction, as it was now.

He was walking toward her and she felt her heart beat a little faster as he approached. He was so handsome. He wore only a brief wolfskin clout, the broad expanse of his chest drawing her gaze as a bee was drawn to a flower.

"There's a dance tonight," he said, his tone flat. "Do you want to go?"

She did, but some perverse demon took hold of her tongue, and she heard herself refusing him. He didn't give her a chance to change her mind, simply turned on his heel and walked away.

He was angry with her, Elayna thought. Well, maybe it was for the best. Maybe now he would agree to take her home.

"She refused?" Yellow Spotted Wolf surmised from the look on Wolf's face.

Michael nodded, wondering why he kept trying, wondering why he cared. He had encouraged her to socialize with the other women, to learn his language, to adopt the clothing of his people, but she had stubbornly refused, and after a while he had left her alone, knowing she would have to come to terms with her new environment in her own time and in her own way.

As for the tension between them, he was as aware of it as she was, perhaps more so. He knew that the strong sexual attraction between them could not be ignored forever, and he had the feeling that, once Elayna admitted she cared for him, everything would work out. He only hoped he could keep a tight rein on his emotions until then. He purposefully spent most of his time out of the lodge, away from the constant temptation to touch her, to hold her, to draw her down on the buffalo robes and bury himself in her sweetness whether she was willing or not.

"Wolf?"

He was aware that Yellow Spotted Wolf had asked him a question and was waiting for an answer.

"She has a strong hold on your heart, cousin," Yellow Spotted Wolf remarked with a grin. "I will talk to you later, when your mind is not on your woman."

Michael nodded and Yellow Spotted Wolf walked away, heading for a group of young men who were playing the hoop and pole game.

He glanced at his lodge. Elayna had gone inside, and he stared at the doorway, wondering if there would ever be a time when his mind wasn't on Elayna. It was hard, staying away from her. During the day he spent long hours listening to the old men talk of ancient battles, of buffalo hunts and horse raids against their ancestral enemies, the Crow and the Pawnee.

He prayed each morning to the Great Spirit, praying that he might stay here, with the people he had grown to love, with Elayna, who was like a fire in his blood, a thirst he could not quench.

He spent much of his time with Yellow Spotted Wolf. It was hard, sometimes, to remember that the tall, good-looking young man was his great-grandfather. Yellow Spotted Wolf was an exceptional warrior. Though he was only sixteen, his expertise with bow and arrow and lance were unsurpassed. His horsemanship was superb, his courage already proven on a number of occasions. Many families hoped that he would take one of their daughters to wife when the time came, for Yellow Spotted Wolf seemed destined for greatness, like Sitting Bull and Crazy Horse. He had taken part in the Sun Dance, he had counted coup on a living enemy, he had taken the scalp of a Pawnee chief.

There had been many times when Michael had started to tell Yellow Spotted Wolf who he was, but somehow he could never find the right words, though he longed to share his secret with someone else. He tried to imagine what he would say if someone came to him, claiming to be from the future, and he knew he'd never believe it. Never. And so he kept putting it off until it no longer seemed important. He was here with Elayna, and that was all that mattered.

And so the balmy days of summer passed and Michael's admiration for his great-grandfather grew, and with it his love and admiration for the Cheyenne people.

His people. They were warm and caring, generous and kind. There were no poor among them; widows were provided for, and good hunters shared their kill with those in need. And as his affection for his people grew, he knew an overwhelming sadness that their way of life would not last. Already the buffalo were decreasing in number because the whites were determined to hunt them to extinction. Settlers in ever-growing hordes were headed westward, drawn by the lure of fertile farmland and a better life. The railroad was leaving smoky tracks across the Great Plains, the Army was determined to subdue all the tribes, to move the Indians off their homeland to make way for the land-hungry whites.

But for now, for this one last summer, life was good.

Chapter 25

Elayna walked slowly along the riverbank, her thoughts drifting toward home. She wondered how her father was getting along, if her best friend, Nancy Avery, had married Sergeant O'Farrell, if the Army was still searching for her, if Lance was still waiting, hoping for her safe return.

Lance. Even if she was rescued and returned to Camp Robinson, she could never marry Lance, not now. And it was all Michael Wolf's fault. He had stolen her virginity. She was ruined now. Damaged goods. No self-respecting white man would want her.

The thought did not distress her as much as it should have, but she didn't stop to wonder why. Instead, she found herself thinking of Michael.

There were times when she yearned for the comfort of his arms, for the sound of his voice murmuring soft Cheyenne words of love in her ear, but she knew if she surrendered now, she would never be able to leave him. And she did not belong here; she would never belong here. With an effort, she drew her thoughts away from Michael Wolf.

It was a beautiful day, bright and clear and warm. She paused in mid-stride to watch a sparrow dusting its feathers in a shallow depression beside the riverbank, smiled as she saw a large yellow butterfly alight on the petal of a lavender flower. A chipmunk scampered across her path and disappeared in the underbrush.

Still smiling, she continued walking, her troubles disappearing as she lost herself in the beauty of her surroundings. Leaving the river, she walked through the tall prairie grass, then gasped, her fingers flying to hold her nose, as a skunk strolled past, its tail held aloft.

She breathed a sigh of relief as the striped creature ambled past. The air smelled of pine and sage and earth, the sun was warm on her face, the grass soft beneath her feet.

Wandering aimlessly, Elayna thought about Michael's family. They were kind and loving people. She could sense the genuine love and affection between Mo'ohta-vo'nehe and Hemene, the concern they had for their children, the respect Badger and Yellow Spotted Wolf had for their parents.

She had never imagined that Indians loved

each other. She had thought of them as savages, but living with the Cheyenne had forced her to change her opinion of Indians. Even though she was an outsider, she could see that the Cheyenne people, as a whole, were a warm and caring people. They were gentle parents, rarely resorting to physical punishment when their children misbehaved. They held their old people in high esteem, revered their gods, respected life.

Though she still refused to learn Michael's language, she had picked up a few words anyway. *Mesevoz* meant baby, *nakohe* meant mother, *moheno* was the word for horse, *hotova'a* meant buffalo. It was a strange language, though it had a musical sound on Michael's tongue.

Michael. His image danced across her mind, unbidden but not undesirable. She had been drawn to him from the first, and not just because he was more handsome than any man she had ever known. She had sensed that he was lost, that he needed someone. She had known intuitively that he was a good man, one who cared for other people. Still, there was an air of mystery about him. His name, for instance. Who ever heard of an Indian named Michael? And then there was the way he talked, as if he had been raised by a civilized white family instead of heathen savages.

Elayna frowned. She was certain there was something he hadn't told her about himself, his past, some secret he was keeping. She tried to imagine what it could be, but instead she heard his voice in the back of her mind, softly whispering that he loved her. Did he mean it? And what if he did? It changed nothing. He was an Indian. She was white. She did not belong here, with him, would never belong here. They were worlds apart, and yet the thought of going home, of never seeing Michael Wolf again, filled her with dismay.

She had been walking for over an hour when she came to an abrupt halt, the realization that she was alone and far from camp causing a moment of panic. She had been warned not to stray from the protection of the village. Michael had described the dangers lurking beyond the camp several times, reminding her that enemy tribes were a constant danger. And there were wild animals: wolves and coyotes, bears and snakes and mountain lions.

Elayna shuddered. She had heard the long, blood-curdling cry of a mountain lion back at Camp Robinson. The sound had sent shivers down her spine. But surely there were no mountain lions here, on the treeless prairie.

A chill wind blew across the land, causing the grass to dance gently back and forth. Crossing her arms over her breasts, she started walking back the way she had come, eager to return to the warmth of her lodge.

Michael swung down from his horse and stretched his arms overhead before lifting the deer he had killed from his mount's withers. He grinned as he imagined Elayna's distaste when she saw the deer. Thus far, he had taken his kills to Hemene and she had done the skinning and butchering, and they had divided the meat and hides. But Michael had decided it was time for Elayna to learn how to skin a deer. She did fairly well with rabbits, though she found the task repugnant.

He stepped into the lodge, steeling himself for the argument he knew would be forthcoming.

But the lodge was empty, the fire out, the ashes cold.

Stepping outside, he went to Yellow Spotted Wolf's lodge and rapped on the cover, waiting for permission to enter before he stepped inside.

Mo'ohta-vo'nehe was making a new bridle for his war pony. Hemene was mending one of Badger's shirts. She smiled and stood up as Michael entered the lodge.

"Welcome, Wolf," she said. "Will you eat?"

Michael nodded, knowing she would be offended if he refused. Sitting cross-legged beside Mo'ohta-vo'nehe, he accepted a bowl of berries and a strip of cold meat.

"Ne-a'ese," he murmured. Only after eating did he state the reason for his visit. "Have you seen Elayna?" he asked, his gaze moving from Mo'ohta-vo'nehe to Hemene.

Mo'ohta-vo'nehe shook his head. "Not since last night."

Hemene frowned thoughtfully. "I saw her walking toward the river."

"When?"

"Etaesh'omoes."

Michael frowned. It was near dusk. Hemene

had seen Elayna walking toward the river at three o'clock, over two hours ago.

"*Ne-a'ese,*" Michael said, rising. He smiled at Mo'ohta-vo'nehe and Hemene and left the lodge.

Frowning, he took up his bow and slung his quiver over his left shoulder. Swinging onto his horse's back, he headed for the river. He knew Elayna was unhappy here, but surely she would not be foolish enough to try and run away, on foot, with no one to guide her, no one to protect her. He shook off the horrible images that came to mind; images of Winter Song lying dead beside the river.

He found Elayna's tracks beside the river and followed her trail as it meandered along the riverbank, then turned away from the water into the tall grass. He found tracks aplenty, but no sign of Elayna.

She had been so sure she could find her way back to the river, but somehow she'd gotten turned around and now she was lost, hopelessly lost. And it was almost dark.

Changing direction, she took her courage in hand, chiding herself for being afraid. How far from camp could she have walked in a couple of hours? She'd been going the wrong way before, but she was on the right track now.

A low growl rose out of the grass to her right. She halted in mid-stride, her gaze swinging toward the sound.

There were three of them gathered around a deer carcass: a large gray male wolf and two smaller females. The male stood up, his blood-stained teeth bared, his hackles raised.

Elayna froze, her heart hammering with fear as the three wolves stared at her through unblinking yellow eyes. She tried to remember what Michael had told her about wolves, but her mind was blank. They were so big. Blood dripped from their fangs, low warning growls rumbled in their throats.

The male took a stiff-legged step forward and Elayna closed her eyes. Too frightened to move, she prayed that the end would come quickly . . .

He had almost given up all hope of finding her when he saw her silhouetted against the setting sun. He frowned, puzzled by her unnatural stance. And then he heard the low-pitched growl.

Raising his bow overhead, he drummed his heels against his horse's flanks and let out a blood-curdling war cry.

Elayna's eyes flew open as the long, ululating cry filled the air. She saw a warrior riding toward her at a full gallop, saw the wolves break and run as the horseman approached. Her first thought was that she was being attacked, but then her knees went weak with relief.

It was Michael.

Her relief was short-lived. His face was dark with anger, his eyes awful to see, and it occurred to her that she would have had a better chance with the wolves.

"What the hell are you doing out here alone?" Michael demanded. "I've told you a dozen times not to wander away from camp. Dammit, didn't you listen to a word I said?''

She'd never seen him so angry. She wished she could summon the energy to holler back at him, but the close call she'd had with the wolves was just sinking in. She looked up at him, mute, wishing she could curl up in his arms, but there was no way she could approach him now, not when he was glaring at her.

Instead of answering him, she walked away, her head high as she blinked back her tears. She'd been scared to death. She didn't want a lecture, she wanted someone to hold her, to comfort her.

"Where the hell do you think you're going?" Michael shouted. He was furious with her for leaving the village, for putting her life in danger, for scaring the hell out of him. He'd never heard of a wolf attacking a man, but there was always a first time. "Dammit, woman, I asked you a question and you'd damn well better answer me."

"I'm going back to camp," she retorted.

Michael snorted. "What makes you think you could find it?"

His sarcasm dried her tears and stiffened her spine. "I'll find it."

"Yeah." Clucking to his horse, he rode up beside Elayna. "Give me your hand."

"No."

"Give me your hand!"

"I'd rather walk, if you don't mind."

"I do mind." Slipping his bow over his shoulder, he reached down and wrapped his arm around her waist, lifting her onto the back of his horse as if she weighed no more than a sack of flour.

She refused to look at him. His arm was like steel around her waist. His hard-muscled thighs cradled her own, his breath was warm against her cheek. She tried to draw away from him, but he tightened his grip on her waist, keeping her back pinned against his chest.

It was dark now. She stared straight ahead, wishing she could rest her head against his shoulder and pour out all her pent-up fears. She wanted soft words of reassurance, but she was too proud to give in. She wanted him to make the first move.

Michael drew in a deep breath, his nostrils filling with the scent of woman. Strands of her hair brushed against his cheek, her back was warm against his chest.

He thought of taking her there, in the high grass, and easing the awful aching need her nearness aroused in him. But she had rebuffed him too often in the past. And he did not want to take her by force. He wanted her warm and willing, her lips softly inviting his kisses, her body yearning for his touch.

"Katum!" He swore softly in Cheyenne, wondering if Elayna O'Brien would ever admit she cared for the man who would not let her go.

Chapter 26

He woke to the sound of crying. Sitting up, he listened for a moment. It was Elayna, sobbing as though her heart would break, the sound muffled beneath her sleeping robes.

Rolling out of his blankets, he knelt beside her. "Elayna, what's wrong?"

"I'm so unhappy," she wailed, and a fresh flood of tears washed down her cheeks.

With a sigh, Michael gathered her into his arms. With gentle hands he stroked her back, murmuring to her, telling her he understood. But did he? What kind of man was he, to keep a woman against her will? Of course she was unhappy. If he had any decency at all, he would take her home.

And yet, he did not want to let her go. He

remembered lying in the bottom of the ravine, badly wounded and on the verge of unconsciousness, remembered seeing a woman walking toward him through a white world, and a voice whispering in his ear, *She is waiting, waiting for you.*

The woman had been Elayna. He could not be mistaken about that. Or was he? Maybe he had substituted her face for that of the woman in his vision because he had wanted to justify his desire for her. Hell, maybe he'd imagined the whole thing.

Fact or fantasy, one thing remained clear, he had to take Elayna back to her father. It was where she belonged, where she yearned to be.

Tenderly he tilted her face toward his, and the utter misery he saw in her eyes stabbed at his heart.

"Don't cry, honey," he said quietly. "I'll take you home tomorrow."

They left at first light, just the two of them. Elayna's farewells had been brief. She had bid Yellow Spotted Wolf and his family goodbye, thanking them for their kindness, but in her mind she had already left them behind. She was going home. Home to her father. Home to civilization, and soft beds and cold milk. Home. Where she belonged.

She stared at Michael's back as they rode across the flat grassy plain. He hadn't said a word to her since they left the village, nor did he say anything when they stopped for lunch, or when they bedded down for the night.

He prepared their meals, laid out their bed-rolls, built the fire, looked after the horses.

His silence made her uncomfortable, and then it made her angry. Crawling into her blankets, she closed her eyes and willed sleep to come. Instead, she lay awake, gazing at Michael through the veil of her lashes. He was sitting cross-legged beside the fire, his hands resting on his thighs.

She let her gaze wander over his face, unconsciously memorizing his features, the color of his skin, the spread of his shoulders.

She felt his eyes swing in her direction, felt her stomach quiver at the force of his gaze. The heat of it. The hunger . . .

With an effort she drew her gaze from his, turned her back toward him, and closed her eyes.

She was going home.

They were halfway to the fort when they rode down a steep hill and came face to face with thirty cavalrymen.

Michael cursed under his breath as he reined his horse to an abrupt halt. His first impulse was to make a run for it and hope he could outride the troopers, but there was no way to outride a bullet. And there was Elayna to consider. He couldn't take a chance on her getting hit by a bullet meant for him.

And then it was too late to run. He was surrounded, his weapons taken, his hands tightly bound behind his back.

He watched as a tall, blond officer lifted

Elayna from the back of her horse, saw Elayna's smile of pleasure as the lieutenant took both her hands in his. And then he heard a harsh bark of laughter as Sergeant Saunders swaggered into view.

"Major Cathcart's gonna be real pleased to have you back," the sergeant drawled. "Yessir, real pleased."

Cathcart, Michael thought bleakly. *Damn*.

Lance smiled at Elayna as he handed her a tin plate filled with beans and bacon. "Sorry about the grub. It's the best we've got till we get back to the fort."

"It smells wonderful," Elayna replied. "And so does the coffee."

Lance nodded, then turned to stare at Michael Wolf. "Did he treat you all right?"

"Yes. I'd rather not talk about it."

"He didn't . . ." Lance cleared his throat. "He didn't force himself on you?"

"No," Elayna answered quietly. "He didn't force himself on me." *He didn't have to use force*, she thought, ashamed. *I was only too willing*.

She didn't have to look at Michael to know he was watching her. She could feel the intensity of his gaze. He had refused to eat and now sat with his back against a rock, his hands tied behind his back, his face wiped clean of all emotion.

"What will happen to him?" she asked.

Lance shrugged. "That's up to the major. But I reckon he'll hang." Lance glared at Michael. "I'd like to tie the knot myself. Are you sure you're all right?"

240

"I'm fine. Just tired. If you don't mind, I think I'll turn in."

The next two days on the trail were like a bad dream.

Lance stayed at her side, looking after her comfort, eager to please her, his smiles assuring her that he still cared, and each kind word and each chaste caress was like a millstone around her neck. She didn't deserve his kindness, was no longer worthy of his respect. She had let Michael Wolf make love to her. Knowing it was wrong, she had let him make love to her. How could she have done such a thing?

And Michael . . . He rode straight and tall, his eyes focused on the trail ahead. He didn't eat, didn't speak, didn't look at her. And her heart ached for him, for the loss of his freedom, for the humiliation she knew he was suffering. And she knew that worse things awaited him at the fort.

The third night out, Saunders pulled a whip from his saddlebag and gave an impromptu exhibition of his skill. Each crack of the long, deadly-looking lash sounded like thunder in the quiet of the night.

Elayna's gaze kept straying toward Michael. His face was impassive. Only the twitch of a muscle in his jaw showed that he understood that Saunders was reminding him of what was in store when they reached the fort.

Sleep was a long time coming that night. Her dreams were filled with grotesque images of Michael . . . Michael being brutally whipped . . .

Michael standing on the gallows, an enormous rope around his neck. And she was there, too, her hand ready to spring the trap that would send him plummeting to his death.

She woke in a cold sweat, her body trembling, her mouth dry. She couldn't let him hang. Lifting her head a little, she glanced around the camp. There were only two sentries. They stood together, talking quietly as they shared a cigarette.

Rising, Elayna smiled and waved, then indicated she needed to step into the shadows. One of the troopers nodded that he understood, then turned back to his companion.

Moving quickly, Elayna disappeared into the darkness; then, as stealthily as she could, she crept toward Michael.

She had thought to find him asleep, but he was lying on his side, awake, trying to loosen the ropes that bound his wrists. He didn't move as she crept up behind him and began to untie the rope.

"I'll distract the guards while you get away," she whispered as she released his hands. "Be careful."

He turned to face her, his expression unreadable in the darkness, yet she could feel his eyes on her face.

"Come with me."

"No."

He did not ask her twice.

She glanced over her shoulder to check on the

whereabouts of the sentries, and when she looked back, Michael was gone.

She knew a moment of regret, knowing she would never see him again, and then she stood up and walked toward the sentries, praying that Michael would get safely home.

What happened next happened very fast.

The two sentries turned toward her as she approached them.

"Cold, isn't it?" she said, hoping to engage them in conversation until Michael had a good head start.

"Yes, ma'am," Trooper Hutchins agreed. "Shall I build up the fire for you?"

"No," Elayna said quickly. Darkness was the only protection Michael had. "It isn't that cold."

She was congratulating herself on a job well done when Michael stepped out of the darkness behind the troopers. Before she could react, he brought a rock down on the back of the head of the sentry nearest him, grabbed the man's rifle, and jammed the barrel into the back of the second trooper before the unconscious soldier hit the ground.

"Not a word," Michael warned Hutchins. "Hand me your rifle and that knife, then get belly down in the dirt."

The trooper did as he was told, his face a sickly shade of gray as he lay face down on the ground.

Using the same rope that had bound his own hands, Michael secured the trooper's hands behind his back, then jammed his headband into the trooper's mouth.

Elayna watched as Michael went to the picket line and quickly gathered the reins to all the horses, save one. And she knew he had left that one for her, so she wouldn't have to walk to the fort.

Michael was swinging onto his horse's back when Lance sat up. In a glance, the lieutenant saw the two sentries on the ground, and then he saw Michael. Drawing his sidearm, he fired at Michael, instantly awakening the whole camp.

In seconds, every soldier was firing in Michael's direction.

Elayna screamed, "No, no!" as she threw herself at Lance, who shook her hand off his arm. Soldiers were running everywhere, some still firing in the direction Michael had gone even though he was out of sight.

And then she was running, too, running for her horse.

She heard Lance shout her name as she grabbed a handful of the horse's mane and pulled herself onto its back. A trooper materialized out of the shadows to her right, his hand reaching for her horse's bridle. Instinctively she kicked out at him, her heel catching him in the chest and knocking him off balance.

And then she was riding after Michael.

She rode for an eternity through the dark night, trusting that her horse would follow the others. She didn't stop to wonder what she would do if she didn't find Michael, nor did she dare examine her reasons for riding off after him when she was almost home. She just rode steadily onward, refusing to consider the very real possibility that she might be riding in the wrong direction.

It was near dawn when she saw the first of the Army horses. Lathered with sweat, they stood in small groups, heads hanging, sides heaving.

But there was no sign of Michael.

She urged her weary horse onward, her eyes searching the ground for some sign of his passing. She saw an occasional hoofprint, and then, as the ground grew softer, his trail became clear and easy to follow.

She found his horse a short time later. Its left foreleg was broken. Its throat had been cut.

Elayna turned away, gagging. And then she saw it, an uneven trail of flattened grass, and a single smear of fresh blood.

Dismounting, she hurried forward, unmindful of the thorny brush that scratched her arms and snagged her skirt. The trail led slowly upward, the hillside dotted with trees and brush and an occasional boulder. She held her skirt off the ground with one hand, her horse's reins in the other.

She'd gone about a quarter of a mile when she rounded an outcropping of rock and found herself staring into the business end of a Winchester rifle.

"Michael," she breathed. "Thank God."

"What the hell are you doing here?" he growled.

What the hell *was* she doing there? She'd wanted to go home, had begged Michael to take her home. Why had she followed him?

"I . . . I thought you'd been shot," she stammered. "I had to be sure you were all right."

"I'm fine. Go home."

He lifted a hand to his head, then shrugged. "It's nothing. I must have hit my head when my horse fell."

Elayna stared at him. He was sitting down, his back against a large rock. He was holding the rifle in his left hand, the barrel propped on his bent left knee. For the first time, she noticed the tight lines of pain around his mouth. His breathing was shallow and labored.

"What is it?" she asked, frowning. "What's wrong?"

"Go home, Elayna," he said in a tight voice. "You wanted to go home. Now go."

"Not until you tell me what's wrong."

"That damn horse landed on me when it fell. I think I might have busted my shoulder and a couple of ribs."

"Let me look at it."

He nodded as he laid his rifle aside. "Go ahead."

As gently as she could, she examined his shoulder. It was badly bruised, the skin already discolored, but it wasn't broken. Neither were his ribs, though his midriff was also badly bruised and discolored.

She grinned wryly as she lifted her skirt and tore the last few ruffles from her petticoat, wondering what she'd have used for bandages if fashion hadn't dictated the wearing of ruffled petticoats.

She placed Michael's right arm in a sling, bound his ribs for support. He was hurting, she mused, but as sore as he was now, it would be worse by tomorrow.

"You'll have to rest for the next three or four days," she said, smoothing her skirt down over what was left of her petticoat. "And you'll be stiff for a week or so, but at least nothing's broken."

"We can't stay here for three or four days."

"Why not?"

"Think about it."

He was right. They had no food, no water, no matches for a fire.

"You won't be able to ride for at least a day or two," Elayna said, "and even then it's going to hurt like the very devil."

"It hurts now."

"I know, but it's going to get worse before it gets better. You've got some nasty bruises there. They aren't going to heal overnight."

Michael nodded glumly. He'd taken a course or two in First Aid. The surface bruises were already black and blue; it would take a day or two for the deeper ones to surface and when they did, he'd be a sight to see.

"Why don't you take a nap?" Elayna suggested. "I'll see if I can't find some berries or something."

"Take the rifle, just in case."

Michael watched her walk away, wondering why she had followed him.

He was still puzzling over the question as he drifted to sleep.

Elayna sat beside Michael, watching him sleep. They'd eaten the berries she'd found, and then Michael had fallen asleep again. He was hurting, but it would only be for a few days. She thanked God he hadn't been hurt worse, and then, unable to hold them back any longer, she let the tears come, releasing all the hurt and confusion of the past few weeks.

She cared for Michael Wolf, cared for him deeply. Why else had she been so concerned for his welfare back at the fort? Why else had she defied Lance, risked her father's ire and Major Cathcart's wrath by visiting Michael in the guardhouse? And when he escaped, forcing her to go with him, why hadn't she hollered for help? One scream would have brought a hundred soldiers to her defense. Michael would not have harmed her. She knew it now. She had known it then.

She cared for Michael Wolf. The realization had hit her like a shaft of lightning when she saw him riding away from her amid a hail of bullets. He could have been killed, and it would have been all her fault.

And yet, admitting she cared for him solved nothing. He was still an Indian. She was still white. But somehow those differences no longer seemed as important as they once had.

Chapter 27

Michael was stiff and sore in every muscle the next day. His entire upper body was black and blue, and his shoulder hurt like sin.

Elayna went looking for more berries but returned empty-handed, and it was then that Michael offered her his knife.

"Go cut some meat from my horse," he told her.

"I can't."

"We've got to eat something, and that's all there is."

"Raw? I couldn't."

"I'll try and start a fire. And don't forget to take the rifle."

Face grim with determination, Elayna

mounted her horse and rode down the brush-covered slope to where Michael's horse lay rotting in the sun. She stared at the fly-blown carcass for several minutes and knew there was no way she could cut into the bloated carcass, let alone eat the meat, raw *or* cooked.

But they had to eat something. Her stomach was growling even now, but more urgent than the need for food was the need for water. Surely there was a stream or a waterhole nearby.

She rode past the dead horse, her gaze sweeping the plains for some sign of water, and then she gave her horse free rein, hoping it would find water, but the mare dropped her head and began cropping the sparse yellow grass.

Discouraged, Elayna was about to turn back when she saw the horsemen. There were two of them. For a moment she feared they were Indians, but as the riders drew closer, she saw they were white.

Miners, Elayna thought, her spirits rising. Perhaps they'd have some food and water to spare.

"Well, hello there, girlie. What're you doing out here all alone?"

Elayna stared at the man, her relief quickly turning to apprehension. He was big and broad-shouldered, with a long scar across his left cheek. His hair was long and dirty, his buckskins stained with filth.

The second man was reed-thin. His hair was black and greasy, his close-set brown eyes malevolent.

Elayna felt her blood turn cold when she saw the long black scalps hanging from the thin man's saddlehorn.

"What's the matter, girlie?" the first man asked with a leer. "Cat got your tongue?"

The second man grinned. "I'll have her hollerin' with pleasure, Ed, just you wait."

"*You* wait," the man called Ed retorted, "you was first the last time."

"Like hell, I . . ."

She'd die before she let either man touch her, Elayna thought, and slamming her heels into her horse's sides, she raced back the way she had come.

With a whoop, the two men gave chase.

Elayna pounded her heels into the mare's sides, her heart hammering with fear. Only then did she remember the rifle. She vowed she'd use it if she had to, and prayed it wouldn't be necessary, because she knew she'd never be able to pull the trigger, to take a human life. Not even to save her own.

She was breathless with fear when she reached Michael. Sliding from her horse, she ran toward him.

"They're coming!" She clutched the rifle to her breast, her chest heaving.

"Who's coming?" Michael asked, but before Elayna could reply, the two men were there. They pulled their horses to an abrupt halt when they saw Michael.

"Well, I'll be damned," Ed exclaimed. "Looks like we got us another scalp, Clem."

"And a woman," Clem mused. "Put the rifle down, honey. We ain't gonna hurt ya."

What happened next was forever burned in Elayna's mind. It happened so fast, and yet it seemed they were all moving in slow motion, she saw everything so clearly.

The man called Ed drew his Colt and aimed it at Michael, who was struggling to his feet while the man called Clem dismounted and started toward her.

But it was Michael who was in danger. Without thinking, she swung the rifle around and squeezed the trigger, a sob rising in her throat as she saw the awful red stain that spread across Ed's chest before he toppled to the ground.

But the horror was not over. She felt a tug at her side as Michael wrenched his knife from her skirt pocket and hurled it at Clem. It sank to the hilt in the man's chest and he stood there, staring at the quivering handle, for stretched seconds before he crumpled to the ground at Michael's feet.

For a moment, time seemed to stand still, and then, with a low groan, Michael dropped to his knees, his left hand cradling his right arm.

Elayna stared at Michael, and then at the rifle in her hands. She had killed a man. The bile rose hot and thick in her throat and she dropped the rifle and turned away, retching violently.

She had killed a man. She closed her eyes, but the memory was permanently seared in her mind: the weight of the rifle in her hands, the weapon's recoil as she squeezed the trigger, the

sound of the gunshot, the acrid smell of gun-
smoke, and the blood . . .

Michael drew a deep breath, willing the pain
in his shoulder to subside as he gained his feet
and went to stand beside Elayna. Placing his left
arm around her shoulder, he drew her close.
"It's all right."

"No." She was crying now, silent tears that
burned her eyes but did nothing to ease her
guilt.

"You saved my life."

The words were softly spoken, filled with
gratitude. And truth.

She stayed in his arms a long time, content to
be held. And then she felt him tremble against
her and she remembered that he had been hurt.
She thought of the strength needed to throw the
knife that had killed Clem, the strain on his
bruised shoulder, and a rush of gratitude filled
her heart. She had saved Michael's life, but he
had saved her from something far worse than
death.

"Sit down," she urged. "Your shoulder . . ."

"I'm all right."

"Please?"

"Later." He glanced at the dead men. "Let's
get out of here."

He didn't have to ask her twice. She helped
him mount Ed's horse, saw the pain darken his
eyes as he eased into the saddle. She picked up
the rifle, took up the reins of Clem's horse, and
then mounted her own mare and followed Michael down the slope.

They rode for over an hour, heading south toward the Platte. Camp Robinson lay in the opposite direction, and Elayna felt a twinge of regret as they rode further away from her father. She would have liked to see him, if only for a little while, to assure him she was all right. But then she looked at Michael and in her heart she knew she was where she belonged. Lance would tell her father she was alive and well.

She chuckled softly. Her father would never believe she had gone with Michael Wolf willingly this time. Not in a million years.

Chapter 28

Lance was scowling blackly when he left the major's office, his ears still ringing with Cathcart's verbal abuse. He'd been in the Army for ten years, he mused, and served under Cathcart for eight, and this was the worst dressing down he'd ever received.

Pausing on the porch outside the major's office, he glanced across the parade ground at the infirmary. He wasn't looking forward to talking to Elayna's father about what had happened, but putting it off wasn't going to make it any easier.

Swearing softly, he walked down the stairs and headed toward the infirmary. Cathcart had given him twelve hours to rest up before he rode out again.

"And don't come back without those horses," Cathcart had warned. "And O'Brien's daughter, too, dammit!"

Lance shook his head ruefully. It had taken him and his men eight days to walk back to the fort. Eight back-breaking days of packing their saddles and gear across miles and miles of sun-baked prairie, each man praying that they wouldn't run into a Sioux war party.

He found O'Brien in the operating room, filling out a requisition for medical supplies.

"Afternoon, doc," Lance said, removing his hat.

Robert O'Brien looked up, his expression hopeful. "Did you find her?"

"Yeah."

"Thank God." A smile lit the doctor's face. "Where is she?"

Lance cleared his throat. "Listen, doc . . ."

"She's all right, isn't she?"

"She's fine, but . . ."

"But what? You said she's all right."

"She was with that redskin who kidnapped her."

O'Brien cursed under his breath. "If he laid a hand on her, I'll kill him!"

"She said he didn't, ah, didn't hurt her, but . . ."

"Never mind," O'Brien said impatiently. "I'll let Elayna tell me what happened. Thanks for coming by."

"Wait, doc. She's not here."

"Not here?"

"Just listen a minute. We caught the redskin and we were on our way home when he escaped. It was late and he overpowered the sentries and drove off our horses. All but one."

Lance paused, not wanting to believe what he knew to be true. The Indian had left the horse behind for Elayna, hoping she'd follow him.

"Go on," O'Brien urged.

"Well, there was a lot of confusion and gunfire and before I could stop her, Elayna went riding after that damned Injun."

"She went after him?" O'Brien shook his head in disbelief.

"Yeah. We couldn't go after her on foot."

O'Brien stared at Lance. Could it be true? He thought back, remembering how interested Elayna had been in the Indian's welfare. And she had been in the guardhouse the night the Indian escaped. Had it been planned ahead of time?

"I'm sorry, doc."

O'Brien nodded. "Thanks for coming by, lieutenant."

Lance settled his hat on his head and started for the door. "We'll be leaving at first light," he called over his shoulder.

O'Brien watched the young man leave the room, and then he let out a long sigh. "Bring her back to me, boy," he murmured softly. "Please, just bring her back to me."

Chapter 29

They found shelter in a stand of tall trees. There was water in a narrow winding stream that was only a few inches deep, but the water was cool and sweet.

The miners' packs yielded a veritable treasure: an assortment of tinned meat and fruit, cooking utensils, two tin plates and cups, a pair of knives and forks, a sack of coffee and another of tobacco, a dozen potatoes that had started to sprout, several boxes of matches, and three bottles of whiskey. There were also two bedrolls and a couple of blankets.

Once they were settled, Michael took one of the bottles of whiskey, drank half, and then went to sleep.

Elayna gazed at Michael affectionately. The

first thing he had done when they arrived was dig a hole in the soft soil beside the stream and bury the scalps that had been hanging from Clem's saddlehorn. He had handled the scalps reverently as he laid them in the earth, as if they were more than just bits of hair.

He was a remarkable man, she thought, remarkable indeed, but there was work to be done and she wasn't going to accomplish anything if she stood there admiring him all day, as pleasant as that might be.

It was time to set up house. She gathered stones and made a pit for the fire, sorted through the canned goods, shook out the bedroll that would be hers, wrinkling her nose at the smell of stale sweat and tobacco. She gave it one more good shake, then spread it over a bush in the sun, thinking she would do the same for Michael's bedroll when he woke up.

Going to the stream, she filled the battered coffee pot with water and filled the canteen that had been tied to Ed's saddle. Returning to camp, she dumped a handful of ground coffee in the pot and set the pot on a rock while she gathered kindling for a fire.

Then she sat down and observed her handiwork, pleased with what she'd accomplished. The camp was neat, the fire was ready to be lit. The horses were grazing nearby. And Michael was sleeping peacefully. It was what he needed most, rest and more rest.

He was still asleep when the sun went down. Elayna huddled near the fire, wishing Michael would wake up. There were sounds in the night, rustling in the underbrush. She told herself there was nothing to fear. Wild animals would not approach the fire. Noises could not hurt her.

But she wished Michael would wake up.

To busy herself, she fixed something to eat, drank a cup of coffee, glancing at Michael again and again to see if he was awake, but he slept like the dead.

She ate quickly, then rolled up in her blankets beside Michael. She felt better just being close to him.

In minutes she was asleep.

He woke slowly, his head aching from too much whiskey taken on an empty stomach.

Elayna was asleep beside him, her head pillowed on his shoulder. He wondered again why she had followed him. She had been unhappy with the Cheyenne, so anxious to go home. And then, when she had the chance to go back to her own people, she had run after him instead. Why?

She came awake then, and he saw the answer to his question in her eyes.

He murmured her name, and then he kissed her, slowly, deliberately, and she was kissing him back, her tongue sliding over his lips.

She sat up, facing him as she leaned across his chest, her hair falling around him like a red silk waterfall as she kissed him again, a wave of desire uncurling within her like a leaf unfolding in the sun.

"Oh, Michael," she murmured, "I've been

such a fool." She buried her face in his shoulder, wondering why she hadn't realized sooner that she loved him. She had been drawn to him from the first, wanting him, and hating herself because of it. He had been kind to her, putting up with her tantrums, ignoring her sour looks, eating the tasteless meals she had prepared for him without complaint. He had offered her a change of clothing so she wouldn't be so conspicuous, had tried to teach her his language so she could communicate with the other women, and she had scorned his efforts, and in so doing had only made herself more miserable.

Michael took her chin in his hand and lifted her head. "What is it?"

"Oh, Michael, I've behaved like a shrew and you've been so kind to me. You even offered to take me home, and now you're hurt and it's all my fault. Can you ever forgive me?"

"There's nothing to forgive."

"I wish . . . never mind."

"What do you wish?"

"That you weren't hurt."

"Oh?" he asked, grinning. "Why is that?"

She shook her head, too shy to say the words aloud. But he knew what she wanted. He had always known.

"Soon," he promised, drawing her down beside him. "Soon."

They rested in the shelter of the trees for five days while Michael recovered. They were days Elayna cherished, long, lazy days spent getting to know each other better. She told Michael about growing up as an Army brat, moving from post to post. She told him about her mother and how she'd had the "sight." Elayna knew that most people thought it was nonsense, but Michael believed it was real, a gift from the spirits.

Michael told her about his parents, how his father had become a slave to the white man's whiskey, how his mother had died of a broken heart soon after his father's death.

He began to teach her the Cheyenne language. At first she was certain she'd never master his native tongue, but they practiced it for several hours each day, and by the time they were ready to leave, she had learned several words and useful phrases: *pave-eseeva* meant good day, *e-peva'e* was Cheyenne for It's good. *Ne-pevo-mohta-he* translated into How are you? And *Na-ho'e-ohtse* meant I've come visiting.

Knowing some everyday Cheyenne gave her a feeling of confidence. Now she would be able to communicate with Michael's family, at least a little. And she would keep learning and practicing his language until she could speak it fluently.

Seven days after his accident, Michael felt well enough to travel and decided they would start for home the following day.

That last night in the shelter of the trees, Elayna lay next to Michael, her head pillowed on his shoulder. She was aware of his arm around her waist, of his hair brushing against her cheek, of his thigh pressed against her own.

"How do you feel?" she asked.

"Better."

"Are you sleepy?"

"A little."

"Oh."

Michael grinned into the darkness. "Why?"

"Oh, no reason."

He chuckled softly, knowing what she wanted. It had been hard, not touching her while he waited for his bruises to heal. Being near her every minute of the day, watching her as she prepared their meals, listening to her laughter, it had been hell keeping his hands off her.

"It's a pretty night, isn't it?" she said, wishing he could read her mind.

"Elayna."

She heard the question in his voice and felt her heart begin to pound in anticipation. Of course he knew what she wanted. Hadn't she seen the longing in his eyes?

"Yes, Michael?" Joy was bubbling inside her. She felt her cheeks grow hot as he turned on his side and gazed into her eyes.

"Are you sure?"

Elayna nodded, her heart soaring as he kissed her, lightly at first, his tongue darting out to tickle her lips, dipping playfully, provocatively, into her mouth. She wrapped her arms around his neck, welcoming his kisses, his nearness.

His hands were gentle as he removed her chemise, so gentle, and yet she could feel his fingers trembling against her skin, trembling with the same desire that had plagued her for so long.

They undressed each other leisurely, not wanting to rush the moment, wanting to savor each new discovery. And then they were lying in each other's arms, with nothing but desire between them. Michael kissed her slowly, his lips warm, patiently demanding. His hands slid over her flesh, his touch like a soft flame that heated her blood and made her heart sing. And she was touching him in return, all shyness swept away in the magic of the moment. She gloried in his hard-muscled flesh, and in the harsh rasp of his breathing as her untutored hands brought him pleasure. He was beautiful, she thought, the most beautiful creature she had ever seen. Even the ugly scars that crisscrossed his back were beautiful because they were his.

As she would be his, from this night forward.

She murmured his name as his flesh joined with hers, filling her, so that they were no longer two separate entities but one being.

"*Nemehotatse*," Michael murmured, his breath warm and seductive against her ear.

"*Nemehotatse*," Elayna repeated. "What does it mean?"

"I'd have taught it to you long ago if you hadn't been so stubborn," Michael replied with a roguish grin. "It means I love you."

"What a beautiful word," Elayna said, caressing Michael's cheek. "How do you say Wolf?"

"*Ho-nehe*."

"*Nemehotatse, Ho-nehe.*

He smiled into her eyes, his hands cupping her face as he kissed her deeply, fervently, passionately.

And in that kiss was the promise of forever.

Yellow Spotted Wolf was standing outside his lodge when Michael and Elayna rode into the village.

"Ah, cousin," Yellow Spotted Wolf said, grinning broadly as Michael approached him. "I had a feeling you would not come back alone."

"Did you?" Michael replied as he dismounted and helped Elayna from her horse.

Yellow Spotted Wolf nodded. "One had only to see the two of you together to know you would not be happy apart."

"We'll never be apart again," Elayna said solemnly. "Never again."

Elayna took a new interest in village life. She discarded her dress and corset and chemise in favor of a soft doeskin tunic. It was wonderfully comfortable, though she felt almost naked without her corset and chemise. Naked and a little bit wicked to be wearing so little. She put away her shoes and stockings and discovered that Cheyenne moccasins were the most comfortable footwear in all the world. She made an effort to improve her cooking, experimenting with wild herbs and seasoning, asking Hemene for recipes that Michael might like. She kept their lodge tidy so that Michael would not be ashamed of her when his relatives came to visit.

And they came often now, especially Yellow

Spotted Wolf. It was easy to see that Michael loved the young man, yet she often had the feeling that he was holding something back, that there was something he wanted to tell Yellow Spotted Wolf and just couldn't find the words. But when she asked Michael about it, he shook his head and told her she was imagining things.

She made an effort to be friendly with the women, and they began to include her when they went to gather wood or water. They were not savages after all, she discovered, but hard-working wives and mothers who wanted only the best for their husbands and children. They were loving daughters and sisters, loyal friends, and yes, fierce fighters when necessary. Much like women the world over.

Elayna felt a special affection for Soaring Eagle's wife, Sunflower Woman, who was about the same age as Elayna, and for Yellow Spotted Wolf's mother, Hemene. Elayna tried to apologize to them for her earlier rude behavior, but they stilled her words with hugs and assured her that they understood and it was forgotten. They were friends now, and that was all that mattered.

Sunflower Woman was one of the most cheerful, pleasant people Elayna had ever known. She never said an unkind word, rarely complained, and had only the highest praise for her husband. She was pregnant and anxious to present Soaring Eagle with a son.

Hemene was the soul of kindness, loved by everyone, old and young alike. New mothers went to her for advice, new brides sought her counsel, children tagged at her heels. She was a fine seamstress, and her handiwork was prized by the other women in the tribe.

Elayna's days were filled with hard work, and constant exposure to the sun tanned her skin, but she had no complaints and as the days passed, and her love for Michael deepened and increased, she thought less and less of her old home. Michael was her home now. His people were becoming her people.

She smiled as a verse she had learned in Sunday school came to mind. "Whither thou goest, I will go; and where thou lodgest, I will lodge; thy people shall be my people, and thy God my God . . ."

The passage was from the Book of Ruth, she mused, but she had always thought the words sounded more like a woman speaking to her lover than a daughter-in-law speaking to her mother-in-law. Nevertheless, they were beautiful words and captured exactly the feelings of her heart.

She gazed into the distance, wondering when Michael and Yellow Spotted Wolf would return. They had gone hunting early that morning and she was missing Michael more every minute they were gone. She went into the lodge and began to brush her hair, wanting to look her best when he returned.

Michael and Yellow Spotted Wolf were stretched out side by side on a sun-bleached patch of grass near the river a few miles from the village. The hunt had been unsuccessful and they had stopped on the way home for a leisurely swim.

Michael sighed as he crossed his arms under his head and gazed up at the vast blue sky. Somehow the sky seemed bigger here than it had in Los Angeles, wider, deeper, its color a more vivid shade of blue. He wished fleetingly for a cold bottle of beer, and then, somewhat wistfully, he ticked off the things he missed most: a hot shower, a fast car, a quick trip to the beach after a hard day, a pizza smothered in pepperoni and olives . . .

He pushed such thoughts from his mind as he realized that Yellow Spotted Wolf was speaking to him.

"I'm sorry," Michael apologized, sitting up. "I wasn't listening."

Yellow Spotted Wolf was also sitting up. He gestured at Michael's chest. "You have not been a participant in the Medicine Lodge Ceremony."

Michael shook his head. The Medicine Lodge was similar to the Lakota Sun Dance. When a man participated in the Medicine Lodge Ceremony, he offered his blood and his pain to the spirits in the hope that the gods would grant him the desires of his heart, be it help in times of trouble, or prosperity for the People, or the fulfilling of a promise previously made.

Yellow Spotted Wolf grunted softly. "I do not think you lack the courage," he mused. "Have you never felt the need to sacrifice your blood to *Heammawihio*?"

"I have never had the opportunity," Michael replied, ignoring the small voice in the back of his mind that questioned whether he did indeed possess the kind of courage needed to undergo such torture. Was he strong enough to endure having skewers inserted into his flesh? Did he have the tenacity to hang from the Medicine Lodge pole until the skewers tore loose, freeing him from the pole and the pain? He knew that the white man viewed the Sun Dance ceremony as barbaric; but to the Lakota and the Cheyenne and the other Plains tribes, it was a deeply religious experience.

Michael glanced at Yellow Spotted Wolf. He had often touched his great-grandfather's scars as a small boy, marveling at the old man's courage, wondering, even then, if he himself would be brave enough to endure the sacred ritual. It had been an unanswerable question back then, because his people no longer practiced the Medicine Lodge in the old way.

But he was here, now.

"You are young to have endured the Medicine Lodge," Michael remarked.

"I was fifteen summers," Yellow Spotted Wolf boasted. "Already a man."

Michael grinned. It was a tale he had heard countless times, and he was suddenly eager to hear it again.

But Yellow Spotted Wolf did not go on with his story. Instead, he cocked his head to one side. "Have you sought a medicine dream?"

"Yes."

"Was it good?"

Michael chuckled softly. "It changed my life."

Yellow Spotted Wolf did not ask Michael what he had seen, for such sacred things were not spoken of except to one who was holy.

"We should be getting back to camp," Michael remarked, rising to his feet.

"You are anxious to return to your woman," Yellow Spotted Wolf said with a knowing grin.

"Yes," Michael agreed, and the thought of holding Elayna filled him with pleasure. "Come on, I'll race you back to camp!"

But Yellow Spotted Wolf only laughed and shook his head. You could not win a race against a man whose woman was waiting for him.

Chapter 30

They were lying side by side under a clear summer sky. The moon hung low, a great golden scythe surrounded by countless twinkling stars. A gentle breeze whispered through the cottonwoods, sharing the secrets of the night.

Elayna's head rested on Michael's shoulder, and she thought she had never known such contentment, such a feeling of belonging. She liked living with the Cheyenne, she liked their customs, their friendliness, their belief that all life was part of the whole. They had a great reverence for the earth, for all living things.

She turned her head and gazed at the man beside her. How was it possible that she could have grown to love him so completely in such a short time? They lived together in sweet harmony, grateful for each new day. He was a warrior, with a warrior's inborn pride. He possessed a deep inner strength, an assurance of who and what he was. He was adept with the bow and the lance, he rode with the ease and agility that seemed to be inherent in the Cheyenne. He excelled at the hoop and pole game; no one could best him at wrestling. She never grew tired of watching him, whether at work or play, for he was the most beautiful man she had ever known.

She felt her heart swell with joy as Michael raised up on one elbow and smiled down at her. "You're very quiet this evening."

"I was just thinking how happy I am to be here, with you."

He felt a little twinge of guilt as he recalled how she'd come to be there in the first place. "Do you ever miss your other life, back at the fort?"

"No, although I miss my father. I wish . . ."

"What?"

"Nothing."

"You'll see him again, I promise."

"How?"

"I don't know. You'll just have to trust me."

"I do."

He gazed into her eyes, and his love for her drove everything else from his mind. He was here, in this place, with the woman he loved, and he needed nothing else, only time. And as he bent his head to kiss her, he prayed that the *Maiyun*, those mysterious powers that controlled the affairs of men, might grant him a long life with his woman.

He rose early the following morning and went to the river to bathe. The water was cold and invigorating, and he swam briskly for about ten minutes before he climbed out of the water and stood on the shore. Lifting his arms above his head, he offered a morning prayer to *Heammawihio*, thanking Him for a new day, for Elayna, for health and strength, for life itself. Back in L.A. he had never felt the need for prayer, but here, in the land of his ancestors, praying was as natural as breathing.

Elayna had breakfast waiting when he returned to the lodge and they shared a quiet meal. Michael reached out often to caress her cheek or touch her hair, unconsciously reassuring himself that she was there, that it was all real and not just a dream.

After breakfast they went outside to sit in the sun. Elayna was working on a pair of moccasins, her brow furrowed in concentration as she sewed the sole to the heel; Michael sat beside her, sharpening the head of his lance on a whetstone.

Shortly before noon Michael left to visit Yellow Spotted Wolf. Minutes later Sunflower Woman stopped by to see Elayna. They were discussing Sunflower Woman's pregnancy when Red Shield stepped out of his lodge and announced that his eldest daughter had become a woman. To celebrate, he was giving a horse away.

Elayna looked at Sunflower Woman, her expression somewhat stunned. "Do fathers always make such a big to-do about . . . about . . ." She blushed. "You know."

Sunflower Woman nodded. "His daughter, Pretty Flower, will be of marriageable age soon and able to bear children to increase our tribe. It is an important day for his family, and for our people."

"But to tell everyone . . ." Elayna shook her head.

"Is it not the same with your people?" Sunflower Woman asked.

"It's very different," Elayna explained. "Among my people, such things are not discussed. To tell others is unthinkable."

Sunflower Woman frowned. "The whites are very strange indeed. Red Shield is proud of his daughter, pleased that she is about to be a woman."

Sunflower Woman cleared her throat. "There is something I think we must discuss," she began slowly. "Has Ho-nehe spoke to you of the Moon Lodge?"

"Moon Lodge?"

Sunflower Woman nodded. "Among our people, there are certain taboos against women when the time of women is upon them. Pretty Flower will be expected to stay in the Moon Lodge for four days. She must not touch any weapons or eat boiled meat. And she must be purified before she returns to her father's lodge."

"Are all young girls expected to do this?"

"Yes," Sunflower Woman said. "And married women as well."

"But why?"

"It is the custom. Her brothers will not eat or drink from any dish she has used lest they be injured in the next battle."

Elayna bit back the urge to laugh at such superstitious nonsense, knowing her laughter would offend Sunflower Woman.

"Will I be expected to go to the Moon Lodge too?"

"Yes."

"But I don't possess any evil magic that will cause Michael harm," she protested.

"It is the way of our people," Sunflower Woman repeated. "And it is not so bad in the Moon Lodge. It is a time to rest, to catch up on mending, and to visit with other women."

"I'll do it," Elayna agreed grudgingly. "But I won't like it."

The Fox Soldiers were giving a dance and everyone had been invited. Elayna sat on the women's side of the circle between Sunflower Woman and Hemene, her eyes drawn to where Michael sat across the way. The night was warm and he wore only a brief wolfskin clout and beaded moccasins, moccasins she had made for him, she thought proudly. His skin glistened in the firelight as he danced with the men. She glanced at the black wolfskin clout that had been a gift from Yellow Spotted Wolf and wondered idly who had tanned the hide. There were strict taboos against women tanning certain skins, such as that of the bear, the beaver, the wolf, and the coyote. Sometimes such hides were tanned by captive women; occasionally by men. Women believed that if they tanned bear-skins, the soles of their feet would crack and hair would grow on their faces.

Later, during a lull in the dancing, she asked Michael about the wolfskin, and he told her there was a certain women's society that partici-pated in special ceremonies to remove the an-cient taboos. Hemene was one of those women, and she had tanned the skin. The Cheyenne women believed that any female who dressed a wolf hide without observing the sacred ceremo-nies would become palsied.

"Do you believe such things?" Elayna asked, laughing softly. "Do they? You don't really be-lieve I'd start to grow hair on my face if I tanned a bear skin?"

"It doesn't matter what I believe," Michael hedged. "The women believe it. Look." He pointed at the warrior who was stepping into the dance circle.

"Who's he?"

"Hohkeeke. He's going to do the hoop dance."

"Hoop dance?"

"Watch."

The drummers started drumming, and the warrior began to dance. He was beautiful to watch. His breechclout and neck cloth were beaded with bright designs, he wore a crest of dyed horsehair on his head. His body was painted with geometric patterns. But it was his dancing that was truly breathtaking as he maneuvered his head, body, arms, and legs in and out and over and under two hoops, then four, then six, then eight, and with the addition of each new hoop the drumming grew faster and faster. The hoops were made of willow, adorned with bits of feather fluff in a variety of colors. Each maneuver created a different pattern, each more beautiful and more complicated than the last.

"He's remarkable," Elayna murmured as the warrior finished his dance and left the circle, but before Michael could reply, the singers began to sing and a man stepped into the center of the dance lodge and began dancing alone. He carried a stick in his hand and waved it back and forth over his head as he danced. After a few minutes he tossed the stick into the air and shouted, "There goes my wife! I throw her away!"

Elayna tugged on Michael's arm, certain she had misunderstood the man's words. "What's happening?"

"Heovenako has just divorced his wife."

"Just like that?"

"Just like that."

Elayna stared at Michael, speechless.

"It's a disgrace for the woman to be cast aside in such a manner," Michael said, "but I've heard some of the warriors talking. They say she's grown argumentative and lazy, that she refuses to cook for Heovenako. He's a well-known and respected warrior. It shames him to have a wife who does not honor him."

"But to humiliate her in public," Elayna protested. "It seems so unfair."

Michael shrugged, but Elayna could not help feeling sorry for the plump Indian woman who even now was walking out of the dance lodge, her face hidden within the folds of the blanket over her head.

"Come on," Michael said, taking Elayna's hand. "Let's go outside."

The night was cool and quiet after the warmth and noise of the dance lodge. Hand in hand, they walked down to the river and stood looking out over the still water. The sickle moon cast dappled silver shadows on the dark face of the Platte, and as he stood there, Michael felt a sense of peace, a sense of being home. The low beat of the drum could be heard from the dance lodge, and from the distance came the lonely sound of a coyote wailing at the moon.

He studied the profile of the woman beside him. She had been troubled by the scene in the dance lodge; her sympathy for the wife of Heovenako was evident in her eyes.

If Elayna were his wife, he would never throw her away, no matter what she did. If she were his wife . . . if only he could marry her. He'd been wrong to bring her here. No matter if he stayed in the past a year or a lifetime, he had been wrong to bring her here. There was only trouble and heartache waiting for his people. This year, these last few months before the Custer battle, were the beginning of the end for his people. He should take her back to her father now, before it was too late, back where she belonged . . . but he could not part with her. They were both in places where they didn't belong, he thought wryly. She was among alien people, and he was caught in a time that was not his. And he had never been happier.

He murmured her name as he drew her into the circle of his arms, and she came willingly, her face lifting for his kiss, her body pressing against his, her sweet curves and full breasts a perfect complement to his lean, hard-muscled frame. Her eyelids fluttered down as he kissed her, and he was overcome with a searing need to possess her, to taste and touch each inch of honeyed flesh, to make her his woman, for this moment and all eternity.

The grass was cool and damp against his heated flesh as he lowered her to the ground and quickly stripped away his clout. His eyes were filled with promise, his hands swift and urgent as he unfastened the ties on her dress and slid the soft buckskin over her shoulders. He shuddered with pleasure as her hands caressed him, stoking the fires of desire. He unbraided her hair, letting his fingers trail through the silken strands, and then he kissed her, drinking deeply of her sweetness, his senses reeling as her nearness filled every need.

He drew a deep breath, and her scent surrounded him; he touched her, lightly stroking her breasts, and felt the heat of it fan the fire in his loins.

He gathered her into his arms and then he kissed her again, his tongue delving into her mouth, exploring the silken recesses, savoring the velvet of her tongue against his. He stroked her hips, her thighs, the smooth satin of her back and breasts, and each touch, each caress, branded her his woman for now and for always. . . .

Chapter 31

A scream, loud and brittle and edged with pain, sliced through Michael's dreams and brought him instantly awake. He sat up, head cocked to one side, wondering if he'd only imagined it, but then he heard the voice of a woman raised in fear, the shrill war cries of the Cheyenne Dog Soldiers.

Beside him, Elayna sat up, her hand at her throat. "What is it?"

"We're being attacked! Stay here."

He pulled on his clout and sprinted for the village, quietly cursing the fact that he was armed with only a knife.

Rounding a bend in the trail, he burst into the open, his heart pounding as he took in the scene that met his eyes.

Two dozen Pawnee warriors were riding through the village, tomahawks and lances swinging right and left as they tried to escape. They had come in the predawn darkness, undoubtedly to steal the valuable war ponies that were kept near at hand each night, but their presence had been discovered before they could achieve their goal.

He saw Mo'ohta-vo'nehe grappling in the dirt with a shrieking Pawnee. Farther away, he saw Soaring Eagle in hand-to-hand combat with a burly warrior. Everywhere he looked, men were engaged in a struggle of one kind or another, and over the grunts and war cries of the men could be heard the shouts and screams of the women, the wailing of frightened children, the moans of the wounded, and the roar of gunfire. At the far end of the village a lodge was in flames.

As he ran toward his own lodge, Michael saw a Pawnee warrior strike Two Ponies across the back of the head with a war club, saw the blood gush from the fatal wound as Two Ponies collapsed face down in the dirt. And then the Pawnee fell from his horse as Red-Furred Bear's arrow found its mark.

By the time Michael reached the center of the camp, six of the Pawnee were dead. Two others were mortally wounded, and these were at the mercy of a handful of boys who were not yet warriors.

It was considered an act of bravery to strike a

living enemy, and a couple of the boys darted forward to count coup on the injured men.

He saw younger boys run forward to count coup on the dead men.

"*Nanotomasen!*" cried Ma'o'hoohe as he stuck the body nearest him. "I strike the first coup!"

"*Nahonaovehotaneve!*" hollered Badger. "I strike the second coup!"

"*Nanahahotaneva!*" cried Young Bear. "I strike the third coup!"

Michael ducked as one of the remaining Pawnee raced past him looking for a way out of the village. He felt the tip of the warrior's lance graze his arm as the Pawnee swept past, felt his anger rise as blood oozed from the shallow gash, and then saw Yellow Spotted Wolf and forgot everything else. His great-grandfather and a heavy-set Pawnee were locked together in a deadly embrace as they fought for possession of the long-bladed knife in the Pawnee's hand.

The Pawnee was older, heavier, more experienced. He had inflicted several minor cuts on Yellow Spotted Wolf's arms and chest. Blood trickled from the wounds, streaking his great-grandfather's body like war paint, but Yellow Spotted Wolf seemed unaware of his injuries. He was young and strong and determined, and he fought bravely, valiantly, until the Pawnee made a quick feint to the left, then drove the blade into the younger warrior's side.

Time hung suspended for the space of a heartbeat as Michael stared at the scene before him. The Pawnee, his face streaked with black paint, grinned triumphantly as Yellow Spotted Wolf fell back, the knife embedded in his left side. Yellow Spotted Wolf stumbled backward, his right hand groping for the knife, and then he fell heavily. He made a weak attempt to get to his feet, then fell back and lay still.

Michael screamed with rage as he charged the Pawnee, felt his blood run hot in his veins as he loosed the ancient war cry of the Cheynne, felt his body fill with power as he lunged at the enemy.

The Pawnee ducked and sidestepped, his teeth flashing in an evil grin as he jerked his blade from Yellow Spotted Wolf and wheeled around to face his new attacker.

Michael's haste and anger made him reckless and he charged wildly, his knife slashing from side to side as he rushed the enemy a second time. He felt the tip of the Pawnee's blade pierce his forearm, but his need for vengeance was stronger than pain or fear and he threw his arms around the Pawnee and wrestled him to the ground.

With a wild cry, he plunged his knife into the warrior's belly, driving the blade deeper, deeper. He felt the Pawnee's blood spray over his chest, felt a growing sense of satisfaction as he gave the blade a cruel twist.

Uttering a savage shout of victory, he yanked the knife from the dead man's flesh and sprang to his feet, his eyes seeking another victim for his hungry blade.

But the fight was over. Nineteen Pawnee warriors lay dead on the ground. And now Michael had eyes only for Yellow Spotted Wolf, who lay face down in the dirt in an ever-widening pool of his own blood.

A high keening wail filled the air as Hemene knelt beside Yellow Spotted Wolf.

He can't be dead, Michael thought as he ran toward his great-grandfather. *He can't be dead.*

He knelt beside Hemene and carefully turned Yellow Spotted Wolf over. Blood covered Yellow Spotted Wolf's left side and Michael pressed his hand over the wound to slow the bleeding.

"He's alive," he told Hemene. "Go, quickly, find the medicine man."

Hemene rose to her feet and ran toward the shaman's lodge while Michael sat with Yellow Spotted Wolf. People were hurrying from place to place, looking for loved ones, searching for children, battling the flames that raged at the far end of the village. But Michael saw only Yellow Spotted Wolf, felt nothing but the warm wet blood beneath his hand.

"Hang on, Grandfather," he murmured. "There is nothing to fear. Death will not find you today."

The medicine man arrived a few minutes later, closely followed by Hemene, Mo'ohta-vo'nehe, and Badger. Michael relinquished his place at his great-grandfather's side, but he stayed close by, his eyes damp with unshed tears.

It took a moment for him to realize that

Badger was pressed against his side, his shoulders shaking as silent tears tracked his cheeks.

"He will be all right," Michael said, dropping his arm around the boy's shoulder.

"But there is so much blood. And he lies so still."

"I know, but he will not die, I promise you. He will not die."

Badger nodded, his eyes full of trust. Manfully he wiped the tears from his eyes, determined to be strong and brave, like Ho-nehe.

Michael stared at the blood that oozed from his great-grandfather's side. How much blood could a man lose and remain alive? How much blood had Yellow Spotted Wolf lost?

He can't die, Michael thought dully. *Hell, if he had died here, I'd never have been born.*

But he could not stop the hurt that welled inside him as he watched the medicine man dress the ugly wound in Yellow Spotted Wolf's side.

It was only later, after Yellow Spotted Wolf had been carried to his father's lodge, that Michael remembered Elayna.

Muttering an oath, he ran out of the village toward the river, knowing she must be frightened half to death as she waited for him, wondering what was happening in the village, wondering why he was taking so long to come back for her.

"Elayna!" He called her name as he neared the riverbank. "Elayna, where are you?"

He saw the pony tracks in the dew-damp grass, saw the signs of a struggle, her moccasins lying near the water's edge.

Nineteen warriors had been killed, but five had escaped.

"Elayna!" He shouted her name even though he knew she was gone, and then he was running back to camp, his heart hammering with fear.

Mo'ohta-vo'nehe was standing outside his lodge as Michael ran past. "Wolf, wait."

Michael stopped in his tracks and glanced over his shoulder. "I cannot talk now. The Pawnee have taken my woman."

"I will go with you," Mo'ohta-vo'nehe volunteered. "Get the horses while I tell Soaring Eagle what has happened. He will call the Fox Soldiers together and we will go after your woman."

Twenty minutes later Michael rode out of the camp with Soaring Eagle, Mo'ohta-vo'nehe, and a dozen Fox Soldiers. Back at the village, the Dog Soldiers were in charge of cleaning up and taking care of the wounded, but Michael's thoughts were focused on Elayna. He knew that Yellow Spotted Wolf would be all right. He was fated to live to a good old age. But Elayna was another matter. What if it was her fate to die at the hands of the Pawnee? Had he come back eighty years through time to bring her to her death?

She had never known such gut-wrenching fear. Held face down across the withers of one of the Pawnee's horses, her hands bound behind her back, she watched the ground fly by as her captor whipped his mount again and again. The Pawnee were making no effort to conceal their tracks. The horse raid had been a disaster and now they wanted only to get as far away from the Cheyenne as possible in hopes that the pursuing warriors would give up and go home.

They rode for hours, and each mile seemed like ten. Elayna's body ached from the constant jarring of the horse, her neck hurt, her back felt as though it would break in two at any moment. But worse than the pain was the constant fear of what would happen when the Indians stopped. She was acutely aware of the heavy hand on her back, of the hard-muscled thighs crushing her breasts.

She had heard tales of the Pawnee from the Cheyenne. The Pawnee were a cruel people. Some of the women said they practiced cannibalism. Elayna shuddered with renewed terror as the Pawnee's hand moved up her back to stroke her neck, then slid downward to cup her buttocks. She did not need to understand his words to know what he was saying, or what he intended to do to her when they stopped for the night.

Trembling convulsively, she closed her eyes and prayed that she would die first.

And still they rode, pushing their horses relentlessly. The sun rose high in the sky, beating down upon her back and shoulders and head. Sweat pooled between her breasts, trickled down her back and neck, making her feel sticky and dirty. Dust clogged her nostrils and stung her eyes. But as uncomfortable as she was, as thirsty and hot and tired as she was, she prayed they would never stop.

It was mid-afternoon when the warriors drew their horses to a halt beside a shallow stream. Dismounting, Elayna's captor pulled her to the ground and shoved her toward the water. She inched forward, heedless of the rocks and weeds that bruised her legs and scratched her face. The water was wonderfully cool and she drank greedily, wishing her hands were free so she might rinse her face and arms.

She was still drinking when the Pawnee grabbed a handful of her hair and yanked her to her feet.

He spoke to his companions, and she saw the lust in their eyes, heard the hunger in their voices as they leered at her, pointing at her hair, her breasts.

She took a step backward, the bile rising in her throat as she thought of them touching her bare flesh, their hands pawing her, tearing her clothes, pulling her hair, fondling her breasts.

But it was not to happen now.

Her captor mounted his horse and hauled her up in front of him, and they were riding again. His arm was like steel around her waist, imprisoning her, asserting his ownership. She could feel his breath on her cheek, smell the rank odor of his body, feel the heat of his thighs. Once he raised his hand to her breast and squeezed it, squeezed until tears burned her eyes and she cried out from the pain. His coarse laughter assured her that her worse fears would be realized before the day was gone.

She prayed to die, prayed that the horse would fall and crush the life from her body, but they only rode onward, ever onward, toward the setting sun.

It was the longest day of her life, and over too soon.

At nightfall the Pawnee made camp in a shallow draw. There were five of them, all that was left of the raiding party. They had lost the battle, but they had still come away with a prize, and now they turned their attention toward the white woman. She stood helpless before them, her dark red hair falling in a tangled mass about her shoulders, her face stained with sweat and tears, her eyes wild with fright. Her fear quickened their desire and they closed in around her, slowly circling her like wolves around a wounded buffalo calf.

Courage she did not know she possessed squared her shoulders and lifted her chin. Defiance blazed in her eyes. Defiance and contempt. She was powerless to fight them, powerless to resist. But she would kick and bite as long as there was strength in her body.

She whispered Michael's name as the warrior who had captured her grabbed a handful of her hair and forced her to her knees. A second warrior unfastened the ties of her tunic and let it fall, exposing her breasts and belly.

A chorus of male approval rose on the air, and

then the warrior who had captured her knocked her backward to the ground.

She bucked and kicked, knowing a brief moment of triumph as her heel caught one of the men in the groin, but her struggles were in vain and only made the warriors angry. Her captor screamed at her in Pawnee, then slapped her, hard, again and again.

She tasted blood in her mouth and prayed silently that she would die before he violated her, and when death did not come, she closed her eyes and prayed that they would kill her when they were through . . .

The tracks of the fleeing Pawnee were clear and easy to follow, and the Cheyenne war party rode hard and fast, and yet it seemed to Michael that his horse was hardly moving. He lashed the buckskin again and again, demanding more speed. Mo'ohta-vo'nehe assured him they were making good time, yet he felt as though he were caught in a web, that no matter how hard he tried to go forward, he would never make it.

Knowing they would be pursued, the Pawnee were heading straight for home and Michael knew they had to overtake them soon, before it was too late, before . . . He pushed the thought of what the Pawnee would do to Elayna from his mind, knowing he would go mad if he let himself think of other men touching her, possessing her. He had to remain calm, to save his energy for the fight to come. He would kill every last one of the bastards himself and glory in taking their scalps if they so much as harmed a hair of her head.

They rode for hours, but for once, time had lost all meaning. He was immune to the heat and the dust, hardly aware of his companions or his surroundings.

Just let her be alive. Please, God, just let her be alive. Over and over again, he mouthed the words, beseeching all the gods, red and white, to protect the woman he loved while images of Winter Song filled his mind.

Guilt rode beside him as he urged his horse onward. Elayna would not be here now but for him. How could he ever face her again if she came to harm? How would he live with himself if she were hurt or killed? *Please, God, just let her be alive.*

Some two hours after noon, Soaring Eagle reined his horse to a halt near a shallow stream. The Pawnee had been there not more than an hour ago, he said, his dark eyes scanning the ground. They had stopped only long enough to ease their thirst.

Mo'ohta-vo'nehe glanced at Michael, then pointed at the ground. "There," he said. "They have your woman."

Michael stared at the rocky ground, reading the sign. He recognized Elayna's footprints. In his mind's eye, he saw clearly where the Pawnee had pushed her to the ground, how she had crawled toward the water. Her hands were tied behind her back, and he felt the rage boil up inside him as he pictured Elayna dragging herself through the dirt, the sharp stones digging into her flesh, the weeds snagging her dress and scratching her face.

"Let's go," he said curtly. "We're wasting time."

It was just after dark when they caught up with the Pawnee. The scene that met Michael's gaze was forever burned in his mind, and he knew a moment of blessed relief as he realized they had arrived in time.

There were five warriors. Four of them were holding Elayna down while the fifth stripped off his clout. He was a tall man, his body damp with desire, his eyes glazed with lust as he stared at the white woman writhing on the ground.

With a feral grin, Michael nocked an arrow to his bow and let it fly. The first arrow caught the aroused brave full in the groin; the second pierced his heart.

Before Michael could put a third arrow to his bowstring, the other four warriors lay dead upon the ground.

With a cry, Michael ran forward and lifted the Pawnee's roached scalplock. The sound of Elayna's horrified scream punctuated the night, piercing the red mists of his rage. With a soft curse, he tossed the bloody scalp aside, the need for vengeance forgotten as he ran to her side and drew her into his arms. Wiping the blood from his knife, he cut her hands free, then held her close, rocking her back and forth as though she were a child. He felt her arms go around his neck, felt her body shudder with great racking sobs as fear gave way to relief.

He held her for a long time, afraid to let her go. His hands stroked her hair as he murmured soft words in her ear. Time lost its meaning and he was aware of nothing but the woman in his arms as his heart sent a fervent prayer of thanksgiving toward heaven.

Later, when her tears had dried and her body had stopped trembling, he became aware of his surroundings. Mo'ohta-vo'nehe and the others had carried away the bodies of the dead Pawnee, then withdrawn into the darkness, leaving Michael and Elayna alone. A waterskin was on the ground beside them, together with a bundle of pemmican, some jerky, and a blanket.

He smiled to himself, thankful for the thoughtfulness of his friends, as he draped the blanket around Elayna's nakedness.

"Are you hurt?"

Elayna shook her head. "I was scared. Oh, Michael, I've never been so scared."

"I know."

She drew back a little, her eyes moving over him. There was blood on his hands and arms, splashed across his chest.

"You've killed a man." Her words were flat and empty, yet he sensed the pain lurking beneath.

"And taken a scalp." He gestured at the bloody thing lying a few feet away.

Elayna pressed a hand over her mouth, afraid

she might be ill. She could not block the image of Michael bending over the dead Pawnee, his knife lifting the Indian's scalplock.

There was a long silence between them as they pondered what he had done. Elayna's first reaction was revulsion, but that was quickly swallowed up in a sense of pride in Michael, in his ability to protect her. He had fought for her, rescued her from a fate more terrible than anything she had ever imagined.

She drank from the waterskin he offered her, but had no appetite for the food Mo'ohta-vo'nehe had left for them. Now that her thirst was satisfied, she wanted only to be held and comforted.

Michael gazed into the darkness, his fingers toying with a lock of Elayna's hair. He had killed two men and taken a scalp. Michael Wolf, the car salesman, was shocked by such barbaric behavior. Michael Wolf, great-grandson of Yellow Spotted Wolf, knew only a keen sense of pride, of exhilaration. He had acted with courage in the face of danger and death. No quality was held in higher esteem by the Cheyenne than courage under fire.

"If you don't feel like traveling, we can spend the night here," Michael remarked after a while.

"I'd rather go home," Elayna said. And when she said home, she meant the Cheyenne village and not Camp Robinson.

Michael knew it too, and his smile was warm as he helped her dress, then lifted her onto the back of his horse and vaulted up behind her. His arm was tight around her waist as they rode away from the Pawnee camp.

Behind them, like shadows on the wind, rode Mo'ohta-vo'nehe and the Fox Soldiers.

There was a scalp dance the following night. Just the name filled Elayna with revulsion, yet morbid curiosity prompted her to say yes when Michael asked her if she wanted to go.

The dance took place in the center of the village and was directed by a small group of men called the *Hee-man'eh*, which meant half man, half woman. They were a strange lot, and they made Elayna uncomfortable, but they were favorites with the young people. Prior to the dance, the *Hee'man'eh* went from lodge to lodge, entreating each family to send some firewood to the center of the camp.

As the singers and drummers began their songs, the *Hee'man'eh* lit the fire, which was built in the shape of a lodge. As the singing began, the people gathered, everybody painted red and black. All the older people wore black paint. The men were shirtless. The drummers stood in a row facing north, the young women faced the young men, the old men and women took their places facing west. Only the *Hee'man'eh* were permitted in the center of the circle.

Elayna had decided not to participate, but Michael insisted. Watching the girl beside her, Elayna danced in line toward the center while the young men walked around behind the drummers and then placed themselves behind their sweethearts. Elayna smiled at Michael as he took her arm, and they danced the sweethearts' dance.

It reminded Elayna of Halloween. The people all looked like demons as they danced around the fire. She had agreed to wear a streak of red paint on her cheek; Michael had painted the lower half of his face black and he looked alien and fierce. A jagged red slash ran from his right shoulder to his left hip, reminding her of the blood that had stained his chest when he killed the Pawnee.

After dancing for a time, they returned to their places and stood facing each other again. And now the *Hee'man'eh* danced before the drummers, holding long poles to which the scalps were fastened. At the other end of the circle, the old women were dancing.

Michael grinned as one of the *Hee'man'eh* waved the scalp pole at a couple of young boys who were trying to sneak into the dance circle. The boys took one look at the waving scalps and ran back to their lodges.

Later there was a match-making dance, and then something called the slippery dance, followed by the last dance, which was called the galloping buffalo-bull dance.

Elayna was thoughtful as they walked back to their lodge. She had expected some kind of wild gyrations with a lot of yelling and screaming, but once again the Cheyenne had surprised her.

Finally, lying together under the buffalo robes, Elayna asked the question that had been haunting her all day.

"What was it like?" she asked. "What was it like to take that man's scalp? How could you do it?"

"He was the enemy," Michael replied, and he felt again the terrible rage that had consumed him when he saw the Pawnee staring down at Elayna. It had been a good feeling, taking the Pawnee's life, robbing him of his scalp so that he would wander the next world in shame and sorrow.

"But to take a scalp," Elayna said, shuddering. "It's so . . . so barbaric."

"Maybe," Michael agreed. But it had not seemed barbaric. He had lifted the Pawnee's scalp as if he had done it a hundred times before. He had felt the blood on his hands, and it had satisfied a deep need. Elayna had been avenged. And so had Winter Song.

He turned on his side and took Elayna in his arms, one hand drawing her against him so that her breasts were crushed against his chest, her hips molded to his, her belly cradling his manhood.

Elayna breathed a sigh of sweet contentment as Michael bent to kiss her. She was in his arms again, safe and warm, and she knew there was no place on earth she'd rather be.

Chapter 32

Michael went to see his great-grandfather early the following morning. Yellow Spotted Wolf smiled weakly as Michael sat down beside him.

"My father tells me you saved my life," Yellow Spotted Wolf remarked.

"Yes."

Yellow Spotted Wolf nodded, his eyes searching Michael's face. "I would ask you a question," he said slowly. "When I was wounded by the Pawnee, you knelt at my side. You called me Grandfather and told me I had nothing to fear."

Michael nodded, his heart hammering as he waited for the inevitable questions, the disbelief.

"Why did you call me Grandfather when I am younger than you? Who are you, Wolf? Why do we look so much alike? Why do I feel that I have always known you?"

"I do not think you will believe the answer," Michael said. "Sometimes I do not believe it myself."

"Tell me."

"I have come here from a great distance across time and space."

Yellow Spotted Wolf nodded. He tried to concentrate on Wolf's face, to listen to his words, but the world seemed out of focus and he knew that the medicine old Red-Furred Bear had given him was starting to take effect.

"Why have you come?" he asked.

"It was my great-grandfather's last wish that I seek a vision to guide me through life."

"He was a wise man."

"Yes."

"And did you receive a vision?"

"Yes. And you are a part of it."

"Have you come here from the future, then?"

"Yes."

"Tell me, Wolf, what does the future hold? Will we win the battle against the white-eyes?"

"No. But next year we will win a great victory at the Little Bighorn. Sitting Bull will offer one hundred pieces of his flesh during the Sun Dance when the Lakota and the Cheyenne gather together, and in return he will receive a vision wherein he will see hundreds of white men falling at his feet. The battle he sees will be against Custer at the Greasy Grass."

Yellow Spotted Wolf smiled indulgently.

"You do not believe me?"

"No, but it is a good story."

"If you believe nothing else I have told you," Michael said fervently, "you must give heed to what I say now. You must not let Badger near the battle."

"Badger? He is only a boy."

"I know, but he will follow you to battle if you do not listen to what I say, and he will be killed. Promise me you will keep an eye on him that day."

"I promise," Yellow Spotted Wolf answered. "Tell me, Wolf, will I die in this battle at the Greasy Grass?"

"No. You will live a long and healthy life."

Yellow Spotted Wolf nodded, then his eyelids fluttered down.

Michael gazed at his great-grandfather for a long time, praying that Yellow Spotted Wolf would remember his warning.

"Rest well, Grandfather," Michael murmured, and left the lodge.

"Grandfather?" Yellow Spotted Wolf repeated softly, and the word followed him to sleep.

It was September, what the Cheyenne called *Wah-kamuneishim*, the month of the Plum Moon.

Near the end of the month, a runner from Sitting Bull's camp arrived at the village. He had news, troublesome news, and that evening there was a council meeting. Mo'ohta-vo'nehe told Michael about the meeting when it was over.

That night, lying under the buffalo robes,

unable to sleep, Michael thought about what Mo'ohta-vo'nehe had said, and to that he added what he remembered from the history books. The problem, as he understood it, had to do with the Treaty of 1868, which stated that the government would provide clothing and other necessities of life to the Sioux for thirty months from the date of the treaty, and would continue to provide meat and flour for a period of four years while the Indians learned to adjust to the ways of the white man.

The latter provision had expired in 1871, and since the government did not feel it could continue to support the Sioux, who had shown little or no interest in farming, it had been decided that the government would supply the Indians with food for an extended period of time, and the Indians could pay for these supplies by ceding the Black Hills. Some people felt the arrangement was more than fair: the Indians would receive the food they needed, and the Americans would finally get the land they had coveted for so long. The few who disagreed with this line of reasoning were in the minority.

A council had been scheduled for September 1 at the Red Cloud Agency, and the Indians at the other agencies had been notified and invited to attend. The council did not go well, according to the runner sent by Sitting Bull. Many of the Indians refused to participate; those who did attend were divided in their opinions. Some were willing to sell the Black Hills for a great deal of money; others refused to sell at any price. In the end, the government offered the Indians four hundred thousand dollars a year for the mining rights, or six million dollars for outright purchase of the Hills, but that had been less than the Indians wanted, and the council had come to an end.

Sitting Bull had refused to attend the meeting; so had Crazy Horse, but the war chief of the Oglala had sent a message, which said in part: "Are you the Great God that made me, or was it the Great God that made me who sent you? If He asks me to come to see Him, I will go, but the Big Chief of the whites must come to see me. I will not go to the reservation. I have no land to sell . . ."

Michael gazed at the dark triangle of sky visible through the smokehole of the lodge. Miners were continuing to pour into the Black Hills, and the Indians continued to harass the wagon trains and settlers they found on the roads. And everybody knew it was going to be war . . .

War, he thought bleakly. It would come next year, and the Indians would win their greatest victory, but in the end they would lose, and in less than three years there would be no more Indians hunting in the Paha Sapa, no more warriors riding wild and free across the broad grassy plains, no more Cheyenne lodges pitched along the peaceful shores of the South Platte.

He turned his gaze to Elayna sleeping quietly beside him, and he wished he did not know what the future held so that he might enjoy the next few months in blissful ignorance unaware that the good days, the good times, were fast coming to an end.

He wondered if she would be strong enough to stay with him when the bad times came, when the Cheyenne were forced onto the living hell of the reservation, when food was scarce and the snow was deep and the cries of the sick and the dying drifted on the wind. The soldiers would look at her with contempt because she lived with an Indian. They would leer at her and call her ugly names.

He stirred restlessly beneath the covers, troubled by his thoughts, and then he felt Elayna's hand on his arm, heard her voice heavy with sleep as she murmured his name, and he knew he could endure any hardship so long as she was there beside him.

He gathered her close, his face pressed to her shoulder, feeling the worry and the tension drain out of him as she stroked his back, her lips moving in his hair as she whispered that she loved him.

Her nearness and the sound of her voice drove the demons away, and he fell asleep in her arms, her name like a prayer on his lips.

The following morning the aged warrior who announced the camp news brought word that the village would be moving the next day. They would trail the buffalo for one last hunt, and then they would seek a place to spend the winter.

The people spent that day getting ready for the

move, and by mid-morning the next day the village on the Platte was gone, with only the blackened ashes of old campfires and the debris of daily living left behind.

It was a happy time. The warriors, mounted on their best ponies, rode ahead, their watchful eyes scanning the plains. The women and the travois ponies came next, followed by the vast Cheyenne horse herd. Yellow Spotted Wolf lay on a travois. He had argued that he was well enough to ride, but the medicine man would not hear of it, and neither would Hemene, and so Yellow Spotted Wolf rode on the travois, complaining loudly to anyone who would listen that old Red-Furred Bear was trying to make a woman of him.

Toward noon, Michael fell back to ride beside his great-grandfather. His heart swelled with gratitude as he listened to Yellow Spotted Wolf's complaints. The warrior would recover, of that there was no doubt.

They made camp along the Sweetwater River in Wyoming Territory. Yellow Spotted Wolf had recovered most of his strength by the time the camp was settled, and he sought Michael's company often, wanting to hear more stories of the future, even though he refused to believe them, refused to believe the Cheyenne would be defeated by the *vehoe*.

They had been camped at the Sweetwater about a week when the council decided the time was favorable to hunt the buffalo.

That night several of the warriors who were

going on the hunt performed the buffalo dance to ask the Great Spirit to bless the hunt and bring the buffalo close to camp.

Elayna watched, fascinated, as the warriors danced, their movements imitating the behavior of buffalo grazing and pawing the ground.

The dancers wore leggings and breechclouts adorned with beaded symbols. Their moccasins and armbands were also beaded in colorful designs. Below their knees they wore leg bands to which bells had been fastened. On their wrists were cuffs made of buffalo hair. Each dancer carried a brightly painted bow and rattle. But most impressive was the buffalo horn headpiece that covered each dancer's head, shoulders, and back. A buffalo tail was fastened to the back of each man's belt.

The following morning a handful of warriors rode out in search of the buffalo. They returned late that afternoon with good news. A small herd had been found nearby. The location of the herd was given and the men were admonished to avoid that area lest the animals be disturbed or frightened away. Any warrior foolish enough to set out on his own in violation of the council's edict would be severely punished. Warriors who violated tribal laws were beaten; sometimes their lodges were destroyed, or their horses killed.

But no one violated the law, and Michael and Yellow Spotted Wolf rode out of the village side by side early the next morning.

Michael could hardly contain his excitement

as he contemplated killing his first buffalo. He had killed other game—deer and elk, rabbits by the dozen—but a buffalo! That would be a prize indeed.

His horse pranced beneath him and Michael felt like laughing out loud. It was good to be alive on such a glorious morning, good to be in the company of men he respected.

"Even the horses are eager for the hunt," Yellow Spotted Wolf remarked as his own mount tossed its head and pulled against the reins.

Michael grinned. They would dine on fresh buffalo meat before the day was out.

He drew a deep breath, his nostrils flaring as his lungs filled with the cool fresh air. It was fall, and the air was clean and crisp. The leaves were changing on the trees, putting away their emerald gowns for dazzling coats of red and gold and orange.

The warriors rode in silence, every eye looking ahead, eager for the sight of the great curly-haired beasts that provided the Cheyenne with virtually everything they needed for survival.

It was just before noon when Red Tail Fox held up his hand, signaling that he had spotted the herd. The Indians split into two columns and rode around the herd, surrounding the buffalo.

Michael's heart was beating wildly as he nocked an arrow to his bowstring. His horse pranced beneath him, as eager for the hunt to begin as was the man on his back.

Red Tail Fox loosed the first arrow, killing a

fat cow near the edge of the herd. A horse whinnied, a second arrow whistled through the air, and suddenly the herd was racing away. Tails high, heads down, the buffalo ran, the sound of their hooves like rolling thunder.

Yellow Spotted Wolf uttered a shrill cry as he put his horse after the herd, and Michael did likewise. Dust boiled up, filling his nostrils, clouding his vision.

His horse had chased the buffalo before, and it carried Michael alongside the stampeding herd. Guiding his horse with the pressure of his knees, Michael rode up on the right side of the cow he had chosen, sighted down the shaft, and loosed an arrow. The cow snorted as the arrow pierced its heart, then fell heavily to the ground.

A triumphant cry rose in Michael's throat as he urged his horse onward. Ahead he saw Yellow Spotted Wolf chasing an enormous bull, and he forgot about killing another buffalo himself as he watched his great-grandfather. Man and horse moved as one, riding just behind the bull's shoulder. Yellow Spotted Wolf carried a lance, and as Michael watched, he drove it into the animal's heart. The sound of his great-grandfather's kill cry was a sound Michael would never forget.

Lifting his own voice in a cry of exultation, Michael turned back to the hunt. He had nocked an arrow to his bow and was sighting down the shaft when a big bull came up on his left and raked its horn across his horse's belly.

The horse screamed and went down, pinning Michael beneath its bulk.

Time. It seemed to slow to a crawl. He saw the scarlet tide pouring from his horse's belly, smelled the dust and the blood and his own fear as he waited to be crushed beneath the last of the stampeding herd.

But death did not come. The herd divided, flowing in two dark brown waves around the carcass of the horse.

His heart was still pounding furiously when Yellow Spotted Wolf rode up and dragged him out from under the horse's belly.

"Close call," Yellow Spotted Wolf said, laying his hand on Michael's shoulder.

"Yeah," Michael agreed. "Too close."

And now the hunt was over and the butchering began. The women rode out, identifying their husband's kills by the markings on their arrows and lances. Children who had never been present at a chase before were taken aside and blood was smeared over their cheeks.

Michael knew a sense of pride as he watched Hemene help Elayna butcher his kill. The scent of dust and sweat and fresh-spilled blood hung heavy in the air as the butchering began. The tongue and the nose were delicacies, as was the liver when sprinkled with gall. The small intestines would be filled with chopped meat and roasted or boiled. The marrow bones were split and the contents eaten on the spot.

Elayna gagged and looked away as one of the

warriors ate the heart cut from a young calf. Michael had told her that, except for the bones and the hooves, the whole animal was used for food in some form or another. She had thought he was exaggerating, but as she watched the Indians savor the liver and the marrow, she knew he had been telling the truth. Even the blood would be cooked until all the moisture was gone and it was hard, like jelly.

She had learned, in the few short weeks she had lived with the Cheyenne, that they ate all manner of things that made her stomach queasy: young wolves and coyotes, puppies, wildcats and panthers, badgers and skunks, even their horses when necessary.

It took hours of work to skin a buffalo, butcher the meat, tan the hides. And it was all woman's work. Elayna had never toiled so hard in her life as she did that day, working beside Hemene. She knew Michael had thought the hunt great fun, but she found no pleasure in it, nor in the blood that stained her hands and skirt.

There was a feast that night. The Cheyenne seemed to throw a feast for every occasion, and after the feast there would be dancing, and that was something she had learned to enjoy.

And after the dancing, she followed Michael into the privacy of their lodge. Whatever differences lay between them were forgotten in the warm cocoon of darkness that surrounded them. There was neither red nor white now, only two people in love—a man caught up in a time that was not his and a woman living among an alien people, and yet both were content to be there.

Michael made love to Elayna tenderly that night, his close brush with death making whatever time he had left with her all the more precious, her love that much sweeter. He hadn't told her what had happened, how easily he might have been killed, only that his horse had gone down and had to be destroyed.

But now they were alone and she was in his arms and he told her with each gentle kiss and lingering caress that he loved her, that he would always love her.

Elayna gloried in his touch, in the rough satin of his skin as her hands kneaded his back and shoulders. She moaned with sweet ecstasy as he kissed her again, their breath mingling, becoming one, as their souls were one.

They came together like two halves of a perfect whole, each kiss adding fuel to the fire between them until they reached that one golden moment when his pleasure melded with hers, and hers with his, making them truly one heart, one soul, one flesh.

And for that moment, there was no thought of tomorrow, only the magic and the wonder of now.

Chapter 33

Sleep did not find Michael that night. Instead, he recalled how close he had come to death that afternoon when his horse went down. He remembered the fear that had gripped him when Elayna had been kidnapped by the Pawnee, his sense of helplessness, of loss. He had made her his woman, yet she was not truly his, would never be his until he could call her wife.

Time might separate them, death might part them, but for whatever time they would have together, he wanted Elayna to be his wife in every sense of the word.

He watched her all through the night, his eyes seldom leaving her face. He loved her, and it had been worth a trip back in time to find her, to find himself.

He kissed her gently as she woke up. Smothering her questions with kisses, he told her to get dressed while he got their horses.

Elayna's stomach was all aflutter as she pulled on her tunic and moccasins, then brushed her hair. Where were they going so early in the day?

Michael refused to answer her questions, and a short time later they were riding downriver.

A stand of lacy cottonwoods and ferns offered a cozy hideaway. Michael lifted Elayna from her horse, tethered their mounts to a nearby sapling, then spread a blanket beneath a tree and drew Elayna down beside him.

Elayna smiled up at him, her dark eyes filled with curiosity. "Are you going to tell me what this is all about?"

Michael lifted his left shoulder and let it fall. "I wanted some time away from the village, just the two of us." He took her hand in his, his thumb massaging her knuckles. "You might have been killed the day the Pawnees attacked us." He shook his head when she started to speak. "Let me finish. There are no guarantees in life," he said ruefully. "No one knows that better than I do. Anything could happen. We might have years together, we might have days . . ."

"Michael . . ."

He placed his forefinger over her mouth. "However long we've got, I want you to belong to me. Only me."

"But I do."

"I'm asking you to marry me."

"Marry you," she breathed, her eyes suddenly moist. "Oh, Michael!"

"I hope those are tears of joy."

"Yes, oh yes." She threw herself into his arms, covering his face with kisses and tears.

"Hemene is making the necessary preparations."

"Oh, she is, is she!" Elayna said, feigning a pout. "Just when did you arrange all this?"

"First thing this morning. The ceremony will be this afternoon."

"Pretty sure of yourself, aren't you?" she teased, joy bubbling up inside her.

"Well, since we've been living together since we got here, I didn't think you'd say no."

His kiss, when it came, was filled with hope and promise for the future. His hands caressed her, and yet he held his desire in check, wanting Elayna to be his wife the next time they made love.

He smiled suddenly and then, before she could guess what he had in mind, he picked her up and carried her to the river's edge.

"No!" Elayna shrieked. "Michael, don't you dare! Oh!" She gasped as he dropped her into the water, which was shallow and very, very cold.

"I'll get you for this," she warned, shaking her fist at him.

"You'll have to catch me first," he retorted with a grin.

Elayna sprang to her feet and gave chase, but Michael quickly outdistanced her and she turned her back to him, pretending to pout.

She sniffed loudly as she heard his footsteps coming up behind her.

"Should I apologize?" he asked, and she heard the laughter in his voice.

"Yes."

"I'm sorry," he said solemnly.

"You promise never to do it again? Well, do you?"

"No," he decided, and picking her up, he carried her into the river and sat down, holding her on his lap.

"I'll be a waterlogged bride if you don't let me dry off soon," Elayna remarked.

"You'll be a beautiful bride, wet or dry."

She had to kiss him for that, and then he was kissing her, and it was a long time before they left the river.

On the bank, she watched him undress, loving the sight of him, more pleased than she'd thought possible at the prospect of being his wife. Mrs. Michael Wolf. Mrs. Elayna Wolf. She smiled as shivers of delight coursed through her. Mr. and Mrs. Michael Wolf. It was too wonderful to be true.

They sat side by side on the grass, letting the sun dry their hair and clothes. It was all Michael could do to keep his hands off her, to make himself wait. Only a few more hours and then she would be rightfully his. He was surprised at how deeply he felt the need to make her his wife.

When they returned to the village, Hemene took Elayna to Mo'ohta-vo'nehe's lodge. Sunflower Woman was waiting for them, and Elayna found herself being purified and dressed by the two women.

"Ho-nehe has chosen well," Hemene remarked as she rubbed the inside of Elayna's thighs with sweet sage. "His bride's skin is as soft and smooth as the petals of the wild roses that grow along the banks of the Greasy Grass."

Sunflower Woman nodded in agreement. "She has fine breasts and good hips. Such women make good mothers."

Elayna blushed furiously, embarrassed by their frankness, flattered by their praise.

"And Elayna has also chosen well," Hemene added. "Ho-nehe will be a good husband, a good provider." She slid a knowing glance at Elayna. "He will warm you well when the nights grow long and cold."

"And fill your belly with children," Sunflower Woman said solemnly, and patted her own burgeoning belly.

The two Indian women smiled at each other as they slipped a tunic over Elayna's head. Elayna marveled at the velvetlike texture of the dress, the intricate beading across the bodice, the delicate fringe that fell from the sleeves. Tiny silver bells had been fastened to the fringe so that each movement was accompanied by the soft tinkling music of the bells.

"It's beautiful," Elayna said. "Thank you."

"I wore it on my wedding day," Sunflower

Woman said. "It was a gift from Hemene. Now I give it to you, and pray you find the same happiness with Ho-nehe that I have found with Soaring Eagle."

Elayna blinked back tears of gratitude as she squeezed Sunflower Woman's hands, too overcome with emotion to speak.

She sat down and Hemene brushed her hair, parted it in the middle, and dabbed the part with vermilion. New moccasins were placed on her feet, and a necklace of tiny white shells was placed around her neck.

Sunflower Woman and Hemene smiled at each other, pleased with their handiwork, confident that Wolf would also be pleased when he saw Elayna.

"He waits," Sunflower Woman reminded them, and the two Indian women escorted Elayna out of the lodge.

A white horse was waiting near the doorway and Hemene and Sunflower Woman helped Elayna onto its back, then led the horse to Michael's lodge.

Elayna felt her cheeks grow warm as she saw the crowd gathered outside their lodge. She saw Yellow Spotted Wolf and Mo'ohta-vo'nehe standing beside Soaring Eagle. But there was no sign of Michael.

When they reached the lodge, Sunflower Woman spread a blanket on the ground, then Yellow Spotted Wolf stepped forward. Lifting Elayna from the horse, he placed her on the blanket and motioned for her to sit down.

Her heart was fluttering in her breast as Yellow Spotted Wolf, Mo'ohta-vo'nehe, Soaring Eagle, and three other men grasped the blanket by the corners. Lifting two sides, they carried her into the lodge.

A small fire burned in the center of the tipi. Michael was standing beside the fire. Elkskin leggings hugged his long, muscular legs; his shirt was made of the same material. A single streak of white paint adorned his left cheek, an eagle feather had been tied in his hair.

He looked very Indian, and very handsome.

The men lowered the blanket to the ground, then Mo'ohta-vo'nehe took Elayna's hand and helped her to her feet.

Elayna gazed at Michael, only vaguely aware that Hemene and Sunflower Woman had entered the lodge. The Indian men and women formed a half-circle around the bride and groom, and then the medicine man, Red-Furred Bear, stepped into the lodge, resplendently draped in a white buffalo robe.

"Ho-nehe and E-layna are now married according to the customs of our people," Red-Furred Bear intoned in a solemn voice befitting the occasion, "but because the woman, E-layna, is white, they wish to marry *wehoevistoma-zistoz*, in the white man's way. So I ask you, E-layna, do you wish to have Ho-nehe for your *nahyan*, your husband?"

"Yes," Elayna murmured, her heart brimming with joy. "I wish to have Ho-nehe as my *nahyan*, my husband."

"And you, Ho-nehe, do you wish to have this woman for your *mazheem*, your wife?"

"Yes," Michael replied, unable to draw his gaze from the love shining in Elayna's eyes. "Very much."

"Then I say to all who are gathered here that Ho-nehe and the woman E-layna are one blood and one heart. May the Great Spirit bless you with many strong sons and daughters."

Red-Furred Bear chuckled softly, his rheumy old eyes alight with merriment. "The ceremony is over, Ho-nehe. You may kiss her now, in the manner of the *vehoe*."

Everything else faded into the distance as Michael took Elayna into his arms. Never had she looked more beautiful. Never had he loved her more. His woman. His wife.

Gently, tenderly, he kissed her.

Elayna's eyelids fluttered down as Michael's lips covered her own. She felt the tenderness in him, the barely restrained passion, the love that flowed between them as strong and deep as the Platte at floodtide. Her heart swelled, her emotions rising to the surface and spilling over in tears of joy. She was Michael's wife. Nothing could part them now.

Gradually Michael became aware of the soft murmur of conversation, of Red-Furred Bear's amused laughter as Yellow Spotted Wolf remarked that he would have to try the *vehoe* manner of kissing soon.

Elayna's cheeks were flushed when Michael finally released her. Hand in hand, they accepted the good wishes of Michael's family and friends.

Sunflower Woman patted her swollen belly and then patted Elayna's stomach and smiled. Elayna smiled back, pleased at the thought of giving Michael a son. Many sons.

Of course there was a feast, and dancing. And singing. Elayna thought the day would never end. Not that she didn't appreciate the kindness and good wishes of the people, only that she was anxious to be alone with Michael. Her husband. The mere word filled her with a rush of excitement and exhilaration.

Husband, husband, husband. She whispered the word to the beat of the drum.

And then, at last, Michael was beside her, taking her hand in his, leading her away from the festivities to the privacy of their lodge.

A low fire burned inside. Sprigs of sweet-smelling sage had been placed beside their sleeping robes.

She felt a sudden shyness as Michael secured the lodge for the night. She was being silly, she thought as she toyed with the fringe on her sleeve. This was Michael. They had shared this lodge for weeks now, had slept together, eaten together, bathed together.

But she was his wife now, and this was their wedding night, and she was as nervous as any new bride. But then he took her in his arms and everything was all right. This was Michael.

He drew her close, his desire evident in the tension in his arms, in the thrust of his manhood against her thigh, in the rasp of his voice as he murmured her name, telling her that she was beautiful, that he loved her, would always love her.

He slid the tunic over her shoulders, the bells tinkling as it fell to the floor, and then he was kissing her, his lips moving over the curve of her shoulder, down the inside of her arm, across her breasts. One hand cupped her buttocks, holding her close against him.

Elayna moaned low in her throat, her skin feverish, her hips arching toward him, her whole body aching to receive him. Too weak to stand, she drew him down on the buffalo robes and tugged at his shirt, impatient to feel his bared flesh against her own.

Her haste made her clumsy and he chuckled softly as he shrugged out of his shirt, clout, and leggings. Elayna smiled at the unmistakable proof of his desire, sighed his name as he covered her body with his. Her fingers moved through his hair, slid down his back, caressed the strength of his arms. She gloried in his touch, in touching him.

From outside came the faint notes of a flute, the soft sweet music of love serenading them, whispering into the lodge to mingle with the low crackle of the fire.

She heard Michael whisper her name and she rose up to meet him, her arms drawing him closer, closer. His eyes blazed with desire, his need consuming her as flames consumed kindling. His skin was dark, sheened with perspiration, his hair the color of midnight, warm where it brushed her cheek. He was Man, primal, masterful, yet gentle, and she was Woman, eternal, submissive, yet equal, eager to bear his love, to give life to life.

Her head fell back, her nails raking his back, as his life spilled into her, filling her with warmth, his love making her complete at last. . . .

Chapter 34

She was a married woman. The thought made her smile as she tidied up their lodge, her hands lingering on Michael's wedding clothes. She had not thought it would make a difference, but it did. She was his wife now, and though nothing had really changed between them, everything was different. She belonged to him now, in a way she hadn't before. In the white world, a woman was considered her husband's property. His word was law. A man could beat his wife, abuse her, neglect her, and no one would dare question his right to do so. A woman did not own property. She could not vote. Her children belonged to her husband. Any money she might earn or inherit was controlled by him.

It was different with the Cheyenne. The women discussed matters freely with their husbands, arguing, persuading, and cajoling until they got their own way about tribal affairs. There had been women chiefs, and women shamans, and women who had gone to war. If a couple divorced, the children went with the mother.

She did her best to adapt to the ways of the Cheyenne, knowing she could never go back to her own people now, but the loss of her friends at Camp Robinson seemed a small price to pay for the joy of being Michael's wife. Her only regret was that her father would never know or understand how she felt, would never know how happy she was.

She felt more at home when she joined Hemene and Sunflower Woman at the river that morning. They had accepted her before, but she was one of them now, a wife.

"So, E-layna, what did you do last night?" Sunflower Woman asked innocently, and then burst into gales of girlish laughter as Elayna's cheeks turned bright pink. "Did you tame the wild Wolf?"

"Behave yourself," Hemene chided, her eyes twinkling with merriment. "Can you not see our new wife is weary?"

"She will be weary for many mornings to come," Sunflower Woman predicted.

Hemene shrugged. "Perhaps not. Perhaps it will not take long for Ho-nehe's seed to sprout in her belly."

"Perhaps," Sunflower Woman agreed. She smiled as she placed her hands on her own swollen belly. "Perhaps E-layna is with child even now."

Elayna placed her hands over her stomach. It had not occurred to her she might get pregnant, but it was a very real possibility. And a welcome one.

In the afternoon some of the men gathered together to test their skill with bow and arrow. Targets were placed in trees and there was furious betting and boasting before the contests began. Michael was one of the contestants, as were Yellow Spotted Wolf, Mo'ohta-vo'nehe, and a half-dozen other warriors.

Elayna stood behind Michael, her heart welling with pride for the man who was her husband. No other warrior was as handsome, as tall, as wonderful.

Watching him, she noticed anew how much he looked like Yellow Spotted Wolf. Many of their mannerisms were the same. At one point she saw Mo'ohta-vo'nehe staring at the two of them, his eyes narrowed, his brow furrowed. Mo'ohta-vo'nehe was a remarkable man, she thought, to have taken Michael into his affection so readily. But there was no doubt that Michael was related to the family. Only a blind man could fail to see the resemblance between Michael, Yellow Spotted Wolf, and Mo'ohta-vo'nehe himself.

Her musings were interrupted as the contests began. It was soon evident to Elayna that, as good as Michael was with a bow, he was no match for Yellow Spotted Wolf, and neither was anyone else. Time after time, Yellow Spotted Wolf's arrows hit the target, and Elayna became aware that a number of young maidens had joined the spectators, their dark eyes filled with admiration as they watched Yellow Spotted Wolf win one round after another. She let her gaze wander over the girls, and wondered which one would win Yellow Spotted Wolf's heart.

Michael grinned knowingly as Pretty Flower batted her eyes at Yellow Spotted Wolf. *You're wasting your time*, he thought, and turned his gaze to the young woman standing quietly at his great-grandfather's side.

Blue Fawn was a tall, slender girl with large dark eyes and a sensuous mouth. She spoke to Yellow Spotted Wolf, her eyes aglow with admiration, and Yellow Spotted Wolf puffed out his chest with pride.

Pretty Flower grimaced and quit the field, and Michael laughed out loud, wishing he could hear what Blue Fawn was saying to make Yellow Spotted Wolf swell up like a turkey gobbler.

He saw Yellow Spotted Wolf take Blue Fawn's hand and give it a quick squeeze. Blue Fawn blushed prettily, and then Yellow Spotted Wolf turned away to accept a challenge from Soaring Eagle, and the brief interlude was over.

Michael watched Blue Fawn gaze longingly at Yellow Spotted Wolf, her heart in her eyes. It was Blue Fawn who would win his great-grandfather's heart. They would be married in 1879, and they would have five sons, though only one would live to manhood. And yet, in spite of everything, their marriage would be a good one.

He turned to smile at Elayna, and in his heart he wondered if his own marriage would survive the days to come, if their love was strong enough to overcome the aftermath of the Custer battle, the hardships that would follow.

"Elayna," he murmured, brushing a wisp of hair from her brow. "*Zemehoesz.*"

"*Zemehoesz,*" she repeated. "What does it mean?"

"The beloved one."

Her heart swelled until she thought it might burst, and she forgot all about Yellow Spotted Wolf and who his future wife might be as she followed Michael into their lodge and secured the flap.

The future would take care of itself. For now, she wanted only Michael's arms around her, his lips crushing hers, his voice whispering her name.

Chapter 35

The days were cold and the nights longer as October gave way to *Hik'omini*, the Month of the Freezing Moon.

Michael and Elayna spent much of their time inside their lodge as snow covered the plains with a thick blanket of white. The autumn leaves were gone and the trees stood barren on the hills, their skeletal arms fringed with icicles.

On mild days they ventured outside. The Cheyenne were active, even in the winter, weather permitting. The men went hunting, and sometimes to war. Winter was considered a favorable time to steal horses from the Crow and the Pawnee.

The women often cleared a space among the trees and hung robes or lodgeskins to serve as windbreaks. They would then build a fire and spend a pleasant afternoon sewing or mending. Elayna was included in these gatherings and learned how to do the fancy beading that made Cheyenne moccasins a thing of beauty. She had grown accustomed to wearing doeskin tunics and fur-lined moccasins, and except for the color of her hair, she looked like the other Indian women as she walked through the snow-bound camp bundled in a heavy robe.

Winter was also a time for fun. Men and boys made sleds from buffalo ribs lashed together with rawhide and raced down the icy slopes. The rib sleds could fly down a hill faster than a horse could run. Very small children slid down small hills on pieces of rawhide. Mothers encouraged this, for not only did it provide their children with hours of fun, but it was also a convenient, labor-saving means of wearing the hair off a buffalo hide they wished to use for moccasins.

But the best days for Michael and Elayna were those they spent alone in their lodge. Michael accepted each new day as a gift from God, another twenty-four hours to spend with Elayna, another day with his great-grandfather, with Mo'ohta-vo'nehe and Hemene and Badger. He had a strong premonition that his time with the People was growing short. He had learned their ways, discovered his true heritage, and had a genuine love for the Cheyenne, and for the land they fought for.

He made Yellow Spotted Wolf promise to return Elayna to Camp Robinson if anything happened to him, to tell her who he was and where he had gone.

Yellow Spotted Wolf agreed, his expression skeptical. Try as he might, he could not believe that Michael Wolf was from the future, or that the things he had spoken of would come to pass.

But then, in December, Yellow Spotted Wolf began to believe.

A month earlier, Michael had told him that the Grandfather in Washington would soon send word to the Cheyenne and the Lakota, informing them that they would be considered hostiles if they did not report to the nearest reservation by January 31st. Because of the severe weather, such a thing would be impossible.

And now word had come from the Secretary of the Interior, ordering all Indians to report to the nearest Agency by the end of January.

The chiefs of the Cheyenne shook their heads as they discussed the secretary's ultimatum. There was no way they could comply even if they were so inclined. The snow was deep, the trails impassable for travois ponies.

It was going to be war, Yellow Spotted Wolf mused. Just as Michael had predicted.

In the days that followed, Mo'ohta-vo'nehe and the other chiefs met together often, and eventually it was decided that the tribe would join forces with Sitting Bull and Crazy Horse as soon as possible. There was strength in numbers, Mo'ohta-vo'nehe declared, and if the *vehoe* wanted war, then war it would be!

Michael made a concentrated effort not to

dwell on what spring would bring. Instead, he spent all his time with the two people he loved most in all the world, Elayna and Yellow Spotted Wolf.

He found himself staring at Elayna, committing her face to memory, the color of her hair and eyes, the shape of her mouth, wanting to imprint her image so deeply upon his mind that it would last forever, for he could not shake the feeling that his time was growing short. He memorized the sound of her voice whispering his name, the merry sound of her laughter. He told her often that he loved her, would always love her.

During the long winter evenings the people often gathered in small groups to listen to the old ones tell of days gone by. Sitting snug in one of the lodges, with Elayna by his side, he gained a deeper appreciation for his people, a true understanding of his great-grandfather's beliefs.

"It is better to live in a lodge than a square house," proclaimed Red-Furred Bear one wintry evening. "Our lodges are warm in winter, cool in summer, easy to move. The *vehoe's* house is like a cage, trapping him within its walls, shutting out the sun. The Great Spirit knew that man and animal need to move that they might always have fresh water and grass."

"*Ai!*" Buffalo Calf Horn agreed. "The Cheyenne live within a circle. The Power of the World is a circle, and everything tries to be round. The sky is round, birds make their nests in circles, for their religion is like ours. The sun is a circle,

and so is the moon. The four quarters of the
earth nourish the great circle. The East provides
peace and light, the South gives warmth, the
West gives rain, and the North sends the cold
and the wind for strength and endurance."

"*Ai!*" said Red-Furred Bear. "The life of a man
is a circle from childhood to childhood. I was
cared for by my mother when I was young, and
now that I am old, my children care for me."

The elderly men and women in the lodge
nodded in agreement.

"Even the earth mothers us," remarked an
aged woman with long gray braids and twinkling black eyes. "In the spring I sit on the new
grass in my bare feet and I feel her power seep
into my soul."

Buffalo Calf Horn grinned, revealing a mouth
full of yellow teeth. "The earth is a part of us,
and when we die, our flesh and blood nourish
the earth for the next generation, and that, too,
is a circle."

The soft voices of the ancient ones wrapped
themselves around Michael. He listened to the
old tales, handed down father to son for genera-
tions.

"Listen, and I will tell how the land of our
People was discovered," Mo'ohta-vo'nehe said,
and a hush fell over the tipi. "Long ago a certain
man took flight on the back of an eagle. The
great bird carried him across a wide body of
blue water. The flight took several days, and
when the eagle landed, the man was in a place
of snow-capped mountains and flat rolling

plains. Everything the man needed could be found in this place."

Red-Furred Bear cleared his throat. "I will tie another tale to the last," he said, and told of a long journey from a land of many islands, and how the people crossed a large body of frozen water. Part of the People were left on the other side.

"And they are still there," Red-Furred Bear said, and sitting back, he crossed his arms over his chest.

"Tell us another," Hemene coaxed.

Red-Furred Bear smiled. "Once, long ago, there was a great famine in the land of the People. Two brave young men decided to go in search of the underground hiding place of the buffalo to find meat to feed the People. They painted their bodies before they left on their journey, and begged the Great Spirit to bless them on their way.

"One day, after they had been gone a long time, they plunged into a great waterfall which they believed led to the hiding place of the buffalo. They found an old woman there who took pity on them and gave them corn and buffalo meat to sustain them on their long journey home."

Later, walking hand in hand with Elayna toward their lodge, Michael felt a new sense of belonging, of being a part of the earth. He gazed up at the sky, and the moon smiled down at him.

"Circles," Michael mused aloud. "The earth, the sun, the moon . . ."

"And my love for you," Elayna murmured. "A circle with no beginning and no end."

There was a constant stream of news in the days that followed. Runners and scouts on weary horses fought their way through the cold and the snow to carry word from tribe to tribe. And that word was *war*.

In February, Sitting Bull was officially declared a hostile and was to be warred upon. General George Crook was ordered to go out and bring in Sitting Bull, Crazy Horse, and the others.

In March, word came that Crook had left Fort Fetterman. His head scout was Frank Grouard, a man who had been captured years earlier by the Hunkpapas and adopted by Sitting Bull. But he had returned to the whites, and now he was riding with "Three Stars" against his old friend.

Another runner brought the news that one of Crook's columns under General James Reynolds had attacked a Cheyenne village on the Little Powder River. The survivors had made their way to Sitting Bull's camp on the Powder River some sixty miles away.

Sitting Bull had been enraged when he heard about the battle. He was a man who wanted only peace. He had stayed away from the whites, asking only to be left alone. Now they were forcing him to fight.

"We are an island of Indians in a lake of whites," the runner said, relating Sitting Bull's words. "We must stand together, or they will rub us out separately. Those soldiers have come shooting; they want war. We will give it to them."

A short time later another runner came from Sitting Bull. He carried a message that was being repeated in Indian villages all across the Plains: "It is war!" the Hunkpapa medicine man had decreed. "Come to my camp at the Big Bend of the Rosebud."

War. The word reached not only the hostile Indians, but those on the reservations as well. *War.* The very word excited the young men. They were tired of days with nothing to do, nothing to eat. Red Cloud, an influential Oglala war chief, tried to keep his young men on the reservation, but he was an Agency Indian and his words weighed nothing compared to the war cry of Sitting Bull. Even his own son, Jack Red Cloud, went to join Sitting Bull.

Michael heard the stories, listened to the runners, listened to the words of Sitting Bull, and he knew that it was the beginning of the end.

The Cheyenne were moving again. The chiefs had heard the war cry of Sitting Bull and the cry could not be ignored.

Michael heard numerous complaints from the warriors as they rode toward Sitting Bull's camp on the banks of the Rosebud. The whites were entering the Indians' land in ever-increasing numbers, polluting the rivers and streams, littering the plains with tin cans and bottles, raping the earth for gold.

As the Cheyenne traveled across the flowering

prairie, Michael tried not to think about the future. He tried to enjoy the beauty of the greening grass and trees, to find pleasure in the wildflowers that bloomed on the verdant hill-sides, to savor the sweet scent of newness that was in the air as the earth renewed itself. The sky overhead was vast, blue, limitless, reminding him of the Pacific Ocean and California.

Had he ever really lived there, had a life there? What was he doing here, following a path that would inevitably lead to the Little Bighorn and a showdown with Custer and the Seventh Cavalry? Did he have the guts to become a part of the most famous Indian battle of them all?

He had a sense of being caught up in a whirlpool from which there was no escape. He knew what was coming, and knew it could not be changed. *What will be, will be*, Sitting Bull had said, and Michael feared that it was true. He would fight beside Mo'ohta-vo'nehe and Yellow Spotted Wolf, and he would live or he would die . . .

Michael chuckled softly. Maybe that was why he had been sent back in time, he mused—to spill his blood along the banks of the Greasy Grass.

He shook the morbid thought from his mind as Yellow Spotted Wolf rode up beside him.

"Will there be a battle at the Rosebud?" his great-grandfather asked.

"Yes," Michael answered, surprised by the question.

"Will we win?"

Michael nodded, wondering what lay behind Yellow Spotted Wolf's remarks. His great-grandfather never spoke of the future, or of Michael's knowledge of it.

"It is good to fight," Yellow Spotted Wolf declared enthusiastically. "Good for a warrior to test his courage."

"Is it?"

"*Ai*! This will be your first big battle," Yellow Spotted Wolf mused. "I have ridden against the Crow and the Pawnee, but never against the *vehoe*." He raised his lance over his head and shook it. "I am eager to dip my lance in the blood of the white man, to decorate my coup stick with yellow hair."

Michael shook his head. He did not understand his great-grandfather's eagerness to fight, yet all the young men felt the same. They were eager for a fight, eager to drive the whites from the Black Hills, to reclaim the Land of the Spotted Eagle for the red man.

He was thinking of that later that evening as the Indians made camp.

His gaze wandered over the peaceful camp. Men and women were going about their evening chores, laughing and visiting, looking after their children, caring for the elderly. It was a hard life, Michael thought, and yet it was not without its rewards. The Indians were close to the earth, close to their gods, to each other. They had a oneness with nature that the white man would never have, an understanding of the earth and the elements, a kinship with all living creatures.

He gazed at the vast rolling prairie, at the clear sky, and he wished that somehow history could be rewritten, that the victory at the Little Bighorn would send all the whites back across the Missouri, leaving the Indians forever in peace, to live the life they were meant to live. But it would never be. The whites were too powerful, too well armed, too greedy. They wanted the Black Hills and the wealth it contained, and he knew they would not rest until it was theirs, no matter what the cost.

What will be, will be, he thought again.

But he didn't have to like it, and he was suddenly eager to fight. Even though he knew his people could not win, he was eager to fight for the land that had nurtured Yellow Spotted Wolf. The land that should have been his.

He was unusually quiet after dinner that night, his thoughts melancholy.

Elayna sensed that something was troubling him, but she didn't pry, only sat quietly beside him, her hand resting on his thigh, hoping her presence would help.

"It's beautiful here, isn't it?" Michael mused aloud. "I've grown to love this place as nowhere else."

"Haven't you always lived here?" she asked, and it suddenly occurred to her that she knew very little about the man she had married.

"No." He shook his head. "It isn't fair. My people belong here. What right has the government to make them leave? Time and again the United States has promised land to my people, promised them food and shelter. What promises have they ever kept?"

"Michael . . ."

"My people belong here. They're part of the land." He paused, remembering something Luther Standing Bear had written, a statement that claimed only the white man thought of nature as a wilderness. The Indians didn't think of the grassy plains and timbered hills and flowing streams as wild. Only the white man thought the land was infested with wild animals and savages.

Michael sighed, overcome with despair as he recalled something else, something that Crazy Horse had said. *We did not ask the white man to come here*, the Oglala war chief had said. *The Great Spirit gave us this country as a home. You had yours. We did not interfere with you. . . .*

Damn, he thought, it was so frustrating to know what the future held, and know there was nothing he could do to change it. The strong had always preyed on the weak. Old civilizations were lost and new ones were founded.

Nothing remains the same but the earth and the mountains . . . How many times had he heard Yellow Spotted Wolf murmur those words when life threw him a curve?

"Michael, won't you tell me what's bothering you?" Elayna asked softly, her concern evident in her voice. "Maybe I can help."

"You help just by being here," he replied. "You're the best thing that ever happened to me."

"Oh, Michael . . ."

There was a world of wanting in her voice and in the soft glow of her eyes, in the touch of her hand as it slid over his thigh, heating his flesh. He groaned softly as she leaned toward him, her lips slightly parted, her breath warm and sweet as it fanned his cheek.

He forgot about the past then, forgot about the future. There was only Elayna and the wonder and reality of now.

Drawing her into his arms, he kissed her deeply, the heat spreading through him like wildfire as she slid her hands under his shirt and caressed his back and shoulders. He lowered his head and kissed her neck, her shoulder, the tantalizing curve of her breast.

There was too much clothing between them and he uttered a soft oath as he drew away to shed his clout and leggings and shirt. Elayna quickly slipped out of her tunic, and then they stretched out on the buffalo robes, hands and lips eagerly exploring, gently pleasuring, until urgency overcame gentleness and they came together, driven by a need as old as time, as endless as the stars.

He was power and strength, demanding fulfillment, and she was like Mother Earth, giving nourishment and life. She cried his name as his seed spilled into her and she drew him closer, praying that life would merge with life and she would conceive and give Michael Wolf a son.

He held her close long after their breathing

had returned to normal, needing to be a part of her, to be cradled in her warmth a few minutes more.

He gazed into her eyes, dark and deep and filled with love and the hazy afterglow of passion.

"Nemehotatse, nahyan," Elayna murmured as she brushed a wisp of sweat-dampened hair from his brow. "I love you, husband."

"Nemehotatse, zemehoesz," he replied quietly, fervently. And in that moment he knew their time together was growing short.

Chapter 36

They reached Sitting Bull's camp on the Rosebud the second week of June. It was no longer a Hunkpapa camp but was now composed of Indians of many tribes who had heard Sitting Bull's cry of war and had come to join in the fight against the white man.

Crook was in the field again, camped along Goose Creek. War was inevitable.

Michael stayed close to Elayna, knowing she must feel lost and alone, like a white rose in a garden of red.

That night he took her in his arms, comforting her with his presence. They did not speak for a long while, only held each other close. Michael knew there were things that needed to be said, decisions that had to be made, but he was reluctant to mention the coming battle, or to think of the battles that would follow, the inevitable surrender of his people, the horror of the reservation.

The need to tell Elayna who he was and where he had come from was strong within him, and yet he knew the time was not yet right, and he put all thought of the past and the future from his mind and focused instead on the woman in his arms.

From the distance came the muted sounds of laughter, the steady beat of a drum, the haunting notes of a flute. The dying fire cast dancing shadows on the lodgeskins, the air was sweet with the scent of sage and pine. And woman.

His hand moved up and down Elayna's arm, marveling at her soft skin, at the love she had brought into his life. He had made Yellow Spotted Wolf promise again that he would return Elayna to her father if anything happened to him. Yellow Spotted Wolf had readily agreed. He no longer doubted that Michael was his great-grandson, or that he had come to them from another time and place.

Michael sighed. There was one more thing he had to do, and it was time to tell Elayna so she wouldn't be taken by surprise.

"The Indians are going to celebrate the Sun Dance tomorrow."

"What's that?"

"It's hard to explain, hard for whites to understand. The Sun Dance is a religious ceremony. It's very old and very sacred to my people. Often when a man prays he offers the pipe or tobacco to the Great Spirit, but during the Sun Dance a warrior offers his blood and his pain to the spirits to show his gratitude, or to secure the blessings of the Great Spirit on the tribe. Sometimes a man takes part in the ceremony to acknowledge blessings he has already received, or to ask for a special favor, or a vision."

"What do you mean, he offers his blood? How?"

"There are a couple of ways. Some men offer pieces of their flesh. Other men choose to be attached to the Sun Dance pole by ropes attached to skewers inserted in the muscle over their breasts, here and here," Michael said, pointing to his chest.

"That's barbaric!" Elayna exclaimed, horrified by the mere idea of such an ordeal.

Michael nodded. "I used to think so too."

Elayna stared at Michael. "You're not going to do it?"

"I've got to."

"Why?"

"I can't put it into words. It's just something I've got to do. I may never get another chance." His hand stroked the back of her head. "I've asked Yellow Spotted Wolf to help me."

"You won't change your mind? For me?"

"I can't. I'm going to war, Elayna, something I've never done before." He chuckled softly, sheepishly. "I need all the help I can get."

"And you think God will protect you if you do this dance?"

Michael shook his head, his expression tender as he gazed into her eyes. "I want him to protect you."

Two large tears formed in Elayna's eyes and emotion thickened her throat. "Oh, Michael," she murmured, "please don't go."

"I don't want to, but it's something I've got to do. I don't expect you to understand. I don't understand it myself."

She wanted to beg him not to be a part of it, not to participate in such a heathen ceremony, not to go to war against her people, but she choked back the words. He did not need arguments from her, he needed her love and support, and that was what she would give him.

"The Sun Dance lasts for several days," Michael said, squeezing her hand. "I don't know how much time I'll be able to spend with you, but I'll be thinking about you every minute."

Time, Elayna thought. Once it had been her friend, but now it stalked her like a wolf on the trail of fresh blood.

The days that followed were like nothing Michael had ever experienced. The Indians were keyed up, excited at the prospect of the coming battle. There were many great warriors and chiefs gathered along the banks of the Little Bighorn: Gall and American Horse, Two Moons and Crazy Horse, Sitting Bull and He Dog and Little Wolf.

Sitting Bull was not the leader of the camp; there was no single leader, but he was a man of great importance. Broad-shouldered, his dark eyes flashing with anger, he moved through the camp, exuding confidence in an Indian victory.

"What treaty that the whites have kept has the red man broken?" he asked at one of the many council meetings. "Not one! What treaty has the white man ever made with us that they have kept? Not one! When I was a boy, the Lakota owned the world, the sun rose and set on their land. What white man can say I ever stole his land or a penny of his money? Yet they say I am a thief."

His words were strong, filled with truth, and the young men vowed to fight hard in the coming battle.

But before the battle there would be the Sun Dance.

It loomed before Michael with frightening fascination. Did he have the courage to fulfill the vow he had made to the Great Spirit? Could he endure the pain of the knife without whimpering like a child?

Mo'ohta-vo'nehe sensed Michael's anxiety and suggested that Michael visit the sweat lodge to purify himself for the coming ordeal. Michael agreed, and Yellow Spotted Wolf asked if he might join him and Mo'ohta-vo'nehe.

The sweat lodge was only about four feet high. The frame was made of willow branches covered with hides. Before the sweat began, Red-Furred Bear purified the lodge with sweet grass and sage, and then Mo'ohta-vo'nehe, Yellow

Spotted Wolf, and Michael stripped off their clouts and entered the lodge, naked as the day they were born.

They sat in a semicircle for a few minutes, praying silently. Michael prayed for Elayna, that she would be protected during the coming battle, that she would have a long and happy life. And he prayed for courage to face the Sun Dance, for courage in battle, for courage to face the future, whatever it might hold for him.

A short time later Mo'ohta-vo'nehe's wife, Hemene, began passing hot stones into the lodge, plucking them from the fire outside with two forked sticks. The hot stones were placed in a rectangular hole dug in the center of the sweat lodge. Mo'ohta-vo'nehe sprinkled water over the hot stones, creating dense steam and heat.

As the steam filled the lodge, Mo'ohta-vo'nehe began to chant a courage song, imploring the Great Spirit of the Cheyenne to bless those within the lodge with health and strength, with wisdom and fortitude.

At first, Michael could hardly breathe. Steam and smoke filled the lodge, and he knew a moment of panic, a sense of suffocation as the intense steam filled his lungs with heat.

"Relax," Mo'ohta-vo'nehe said. "Let the steam surround you and fill you until it is a part of you. Empty your mind of all thought."

Michael nodded. Closing his eyes, he willed himself to go limp, to think of nothing but the warmth of the lodge, of what he hoped to gain from participating in the Sun Dance.

He was aware of Yellow Spotted Wolf sitting beside him, of the soft chanting of Mo'ohta-vo'nehe, of the soft sizzle of the cold water on the hot stones. He wondered if Yellow Spotted Wolf was aware of the uniqueness of this moment when the past and the future were joined together.

There was a gentle hiss as Hemene passed fresh stones into the lodge and Mo'ohta-vo'nehe sprinkled them with water.

Michael felt as though he were drifting, weightless, mindless, through a world of silent heat. Sweat poured from his body, draining the strength out of him, leaving him feeling drugged, sluggish, suspended between time and space.

He took a deep breath and his lungs filled with moist heat, firing his blood, filling him with exhilaration. His spirit seemed to soar outside his body, and he felt as though his ancestors were in the lodge with him, smiling at him, offering him their support. He was Cheyenne, a warrior of the People, about to offer his pain and his blood to the Great Spirit.

Yellow Spotted Wolf had been right, Michael mused. A man needed a vision to guide him through life. He thought of his father, a man who had never had a purpose, who had never found a reason for living.

He was drifting, warm and safe, like a baby in its mother's womb. Blurred images danced before him. His father, tall and handsome he had been, a likable, easygoing man until he jumped head first into a whiskey bottle and never came out . . . his mother, filled with love and patience and tenderness, a gentle woman, a beautiful woman with eyes that were always sad. Had she ever been happy? Was she happy now? . . .

He felt a quick stab of pain as the images in his mind sharpened and he saw his mother as he had seen her last, a still figure lying in a crude wooden coffin, the pain in her eyes forever veiled behind closed lids. Was she happy now? . . . Was his great-grandfather happy now? He had a sudden recollection of wrapping a frail body in the Morning Star blanket, of placing the body high in the fork of a tree, and it seemed that Death was all around him, dark and quiet. Was Death the only answer to pain, the only happiness . . .

But Yellow Spotted Wolf was not dead. He was here, in the sweat lodge. Perhaps his father was here too, and his mother.

"Father . . ." He breathed the word aloud, and in his mind's eye he saw Joshua Red Wolf as he might have been had he looked for answers within the heart and soul of the Cheyenne instead of the white man's firewater.

A great sadness overwhelmed him and he felt the sting of tears behind his eyes as he grieved for his father, for the man that might have been, for the love they might have shared.

"Father . . ." He felt a hand on his shoulder and he opened his eyes, his heart pounding. But it was only Yellow Spotted Wolf standing before him. There was a deep and abiding sadness in his great-grandfather's eyes, as if he too had seen the man that Joshua Red Wolf might have been.

Rising to his feet, Michael followed his great-grandfather out of the sweat lodge. They were running now, running toward the river.

The shock of the cold water took his breath away, and then he was filled with a sense of power and well-being such as he had never known.

"You are ready now," Mo'ohta-vo'nehe declared as Michael stepped out of the water.

Michael nodded. He had been reborn inside the sweat lodge. The old Michael Wolf had died, and a new Michael had emerged, a man who knew who he was and what he was. A man at peace with himself.

The Sun Dance pole was cut the following day and erected where the dance would take place. Sitting Bull had let it be known that he would take part in the dancing, but first he intended to offer his flesh to *Wakan Tanka*.

When all the preparations had been made, Sitting Bull sat down on the ground and a warrior known as Jumping Bull knelt beside him. Lifting the flesh of the medicine man's arm, he cut away a small piece of skin. Elayna gagged and looked away, but Michael watched intently, his gaze focused on Sitting Bull. The old warrior seemed immune to the pain. No sign of discomfort showed on his weathered face. He might have been sitting comfortably inside his own lodge, meditating, so peaceful was his countenance.

No sound broke the stillness of the sacred circle save for the whisper of the wind through the trees and the song of the river.

Soon Sitting Bull's arm was covered with blood, and Michael knew that each cut was a prayer for victory. Jumping Bull paused only briefly and then began on Sitting Bull's other arm, his knife flashing slowly and skillfully, until he had cut one hundred pieces of flesh from the arms of Sitting Bull.

A collective sigh of admiration rippled through the people, their dark eyes paying homage to Sitting Bull's courage.

Then it was time for the Sun Dance to begin, and Michael forgot about Sitting Bull's pain as he contemplated his own. He had asked Yellow Spotted Wolf to be his instructor. It was unusual for one so young to be a sponsor, but Yellow Spotted Wolf had endured the Sun Dance, and that was the major requirement.

Too soon it was time for the candidates to be pierced. Michael knelt on the ground, his head thrown back, as Yellow Spotted Wolf pinched up the skin on the right side of his breast and ran an awl through the skin, then quickly inserted a wooden skewer through the incision. The procedure was repeated on the left side, and then the skewers were tied to the end of a rope fastened to the top of the Sun Dance pole.

The pain in his chest was sharp and all-consuming, worse than anything he had imagined, but Michael refused to cry out, refused to show any sign of weakness. It was important that Yellow Spotted Wolf be proud of him. It had always been important.

Bright spots of pain danced before his eyes as he rose to his feet.

He was two years old and he heard his great-grandfather's voice echo through the mists of time: "Do not be afraid," Yellow Spotted Wolf said as he lifted Michael onto the back of his horse. "You are Cheyenne. We were born to ride with the wind." . . .

He was five years old and going to school for the first time. "Do not be afraid," chided his great-grandfather. "You are Cheyenne. The white man cannot hurt you." . . .

He was eight years old and his right ankle had been broken when he fell out of a tree. "Do not be afraid," admonished Yellow Spotted Wolf as the doctor prepared to set the bone. "You are Cheyenne. A warrior endures pain without complaint." . . .

He was sixteen and his father was dead and his mother was dying. And Yellow Spotted Wolf was there, as he had always been there. "Do not be afraid," the old man had said, his own grief heavy in his voice. "We are Cheyenne. Birth and death are but two halves of the same whole, part of the great circle of life."

And now Yellow Spotted Wolf was standing before him again. "There is nothing to fear. Pull against the rope, and keep it taut. The pain will be bad but quickly over if you do not give in to it, if you do not try to cheat the rope by letting it go slack."

Yellow Spotted Wolf placed his hands on Michael's shoulders and gazed deep into his eyes. "Do not be afraid, Wolf. You are Cheyenne. Today your blood will mingle with ours and you will truly be one of us."

Do not be afraid. Michael drew a deep breath, expelled it slowly, and then pulled back on the rope that bound him to the Sun Dance pole, testing the pain. It went through him like molten daggers, hot and sharp and white, burning through his body, dancing behind his eyes.

He closed his eyes and he was a child again, listening to Yellow Spotted Wolf explain what the colors on the sacred sweat lodge stood for.

"White is for life, for light and morning, for spring," his great-grandfather had said. "Red symbolizes fire, heat, summer, the substance of life, our very blood. Green stands for growing life, for youth and happiness. The blue represents serenity, cloudlessness. Black symbolizes victory over an enemy."

"White is for life," Michael murmured, and, opening his eyes, he tugged on the rope again. The increased pain brought tears to his eyes.

All the participants were ready now, and the drumming began. Around and around the pole they danced, sweating and bleeding under the hot summer sun.

Sitting Bull danced with them. Blood oozed from his arms and dripped to the ground to stain the dirt at his feet, and still he danced, his presence lending strength to the other participants.

Michael felt his own spirits lift as he watched Sitting Bull dance. Images imprinted themselves on his mind: the blood flowing down Sitting Bull's arms, the deep abiding love and compassion he saw in Elayna's eyes, the strong, implacable face of Mo'ohta-vo'nehe, the pride reflected on the face of Yellow Spotted Wolf. The air smelled of blood and sweat and dust, of roasting meat and sweet grass, of sage and tobacco. There was the soft shuffle of moccasined feet moving to and fro, the chanting of the medicine men, and over all the steady beat of the drums.

He looked at the faces of the people and he could almost hear their thoughts. *How can we lose when we have warriors like Tantanka Iyotake to lead us?* they seemed to say.

But they would lose. It was inevitable.

Michael threw his head back and gazed upward, silently pleading for health and strength to face the future.

Time passed, and he forgot about the other dancers, forgot the people watching him, forgot about Elayna as he gazed steadfastly into the sun, losing himself in the bright white light as he blew on the eagle-bone whistle that Yellow Spotted Wolf had placed between his lips.

The notes of the whistle were high and sharp and clear, like the pain that ebbed and flowed as he rocked back and forth, trying to free himself from the Sun Dance pole. His tether was like an umbilical cord connecting him to the lifeblood of the Cheyenne, the beat of the drums was like the beat of his own heart.

Time passed slowly. The pain was always there, like the blazing sun that engulfed him in its heat and bathed him in its light.

And still he danced around the pole, his moccasins raising little clouds of dust at his feet. Head thrown back, he stared into the sun, lost in its light as he embraced the pain. He was weightless, mindless, and as he stared into the sun, it changed shape, becoming a small white room that closed him in and shut out the rest of the world. And he was alone. There were tears in his eyes and an ache in his heart. His arms were empty, his heart was empty. He went to the window and gazed out into the darkness, and it too was empty, like his life. Elayna was gone. Yellow Spotted Wolf was gone. And he was alone . . .

He sobbed Elayna's name, fear of losing her stronger than the pain of his lacerated flesh. Elayna, he had to find Elayna.

He tugged on the rope and his skin tore free, releasing him from the pole, and he sank to the ground, felt himself falling, falling, into the sun . . .

Chapter 37

He woke slowly, afraid to open his eyes for fear he would find himself alone on Eagle Mountain, afraid to discover it had all been a dream.

He groaned as someone touched his lacerated flesh, felt a rush of sweet relief as he heard Elayna's voice calling his name.

He opened his eyes to find her kneeling beside him, her beautiful dark eyes filled with concern as she sponged the blood from his chest.

"Are you all right?" she asked anxiously.

"Fine." He reached for her hand and held it tight. She was here. She was real. "I was afraid I'd lost you."

"I'm here," she said, not understanding the fear she saw in his eyes.

"Yellow Spotted Wolf gave me some ointment

for your wounds. He's very proud of you. So is Mo'ohta-vo'nehe.''

Michael nodded, unable to take his gaze from her face as she applied the salve to his wounds.

"The dancing is still going on," Elayna remarked, "and Sitting Bull is still going strong. He's a remarkable man."

Michael nodded. The ointment quickly eased the pain in his chest, but it could not erase the vision of that lonely room from his mind and he clung to Elayna's hand, more certain than ever that their time together was coming to an end.

Yellow Spotted Wolf came to see him the following afternoon. "Where is Elayna?" he asked, glancing around the lodge.

"She went to visit Sunflower Woman."

Yellow Spotted Wolf nodded, glad to have found Michael alone. "You did well," he said. "I am proud to be related to you." His dark eyes glinted with amusement. "I am proud to be your great-grandfather, though it is still hard to believe."

"And I am proud to be your great-grandson," Michael replied solemnly. "No one has influenced my life as you have."

Yellow Spotted Wolf nodded. It pleased him to know he would be an influence for good in his great-grandson's life, and yet it was all so confusing. Michael had come from the future and now dwelt in the past. If he stayed in the past and died here, would he be reborn again in his own time?

Yellow Spotted Wolf frowned. A man could go

crazy in the head trying to unravel such a mystery.

"Is the dance over?" Michael asked.

"Almost. Sitting Bull danced all night and on into this afternoon. He might be dancing still, but two of the tribal elders took him out of the Sun Dance lodge, insisting that he rest. Sitting Bull did not wish to leave, but he was very weak from the loss of blood and the rigors of the dance. As soon as he sat down, he lost consciousness."

Yellow Spotted Wolf paused, his dark eyes thoughtful. "When Sitting Bull recovered, he announced he had seen a great vision in which many horse soldiers fell at his feet."

"Custer," Michael murmured. "He was describing the battle with Custer."

"You know of this battle?"

"Yes. It will take place at the Little Bighorn."

"His vision is a true one, then?"

"Yes. Custer and all his men will be killed. But before that happens, there will be a battle with Crook."

"Three Stars," Yellow Spotted Wolf muttered. "When will this battle take place?"

"Very soon."

"And will we win that battle as well?"

"If I remember correctly, the battle was not really a victory for either side." Michael let out a long sigh. "You must remember to keep an eye on Badger when Custer comes. If you do not, he will be killed in the first wild attack on the camp."

"I will see to him." Yellow Spotted Wolf rose smoothly to his feet. "Rest well."

Michael stared after his great-grandfather, wondering if it was possible to change future events. Would Yellow Spotted Wolf be able to save his brother's life now that he had been warned, or was Badger fated to die? If he, Michael, rode into the battle and somehow managed to save the life of General George Armstrong Custer, would it change anything, or merely prolong the inevitable?

Michael shook his head ruefully. A man could go crazy trying to figure out a thing like that.

The battle with Crook came two days later. Michael was not a part of it, but he heard about the fight in great detail from some of Crazy Horse's young men.

It was about eight o'clock in the morning when Crook's soldiers halted their march in a valley watered by Rosebud Creek, so named because of the thick growth of wild roses along its banks. It was there that Crazy Horse and his warriors found them. There were several brief skirmishes. The Sioux were not fighting for honors or glory now. Those days were gone. War against the white man was not a game to see who could count the most coup or steal the most horses. The Indians were fighting for their lives now, for their freedom. When they charged, they were not thinking of glory or of striking the enemy, but of taking lives.

Crazy Horse had thought the battle won, when a party of reinforcements arrived on the scene. Crook's men began to cheer when they saw that help was on the way, and Crazy Horse retreated. The battle was not a victory, and when Crazy Horse returned to the camp and told Sitting Bull what had happened, the Hunkpapa medicine man declared that the fight with "Three Stars" was not the battle he had seen in his vision.

That fight was yet to come.

It was time for the Indians to move again, time to find fresh graze for the vast pony herd. And so the Sioux and the Cheyenne struck their lodges and headed for the valley of the Little Bighorn.

The war camp on the Greasy Grass was a sight Michael knew he would never forget. The Cheyenne made their camp downriver near the Brule and the Oglala Sioux. At the south end of the valley were clustered the lodges of the Minneconjou, the Hunkpapa, the Sans Arc, the Blackfoot Sioux, the Santee, and the Two Kettles.

Michael guessed the camp to be four or five miles long with perhaps two thousand lodges. Assuming there were two warriors to each lodge, he estimated there were close to four thousand men of fighting age, more than half of them seasoned fighting men. He doubted that there had ever been an Indian encampment of this size before, and he knew with a cold and bitter certainty that he would never see its like again.

There were thousands of horses grazing along

the river flats, and he saw the herd boys moving among them, driving them down to the river to drink, then herding them back to the heavy grassland benches west of the camp.

By nightfall the Cheyenne had erected their lodges and the cook-fires were burning brightly. The warriors strolled through the camp, smoking and talking, renewing old acquaintances, speculating on the battle to come. "Yellow Hair" Custer was coming, "Red Nose" Gibbon was in the field, as was "Star" Terry. The Army was spoiling for a fight, and they were going to get it.

The women also moved through the camp, greeting old friends and relatives, admiring new babies. The young maidens dressed in their best clothes and stood together in small groups, flirting with the young men, while the children ran together in carefree abandon.

Michael tried to hold the memory of each day close, hoarding memories like a miser hoarding gold. He sensed that his time with the Cheyenne was growing short, that death in battle, or a return to his own time, would soon take him from the people he had grown to love, from the woman who meant more to him than his own life.

He spent as much time as possible with Yellow Spotted Wolf, treasuring their time together, increasingly grateful for the man who was his great-grandfather.

He studied the countryside, imprinting the image of the Bighorn Mountains in his mind, trying to memorize the deep blue of the sky, the scent of the earth, the feel of a weapon in his hand, the sound of the drum.

Nights, he held Elayna close. At such times he told himself his feelings of time growing short were born out of his fear of the coming battle. He could not, would not, believe that he had found her only to lose her forever.

He shunned the dances and feasts to stay in his lodge, alone with his woman. They made love with desperate passion, both fearing that each time might be the last.

And later, when he held her in the protective circle of his embrace, he listened to the sounds of the night. How quiet these nights were, with only the whisper of the wind and the call of a nightbird to break the stillness. There were no loud sirens wailing through crowded streets, no horns, no screeching tires to mar the serenity of a quiet summer night. Only the soft crackle of the dying fire, and the gentle breathing of the woman pressed against his side.

Preparations for war increased daily. The warriors were constantly on the go, hunting for meat, traveling to nearby trading posts to trade furs and robes for rifles and ammunition.

Michael was frequently included in trips to the trading posts. His English was far superior to that of the other men. The traders eyed him suspiciously, mystified by his Indian appearance and his ready command of English.

Michael did not trust these men. He knew they cheated the Indians and often sold them inferior goods, but that didn't matter now. It was not flour or beads the Indians wanted, but guns and ammunition, and the traders readily accepted the fine robes and skins in exchange for weapons.

On one such trip Michael bought a pound of coffee, a tin of peaches, a side of bacon, and a dozen potatoes, his mouth watering as he thought of bacon and fried potatoes for breakfast, and lots of hot coffee to wash it down with.

He was about to leave the trading post when he saw the necklace. It was long and slender, fashioned of turquoise and silver. He thought immediately of Elayna, wanting to see it nestled against her throat, wanting to give her something that would last longer than memories . . .

He tried to shake the feeling that his time with her was short, and yet, in his heart, he *knew*, he just knew.

The narrow-eyed proprietor seemed to know how badly Michael wanted the necklace, and he refused to haggle over the price, or accept hides in exchange for the bauble.

"Ten silver dollars," the trader said firmly. "Not a dollar less."

But Michael didn't have ten dollars, silver or otherwise, and so he turned away, his mouth set in an angry line, sorely tempted to strangle the man and take what he wanted.

They were riding toward home when Yellow Spotted Wolf reined his horse close to Michael and pressed the silver necklace into his hand.

"For your woman," Yellow Spotted Wolf said, grinning broadly.

Michael stared at Yellow Spotted Wolf. "How'd you get this?"

Yellow Spotted Wolf shrugged elaborately. "I took it when the *vehoe* turned his back."

"You stole it!"

"It is not stealing when you take from the enemy," Yellow Spotted Wolf replied solemnly, and their combined laughter rang loud and clear over the plains.

He gave Elayna the necklace that night when they were alone. He kissed the back of her neck, his tongue sliding across her skin, before he fastened the clasp.

"Oh, Michael," Elayna said, her voice thick with emotion, "It's beautiful."

"You are," he murmured. His hands slid over her shoulders, unfastening the ties of her tunic, letting his fingertips caress her bare skin.

Elayna shivered with delight as his hands slid down her arms, moved to span her waist as he drew her close to him, his lips seeking hers. His shirt was like rough velvet against her breasts. His kiss lengthened and deepened, igniting tiny fires deep within her. His mouth moved to her neck and she threw her head back, giving him access to her throat and breasts as her hands unfastened the thong at his waist. His clout fell to the floor beside her dress, and she tugged at his shirt, wanting nothing between them.

His hands were impatient as he shrugged off his shirt and removed his leggings, then reached for her again. Her skin was softer than doeskin, more beautiful than the gleaming circle of silver around her neck. He lowered her gently to their bed, whispering to her that he loved her more than his own life, that he would always love her.

They kissed and caressed all night long, their passion building to a crescendo, then slowly waning only to be nourished again, and then again.

Michael knew that many warriors did not lie with their women before a battle, believing that sexual intercourse drained a man's strength and dulled his senses, but Michael needed to feel the warmth of her womanhood enfolding him. He drew strength from her touch, from the knowledge that she loved him above all else.

Just before dawn she placed his hand over her belly. She did not have to say the words for him to know what she was thinking. She was hoping for a child, his child. And in spite of all the hardships and uncertainty that lay before them, it was what he wanted too. A child born of their love, a link that would bridge the gulf of time.

He drew her on top of him, the tips of her breasts brushing his chest, tantalizing him beyond words. He breathed deeply, inhaling the scent of her, the heady, musky scent of passion, of woman.

His mouth sought hers as his flesh melded with hers, and then he laughed softly.

"If you don't get pregnant tonight," he muttered with a roguish grin, "it won't be for lack of trying."

Chapter 38

Custer was coming. The whole camp talked of it day and night. Scouts brought word that Custer had left the fort, and with him were "Star" Terry and "Red Nose" Gibbon. And with the blue-coats rode the hated Crow scouts. Reports of Custer's progress toward the Little Bighorn arrived daily, and daily the preparations for war increased.

Michael's emotions ranged from excitement to dread. The most famous Indian battle of all time was about to be fought, and he would be in the thick of it. It was awesome, frightening, exhilarating.

Needing to be alone to sort out his feelings, he left the sprawling Indian camp, moving downstream until he came to a bend in the quiet river. He came to an abrupt halt as he neared the riverbank, for there, sitting on a flat rock, was Crazy Horse.

Crazy Horse. He had always been a man apart. His hair was not black but dark brown, and his skin was almost fair. As a boy he had been called Curly and often mistaken by traders for a captive.

The Oglala war chief glanced over his shoulder at Michael's approach.

"I did not mean to disturb you," Michael said, taking a step back.

"Come, sit with me," Crazy Horse invited. "I grow weary of my own thoughts."

"What are you thinking?" Michael asked as he sat down beside the Lakota warrior.

"Can you not guess?" Crazy Horse replied with a wry smile. "Yellow Hair is ever in my thoughts."

Michael nodded. Custer was on everyone's mind just now. "Do you expect to win the battle?"

"Of course. Tatanka Iyotake has foreseen our victory."

"Then what is it that troubles you?"

"The other battles, the ones that will come after."

"Our people grow few in number," Michael remarked. "Perhaps it is time to surrender."

"No."

"You cannot fight forever."

Crazy Horse shrugged. "We will fight until the last warrior lies dead on the plains."

"And if you knew you could never win, that the people would go down in bitter defeat, would you still fight?"

"I am a warrior. What else should I do? Sit with the women and cry after the old days?" Crazy Horse stared at Michael, his dark eyes thoughtful. "Why do you ask me these questions?"

"Because I am afraid for you, for our people. I have lived with the white man, Crazy Horse, and they are numberless as the blades of grass on the prairie. You cannot fight them all."

"You are one of us," Crazy Horse mused slowly, "and yet you are not. Who are you, Michael Wolf? Why do you tell me these things? Do you think I do not know what lies ahead?" A great sadness filled the war chief's voice. "I know we cannot defeat the bluecoats. I know that, in the end, we will lose our homeland, our freedom. Your own prophet, Sweet Medicine, foretold the coming of the whites, the destruction of our way of life. But I cannot surrender without a fight."

Michael nodded, his heart suddenly heavy as he heard Sitting Bull's voice echo in the back of his mind: *What will be, will be.*

"A man cannot change his destiny," Crazy Horse remarked. "When I sought my medicine dream, I saw a warrior mounted on a horse that constantly changed colors. The warrior carried no scalps. His body was decorated with hail spots and a streak of lightning. Bullets and arrows flew at him, but they could not touch him. A storm raged around him, yet he passed through it unharmed. People reached out to him, but he rode through them, a red-backed hawk flying above his head. This warrior was the warrior I was destined to become. The white man cannot harm me. Only my own people can bring me down. Until then, I must fight."

Michael felt a chill pass through him as he recalled how Crazy Horse had died, killed by an Army bayonet while his own people blocked his escape.

"A man cannot change his destiny," Crazy Horse said again. "I will meet mine when the time comes."

Michael grunted softly. Looking past Crazy Horse, his thoughts turned inward. Perhaps it had always been *his* destiny to travel back in time, to find Elayna. Perhaps he was meant to be here, in the land of his ancestors. Perhaps he had been born in the wrong time, and he had been sent here because this was where he really belonged. Who could say?

"It is my destiny to lead my people," Crazy Horse said, his voice strong with conviction. "I would have it no other way."

The war chief placed his hand on Michael's shoulder. "It is not my fate to die in battle," he said with a note of regret. "Nor yours. We will both know victory before defeat, *le mita cola*. Let us savor the good things of life while we can."

Chapter 39

June 25th started like any other day. Michael went to the river to bathe with some of the men while Elayna prepared breakfast.

When they returned to camp, sentries brought word that Custer was near.

Custer. For a minute, it was as though all time had stopped. Michael looked at the village, the clear blue sky, the children at play, the warriors sitting outside their lodges, the women laughing, and he knew it was all about to come to an end. Custer was coming.

He saw Sitting Bull striding through the camp. A white missionary lady had once called the Hunkpapa medicine man tender, gracious, and invariably sweet. Perhaps he had been so, once, but no more. He was a man possessed of a deep and abiding hatred toward those who would not leave him and his people alone. He had told his young men to be merciless when they were raiding.

"If you find someone, kill him and take his horse and his weapons," Sitting Bull exhorted. "Spare no one." This from a man who had been known to spare the lives of captives, who had once declared that all prisoners must be freed or adopted into a family so there would be no slaves in his camp.

Gall rode into the village a few minutes later saying they had seen soldiers crossing the divide between the Rosebud and the Bighorn. Shortly thereafter, he had seen Reno and Custer separate their forces. And even while he was talking, a cry went up that the white man was coming.

The sound of shots being fired near the upper end of the village where the Sioux were camped spurred Michael to action and he ran to his lodge and swept a frightened Elayna into his arms.

The moment he had been dreading had come.

"It's Custer," he said flatly. "Stay here and you'll be all right." He buried his face in her hair and let his senses fill with the touch of her, the scent of her. "Promise me you'll stay here."

She was trembling and couldn't stop. He was going to fight, and nothing she could say would stop him.

"Promise me," he said again.

"I promise," she replied. "If you'll stay with me."

"I can't. I've got to find Yellow Spotted Wolf. We've got to find Badger before it's too late."

"Too late for what?"

"I don't have time to explain it to you now." His arms tightened around her as he kissed her with all the love in his heart. "Stay here," he said again. "Custer's men never made it this far."

She looked up at him, frowning. Never made it this far. What did he mean? He spoke as if the battle had already been fought. She wanted to question him, but he was drawing away from her, and she couldn't bear to let him go.

"Michael!" She threw her arms around him and held him close, breathing in his scent, loving the feel of his body next to hers. "Be careful," she whispered. "Promise me."

He nodded, kissed her again, and then he was gone.

"Oh, Michael," she murmured, and then, not knowing what else to do, she dropped to her knees and began to pray.

Outside, the Indian camp was in turmoil. Women gathered their children and ducked into their lodges while the warriors grabbed their weapons and war ponies and hurried toward the battle.

Michael ran toward his great-grandfather's lodge, but he was too late. Mo'ohta-vo'nehe, Yellow Spotted Wolf, and Badger were already gone.

Mounting his horse, Michael galloped downstream to where Custer's men were fighting. He had to find Badger before it was too late.

But it was like looking for a needle in a haystack. Thousands of warriors swarmed along the Little Bighorn, their war cries filling the air. Great clouds of dust were stirred by churning hooves and running feet, adding to the confusion of the battle.

He saw Crazy Horse riding ahead of him, a magnificent warrior mounted on a black horse. Crazy Horse carried no scalps. His torso was decorated with hail spots, a streak of lightning curved from his forehead to his chin.

Michael saw the Oglala war chief lift his rifle overhead, heard him holler *"Hoka-hey,"* heard the other warriors chant the Lakota kill cry, *"Huhn! Huhn! Huhn!"*

The fighting was intense now. He saw soldiers and warriors struggling in hand-to-hand combat, saw dozens of blue-clad bodies lying on the ground. The scent of blood and death filled the air. Once he saw a soldier with fair hair and he wondered briefly if it was Custer, but before he could be certain, he saw Yellow Spotted Wolf fighting with a broad-shouldered trooper. And then Yellow Spotted Wolf was on the ground and the trooper's knife was only inches from his throat.

A cry of rage boiled up inside Michael as he urged his horse toward Yellow Spotted Wolf. Lifting his lance high overhead, he raced toward the two men, his voice piercing the din as he drove his lance into the trooper's back.

A thin, high-pitched wail escaped the soldier's

lips as he fell forward, dead before he hit the ground.

With a shouted cry of victory, Michael grabbed his great-grandfather's forearm and lifted him onto the back of his horse.

"Where's Badger?" Michael hollered. "Is he safe?"

"*Ai!*" Yellow Spotted Wolf replied. "I remembered what you said and I sent him to stay with the horses so he would not be near the fighting."

Michael grinned, but before he could reply, his horse was shot out from under him and he hit the ground, rolling. From the corner of his eye he saw Yellow Spotted Wolf scramble to his feet, and then Michael was fighting for his life as a shrieking white man tried to drive a bayonet into his stomach.

Time seemed to slow and he was aware of the sun on his back, of the intense hatred blazing in the soldier's pale blue eyes. The man grunted as he lunged forward, and Michael smelled the stink of tobacco on his breath, sensed the fear that poured from him like sweat.

He was keenly aware of his own feelings as well. His heart was hammering wildly, perspiration trickled down his back, his palms were damp, his blood hot. He dodged right, then left, then ducked under the soldier's guard and yanked the rifle out of his hands. With a cry born of desperation, he reversed the weapon in his hands and drove the bayonet into the soldier's belly. He felt the blade slice into flesh and muscle, saw the blood flow in the wake of the blade as he jerked it free, saw the fear and the pain that twisted the man's face before he died.

And he knew he had killed the man in vain. The Indians would win the battle, but they would lose the war. Custer would die, and in dying, he would become a national hero, the subject of endless books and movies. Sitting Bull would go to Canada, Crazy Horse would be killed at Camp Robinson, and by the end of the decade virtually all of the Plains tribes would be confined to reservations.

It didn't matter what he did here, on the battlefield. The fate of the Indians would be sealed with Custer's death. All that mattered now was Elayna.

Dropping the rifle, he began to run back toward the village. The fighting was almost over. Only a handful of whites remained alive at this end of the village, though he knew that Reno and his men were entrenched in another part of the valley, fighting for their lives.

Elayna. He whispered her name as he ran.

He didn't hear the gunshot, was hardly aware of the pain as the bullet grazed the side of his head. There was a loud humming in his ears, a sudden weakness in his legs, a burst of light, brighter than the sun, inside his head, and then he was falling, falling, into a deep black void . . . .

Chapter 40

He was gone without a trace. Yellow Spotted Wolf, Soaring Eagle, and Mo'ohta-vo'nehe searched for him until dark, but to no avail. Michael was gone.

"I fear he has gone back to his own time," Yellow Spotted Wolf remarked as he walked Elayna to her lodge.

"His own time? What do you mean?"

Yellow Spotted Wolf shook his head slowly. "I do not know how to explain it to you, E-layna. He was here, yet he was not."

"You're talking in riddles."

"Life is a riddle. The man you knew as Michael Wolf has not yet been born."

"That's impossible. He was here."

"Sometimes we must believe the impossible. I cannot see the wind, yet it is there. Michael was here, and yet he was not. He came to us from a distant time, to fulfill an old man's dream."

Elayna shook her head, refusing to believe such nonsense. Yellow Spotted Wolf was talking about traveling through time, and that was impossible. And yet, if Michael hadn't been killed, where was he? And if he had been killed, why couldn't they find his body?

"Who can explain the Great Mystery of Life?" Yellow Spotted Wolf mused. "In the beginning, I did not believe what Wolf told me, but he knew of events before they happened, and he told me other things, personal things, and then I knew he was who he claimed to be." Yellow Spotted Wolf gazed deep into Elayna's eyes. "Wolf was not my cousin. He was my great-grandson."

Elayna stared at Yellow Spotted Wolf, her mind reeling. Could it be true? She thought of the remarkable resemblance between Michael and Yellow Spotted Wolf, the mannerisms they shared, the close bond between them. Had that bond been forged in another time? Had Michael Wolf come from the future?

It explained so many things, she thought, dazed. His command of English, the fact that he didn't talk like the other Indians, random comments he had made that she hadn't understood.

Tears filled her eyes. She should be glad he wasn't dead, yet he was still gone, separated from her by time instead of the grave. Yet she still felt bereaved. She had loved him and he had been taken from her.

"He belongs here, with me," she murmured. She looked up at Yellow Spotted Wolf, silently beseeching him to make everything right again.

"I believe he would rather be here, with you," Yellow Spotted Wolf said quietly. "He loved you very much."

"Then why was he taken away!" she cried, her heart filled with despair. "It isn't fair."

"I believe Wolf was sent here to discover who he was, and to save my brother's life. He has done those things, and I believe that *Heammawihio* has sent him back to his own time, where he belongs."

But he belongs here, with me. The words were a cry in her heart, and she railed at Fate, wondering at the twist in time that had brought them together only to tear them apart.

Hemene and Mo'ohta-vo'nehe tried to persuade Elayna to stay the night with them, but she refused, wanting to be alone with her memories, her grief. She tried to find consolation in the fact that he wasn't dead, only gone, but his loss was just as permanent, just as painful.

Of course he wasn't dead, she thought, the tears streaming down her cheeks. He couldn't be dead. He hadn't even been born yet.

"Oh, God," she sobbed, "please bring him back to me. I love him so much!"

She prayed all that night, but in the morning, nothing had changed. Michael was gone and the

Cheyenne were preparing to leave the valley. Benteen and Reno were still entrenched in the hills above the Little Bighorn, but Sitting Bull had called off the fight. There had been enough killing. It was time to move on.

Yellow Spotted Wolf came to see her first thing in the morning. "What will you do now?" he asked.

Elayna shook her head. "I don't know."

"You are welcome to come with us," Yellow Spotted Wolf offered. "My family is yours."

"Thank you," she replied, "but I think I'll go home."

Yellow Spotted Wolf nodded. "'Star' Terry and his men will be here soon. They will take you back to your father."

"Yes."

She sat in front of her lodge, watching the Indians break camp. She saw several warriors wearing blue coats and Army hats, others had McClellan saddles strapped to their horses, and still others carried Army-issue rifles or sabers.

To the victor belong the spoils, she thought bleakly.

She saw a little girl playing with a gold watch, saw a little boy toss a handful of greenbacks into the air.

By mid-afternoon the Indians were gone.

The following morning, June 27th, General Terry and Colonel Gibbon arrived in the valley of the Little Bighorn.

The soldiers assumed that Elayna was a captive who had been left behind, and she saw no reason to change their mind. She was too sick at heart to try to explain her relationship with Michael. What difference did it make, now that he was gone.

She wanted only to go home, to forget the sight of two hundred men lying dead under a hot prairie sun, their bodies stripped and mutilated, splashed with darkening blood, the dead horses, the stink of bloated carcasses and decaying flesh, the hordes of hungry flies.

Forget, she thought, forget everything.

She murmured the word over and over in her mind as she rode out of the valley with Terry's column: forget, forget, forget. Forget his voice, his smile, the touch of his hands, the taste of his lips.

Forget, she thought bleakly. Not if she lived to be a hundred.

Her reunion with her father was bittersweet. She was happy to see him again, to assure him that she was well and healthy, but each step away from the Little Bighorn seemed to widen the gulf between herself and Michael. She had felt close to him there, even though he was gone.

She told her father everything, how Michael had taken her to live with the Cheyenne, how she had tried to hate him and couldn't, how he had disappeared after the battle with Custer.

"I love Michael Wolf," she said quietly, fervently. "I always will."

Of course, Lance came to call. He brought her a bouquet of wildflowers, but the closeness they had once shared was gone. She was no longer the innocent, trusting young girl she had once been, and he was a stranger to her now.

Everything she had thought she missed seemed foreign. Her chemise and petticoats and dresses felt cumbersome, her shoes pinched her feet, her bed was too soft. And her heart was empty, so empty.

She began to help her father in the infirmary again, needing something to occupy her mind, to fill the long, lonely days.

She went to visit her friend Nancy, who had finally gotten Sergeant O'Farrell to the altar. Elayna could not help feeling a twinge of jealousy as she listened to Nancy's rosy plans for the future.

Later, walking home, Elayna wondered what her own future held.

She had been home almost a month when she began to suspect she was pregnant. Counting back, she realized she hadn't had her monthly flow for over six weeks. Pregnant. She held the knowledge that she was carrying Michael's child close to her heart, cherishing it. Michael was gone, but she was no longer alone. His child was growing beneath her heart.

Her father did not share her joy. He stared at her for a long moment, his eyes suddenly old.

"Are you sure?" he asked heavily.

"Yes."

He let out a long sigh, his shoulders sagging with despair. "How far along are you?"

"About two months, I think."

He hated himself for the thought that entered

his head. He was a doctor, dedicated to the preservation of life.

But she knew what he was thinking. "I want this baby, Father. It's all I have left of Michael."

"Elayna, you're so young. Have you thought what people will say? And what about the child? What kind of life will it have?"

"I don't want to talk about it," she said, and left the room.

But later, alone, she realized why her father had been so upset. Her child would be a half-breed, born in a land where Indians were despised. People would shun her when they discovered she had loved an Indian, and they would hate her child as well.

She could not let that happen. For days she fretted over what to do, and at last she decided she had to leave Camp Robinson. Feelings against Indians were not so strong in the East. She would go to New York or maybe Philadelphia and have her child there. She would find a job, perhaps in a hospital.

The hardest part was telling her father of her decision.

"Leave?" Robert O'Brien exclaimed. "Where would you go?"

"New York, I think."

"But you'd be alone. How would you live? Who'd look after you?"

"I'll be all right, Father. I can't stay here and be your little girl forever. Surely you can see how impossible it would be to stay. I'd be an embarrassment to you."

"Nonsense! You've done nothing to be ashamed of."

But her mind was made up. She needed to get away, to make a new life for herself, for her child.

But first she had to return to the Little Bighorn. She wanted to walk where Michael had walked just once more, see the river, smell the grass, touch the earth where he had stood. Perhaps if she went back and told him goodbye her heart would find peace.

Part 4

Chapter 41

Awareness returned slowly. He felt a soft gentle breeze ruffle his hair, felt the tickle of a blade of grass against his cheek. Slowly, reluctantly, he opened his eyes.

He was lying at the base of a large white tombstone.

Sitting up, he gazed out over the valley. In the distance he could see where the Indian village had been located. He was on Custer Hill, he thought absently. Markers showed where George Custer, his brothers Tom and Boston, his nephew Autie Reed, and the remnant of the Seventh Cavalry had died. The original graves had been dug in haste on the battlefield, with soldiers being buried where they had fallen.

Later, in 1881, as many graves as could be found had been opened and the bodies reinterred in a common grave around the base of the memorial that listed the names of all the dead.

The Custer Battlefield. He had once seen a brochure that called the battlefield a place where ghosts still walked in broad daylight. The Indians referred to the Park Rangers as ghost herders.

Ghosts. He could almost see them now, the spirits of Custer's men, riding into history and legend. To this day, scholars debated the Battle of the Little Bighorn, schoolchildren studied it, historians pondered it, Hollywood made movies about it, some portraying George Custer as a hero without equal, others branding him an arrogant fool.

Rising, Michael gazed at the markers indicating where Companies E and C had been overwhelmed and defeated. The battle was over, he thought bleakly. It had been over for almost eighty years.

A deep sadness filled his heart. Yellow Spotted Wolf was dead. And Elayna was dead, forever lost to him now.

Had it all been just a dream, after all?

He shook his head, groaned softly as a dull ache quickened in his temple. Lifting his hand to his head, he felt the blood dried in his hair. Glancing down, he saw the scars on his chest, souvenirs of the Sun Dance.

It had not been a dream, after all.

He heard voices and he whirled around, his

heart leaping with hope. But it was not Elayna. It would never be Elayna again.

They were tourists. A man and a woman and three small children. They were staring at him strangely, as though they were looking at a ghost. And that was what he felt like, he mused ruefully. A ghost from the past.

"Pave-eseeva," Michael murmured as he walked past the astonished family. "Good day."

It was over twenty miles to Lame Deer. He'd gone about a mile and a half when a Park Ranger picked him up and drove him to the reservation.

He spent the night in his great-grandfather's house, alone. Sitting on the floor in the living room, he felt the tears sting his eyes, felt the ache in his heart, the emptiness, the loneliness. He went to the window and gazed out into the darkness and it too was empty and alone.

In the morning, he went to the Trading Post and bought a pair of Levis, a blue cotton shirt, and a sack of tobacco. He borrowed a truck from old Two Bulls and headed for the Black Hills, his buckskin leggings, clout, and tobacco pouch folded in a neat bundle on the seat beside him.

He stopped at Johnson Siding to rent a horse and discovered that the big gray gelding and the chestnut mare had wandered home in his absence. He apologized to the man for letting the horses get away from him. Minutes later, mounted on the big gray gelding, he was riding hard for the hills.

He found Eagle Mountain without any trouble. No one had been there since he left, and he found his clothing, boots, wallet, and sleeping bags where he'd left them, along with Yellow Spotted Wolf's battered suitcase.

He stared at the old cardboard valise, wondering how much time had passed since he had prayed for a vision. He wished fleetingly that he'd checked the date before he left Johnson Siding, but it didn't really matter, not now. He thought a good guess would be a week, judging by the horse droppings.

A week, he mused. Was it possible he had lived a year in a week?

Shaking his head, he walked down the hillside to the stand of timber where he had left his great-grandfather's body. It rested where he had left it, high in the fork of a tree, still neatly wrapped in the Morning Star blanket.

He felt a sense of peace as he stood there, a new depth of love and respect for the man who had been his great-grandfather. He understood now why Yellow Spotted Wolf had never been happy on the reservation. He knew why the Sioux and the Cheyenne had never been able to adjust to the white man's way; why they never would.

His people were hunters, not farmers. They had been born to roam the vast sunlit plains, not to squat on a few acres of barren ground and raise crops and cattle. The Cheyenne had been a part of the earth, the sky, the trees, and the grass. The song of the wind was in their blood and in their hearts, and the wind did not sink roots and settle in one place. The wind moved over the face of the land, taking little, leaving little behind.

He bid his great-grandfather a quiet farewell, and then he returned to his campsite. Stripping off his shirt and jeans, he donned his buckskin leggings and clout.

Moving away from his belongings, he raised his arms overhead and offered a prayer to *Heammawihio*, and then he offered tobacco to the four directions, to the sky above and to the earth beneath his feet, and when that was done he prayed again, his voice loud and clear as he beseeched the spirits to send him back to his people, back to Elayna.

He prayed all that day and into the night, and when the sun rose above the mountains the following morning, he was still praying, his voice hoarse, his throat dry, his eyes damp with tears.

He stayed on the mountain for three days, and on the morning of the fourth day he admitted defeat. The magic, the power, whatever it had been, had left him.

He had been sent back to his own time, and here, it seemed, he would stay.

Chapter 42

Los Angeles seemed unusually loud and crowded after the quiet beauty of the plains. The men, clad in suits and ties, seemed overdressed for a warm summer day; the women, wearing layers of clothes and makeup, looked stiff and artificial, like wind-up dolls.

Gerald Walsh had been gruff when Michael returned to work. He had berated Michael for leaving without a word, for failing to keep in touch, for staying away so long, but, in the end, he had patted Michael on the back, offered him condolences on the loss of his great-grandfather, and told him to get back to work.

Work. It had lost its appeal. His office was small and ugly. The phone was a constant annoyance. His car was noisy and confining when compared to a horse, the skies were crowded with airplanes. His bed seemed too soft, his furniture too hard. His suits were bulky, restricting his movements; he thought his ties might strangle him; his shoes were stiff and uncomfortable.

He had never realized how congested the city was, cluttered with houses and factories, with trucks and buses and cars that backfired and tires that squealed. He hated keeping time by a clock, hated the picket fence that enclosed his apartment house, the tall chain-link fences that surrounded vacant lots.

He missed the vast blue prairie sky, the rolling hills thick with buffalo grass, the soft sigh of the wind in the high country. He missed the Cheyenne people, and Yellow Spotted Wolf, and Elayna . . .

Soon after his return to Los Angeles, Melinda had called and they had gone out to dinner and a movie. It had been a dismal evening. The food seemed overcooked, the restaurant smelled of food and wax and the mingled scents of cologne and perfume and dust.

Later, Melinda had asked him what was wrong.

"Is it me?" she had wanted to know. "Have I changed?"

Michael had assured Melinda that what was troubling him had nothing to do with her. She hadn't changed. He had, and nothing was the same any more. And when he kissed her good night outside her door, they both knew it was for the last time.

Elayna. He could think of nothing else as he drove home. What had her life been like after the Little Bighorn? Had she married, had children, lived to a good old age?

Elayna. Elayna.

He took a week off from work and went to Camp Robinson. It was a state park and museum now, famous because Crazy Horse had died there. Elayna seemed very close to him as he walked around the grounds, remembering. He tried to find out what had happened to her, but there was no record of Elayna or her father.

He stopped at Lame Deer on the way home and had a long talk with old Two Bulls, and in the course of the conversation learned that Badger had not been killed at the Little Bighorn. He had ridden with Crazy Horse after the battle, and then fled to Canada with Sitting Bull. He had followed the old chief to Standing Rock when Sitting Bull returned to the United States. He had been at Standing Rock with Yellow Spotted Wolf during the Ghost Dance, and it was there he had been killed, along with Sitting Bull and eleven other Indians.

There was a touch of irony in the fact that Badger had died with Sitting Bull, Michael mused, for Sitting Bull had said the past and the future could not be changed, but Michael had changed a small part of the past by saving Badger's life, and Sitting Bull had died with a man who should have died fifteen years earlier along the banks of the Little Bighorn.

But it was not Sitting Bull he grieved for, or Badger, or even Yellow Spotted Wolf as he boarded the plane for Los Angeles. He grieved for Elayna, for the life they might have shared, for the love that was forever lost to him.

He threw himself into his work when he returned to Walsh Cadillac. He worked seven days a week, twelve hours a day. He frequented the bars along Hollywood Boulevard, drinking in an effort to forget her, but she was ever in his thoughts.

In mid-September he turned in his resignation. Gerald Walsh offered him more money, a new Caddy, a bigger office, if only he'd stay, but Michael just shook his head. He was going home, back to Lame Deer.

The reservation that had once seemed like a prison now loomed as a haven of refuge. He felt the need to be with his own people, to listen to the tales of the old days, the old ways, to hear the language of the Cheyenne.

He left his expensive suits in his apartment, donned a pair of Levi's and a cotton shirt, slipped on his moccasins, and headed for home.

At Lame Deer he moved into his great-grandfather's house. He'd expected to feel lonely, but the spirit of Yellow Spotted Wolf seemed to fill the house. It was there, in the lance that Yellow Spotted Wolf had carried to battle at the Little Bighorn, in the warbonnet that had belonged to Mo'ohta-vo'nehe, in a pair of worn, brittle moccasins that Michael found under the bed.

He went for long walks, stopping to talk to the people he knew. The Cheyenne were wary of him at first. They remembered how anxious he had been to leave the reservation, never returning until Yellow Spotted Wolf called him home.

Gradually Michael won them over. He was no longer a brash, impudent teenage boy, but a man, one who bore the scars of the Sun Dance on his chest. When that fact was made known, the elders of the tribe summoned Michael to a council meeting. The Sun Dance had been outlawed by the white man years ago. How had Michael come to have such scars?

Michael was hesitant to tell them the truth, but in the end he told them the whole story, and when he finished, he felt as though he had discarded a tremendous burden. It felt good to share his experience, to relive the days he'd spent with Mo-ohta-vo'nehe and Yellow Spotted Wolf, and the telling had brought Elayna close once more.

There was a long silence in the council lodge after he finished his story. He had been prepared for their laughter, for their ridicule, their disbelief. But no one laughed. The old ways were still strong in these men, as was their belief in dreams and visions. But, more than that, Michael's words had carried the ring of truth, and they never doubted him for a moment.

Old Two Bulls passed the pipe and as Michael drew the smoke deep into his lungs, he felt as though he had truly come home.

Chapter 43

It was on a warm clear day in late October when Michael returned to the banks of the Little Bighorn. It was here that he had last seen Elayna. He wished now that he had kissed her one more time, told her he loved her, would always love her. There were so many things he wanted to tell her, to share with her.

He reined his horse to a halt where the Cheyenne camp had been. Dismounting, he walked back and forth along the shore, trying to recall exactly where his lodge had stood. Here, perhaps? Or here?

The wind rustled the leaves on the trees, sighing wistfully as it played among the leafy branches.

Standing on the riverbank, he gazed into the distance, and in his mind he could hear again the sounds of battle, the shrill cries of the Indians, the rapid bark of gunfire, the twang of a thousand bowstrings, the frightened whinny of a horse, the sobs of the wounded. He heard Crazy Horse's call to battle: *"Hoka-hey*! It is a good day to die!"* And he heard Elayna's voice, begging him not to go.

Almost, he could hear it now. . . . Heart pounding, he whirled around, but it was only the wind crying through the trees.

Sweat dampened his brow and trickled down his chest, and he felt his mouth go dry.

"Elayna." He murmured her name as he tore off his shirt and flung it aside. He tossed his hat to the ground, then raised his arms above his head and gazed into the sun.

"Heammawihio, help me!"* he implored. "I have no tobacco to offer you, no sacred smoke, only the blood I shed at the Sun Dance pole. Hear me, I beseech thee, send me back to my people, back to the woman who holds my heart."

He paused, listening, waiting. The sun seemed to grow brighter, hotter. She was here. He could feel her presence.

He cried out to the gods again, and as he did so, he removed the knife from his belt and made a long diagonal slash across his chest. "Help me, *Maheo*!" he cried, raking the blade over his chest a second time. "Send me back where I yearn to be."

He cocked his head to one side, listening, and he heard her voice, like a whisper in the wind, calling to him through the mists of time.

She was there. He could feel her presence.

A breeze stirred the leaves, and its touch on his cheek was soft and gentle, like a caress.

She was there. If he only had faith enough to believe, he'd turn around and she would be there.

He drew a deep breath, murmured a silent prayer, and slowly turned around . . .

And she was there.

For a timeless moment they gazed at each other, hardly daring to believe, and then they were in each other's arms, laughing and crying as they held each other close, afraid to speak for fear of shattering whatever magic had brought them together.

After a long while Michael drew back, though he didn't let her go for fear of losing her again. "Are you real?" he whispered. His hands stroked her hair, caressed her cheek.

"Are you?" Elayna smiled through her tears as she drank in the sight of his face, a face she had thought never to see again. Her fingertips explored the two shallow cuts on his chest. "What happened?"

"I was praying, begging *Maheo* to send me back to you," Michael replied, and then smiled. "But he sent you to me instead."

Elayna nodded. She had heard Michael's voice and it had brought her here, to the future, but she was too thrilled to be in his arms again to care where they were, so long as they were together.

"Ne-a-ese, Maheo," Michael murmured fervently.

"Yes," Elayna echoed softly. "Thank you, Father."

Michael felt the laughter bubbling in his chest as he lifted her in the air and whirled her around. "I've so much to show you!" he exclaimed. "So much to tell you."

"Just tell me you love me," Elayna said, her laughter mingling with his.

"I'll tell you and show you, every day of our lives," Michael promised.

And he did.

Epilogue

They sat together on the hillside, watching the sun set in a glorious blaze of pinks and lavenders tinged with crimson.

A baby girl slept peacefully on a Morning Star blanket beside Elayna, a two-year-old boy tumbled head over heels in the grass, squealing with delight as a spotted puppy licked his bare feet.

Elayna smiled at the boy, her heart swelling with love for her son and daughter, and especially for the man beside her.

They had a good life, a full life. Michael taught school at the reservation, but he taught more than reading and writing. He taught the Cheyenne children to have pride in their heritage, to respect the ancient traditions of their forefathers, to honor the old ways even as they learned new ones.

Elayna had visited his class one afternoon and watched with a deep sense of pride as Michael and old Two Bulls performed the Eagle Dance for Michael's class. The dance portrayed the strength and power of the eagle, but it was Michael's strength and power that tugged at her heart and brought tears of joy to her eyes.

"The eagle hears our songs and our prayers," Michael had explained to the class later. "They help to carry our innermost thoughts to *Heammawihio*."

He gestured at the drummer who had accompanied them. "The drum is the heartbeat of our people. It calls us to dance, it calls us to war. The drum speaks to us as we pray and sing and dance. If we listen, it tells us who we are."

Now, sitting beside him, she experienced a deep surge of gratitude for Michael Wolf, for the heritage that made him the man he was, for the love they shared—a love as strong as the eagle that soared overhead, as enduring as the sweet summer wind that whispered through the tall pines.

"*Ohinniyan, wastelakapi,*" the wind seemed to say. "Forever, beloved."

Dear Reader:

I was totally out of ideas and wondering where my next plot would come from when my oldest son suggested I write about a modern-day Indian who goes back in time.

I immediately fell in love with the idea and *A WHISPER IN THE WIND* was born. I only had one real problem with the book, and that was finding the right ending. I wrote it four times.

Originally, Michael stayed in the past, but I didn't like that. (Would he die, and be born again?)

In the second ending, Michael returned to his own time and met Elayna's great grand-daughter, but I wasn't happy with that either. (I wanted Michael to be with Elayna.)

The third draft reunited Michael and Elayna, but I didn't specify whether they were in his time or hers, letting the reader decide. (That didn't work, either. I hate endings like that.)

And so I came up with the existing ending.

Did I make the right choice? I hope you'll write and let me know. My address is:

P.O. Box 1703
Whittier, CA 90609-1703

Madeline Baker

SPECIAL SNEAK PREVIEW!

NIGHT WIND'S WOMAN

BY SHIRL HENKE

"Shirl Henke mesmerizes readers . . . powerful, sensual and memorable!"

—Romantic Times

Enjoy a selection from Shirl Henke's fabulous new bestseller, the historical romance that's bursting with love and adventure!

On Sale In April
At Booksellers Everywhere

Night Wind's Woman

By Shirl Henke

OUR STORY SO FAR . . .

Proud and untameable as a lioness, Orlena had fled
the court of Spain and a forced marriage to an aging
lecher. But in the savage provinces of New Spain, the
golden-haired beauty was destined to clash with
another man—one whom her aristocratic blood
dictated that she loathe, one whom her woman's
heart demanded that she love . . .

Half white, half Apache, he was a renegade who
attacked when least expected, then disappeared like
the wind in the night. He would take his revenge
against the hated Spaniards by holding hostage the
beautiful Orlena.

We pick up the story, on the trail, as Night Wind
takes Orlena back to the Apache camp . . . .

Orlena cursed the plodding, foul-tempered little beast that smelled even worse than she did. After three days without a bath, she was filthy. The hot, parching days in the sun had wind-blistered her delicate golden skin until it peeled painfully; the cold night air drove her to seek the most unwelcome body heat of her captor.

As if conjured up, Night Wind reined in his big piebald stallion alongside her. He inspected her bedraggled condition, finding her distressingly desirable in spite of burned skin, tangled hair and torn boy's clothing. In fact, the shirt and pants outlined her flawlessly feminine curves all too well now that she had discarded the binding about her breasts.

Orlena watched his cool green eyes examine her and felt an irrational urge to comb her fingers through her hair in a vain attempt to straighten it. Instead she said waspishly, "Why do you stare at me? To take pleasure in my misery?"

He chuckled, a surprisingly rich sound, vaguely familiar. Indeed the eyes, too, seemed familiar, but that was only because in his swarthy face such an obviously white feature stood out.

"Look you ahead. Relief for your misery is at hand, Doña. Your bath awaits." He gestured to a dense cluster of scrub pine and some rustling alders. They ringed a small lake of crystal-clear water fed from some underground spring.

Orlena's first impulse was to leap into its cool, inviting depths, but her reason quickly asserted itself. She fixed him with a frosty glare and replied, "A lady requires privacy for her ablutions. Also some clean clothes to wear afterward."

"Unfortunately for you, my men and I travel light. We have no silk dresses in our saddlebags."

"Then you should not have abducted me," she snapped as her burro skittered, smelling the water.

"You should not have worn your brother's clothes and my men would not have taken you by mistake," he replied evenly as he dismounted by the water's edge.

Her eyes narrowed. They were back at the original impasse. "Why did you want Santiago?"

His face became shuttered once more as he considered his plan gone awry. "I did not plan to kill him," was all he would say.

Or ransom him either. Orlena was certain of that much. His motives regarding both of them centered on Conal in some way. Before she could argue further he strode over to the burro and swept her from it, tossing her into the deep clear water. At first she shrieked in shock as her blistered, sweaty body met the icy cold water. But when she began to swim, the cold became refreshing. However, her clothes and boots were a decided impediment. With a couple of quick yanks she freed her boots and tossed them onto the bank.

Night Wind watched her glide through the water like a sleek little otter. He was surprised that she could swim. He had expected her to flounder and cry out to be rescued from drowning. Smiling grimly to himself, he shed his moccasins and breechclout and dove in after her.

"Ladies do not know how to swim, Lioness," he said as he caught up with her in several swift strokes.

She gasped in surprise, then recovered. "Conal

taught Santiago and me when we were children."

His face darkened ominously. "He has taught you much—too much for a Spanish female of the noble class."

"Some Spaniard has taught you also—too much for an Apache male of the renegade class," she replied in a haughty tone as cold as his expression.

He reached out and one wet hand clamped on her arm, pulling her to him. "Come here. Take off your clothes," he whispered.

Her eyes scanned the banks. As if by prearrangement, the Lipan and Pascal had vanished downstream. She could dimly hear them unpacking the animals and making camp, but a thick stand of juniper bushes and alder trees provided complete privacy. She jerked free and kicked away from him, but he was a stronger swimmer. In a few strokes he caught up to her, this time grabbing her around her waist.

"You will drown us both if you are not sensible," he said as he struggled with the shirt plastered to her body.

"I told you the last time you asked me to disrobe that I would never do it for you," she gasped, flailing at him. Blessed Virgin, she could see through the water! He was completely naked! "No!" The cry was torn from her as he finally succeeded in freeing her from the shredded remnants of her shirt.

"You are burned and filthy. If you do not cleanse your skin properly you will become ill," he gritted out as he began to unfasten the buttons on her trousers. She continued struggling. "I am not going to rape you, little Lioness," he whispered roughly.

"I do not believe you," she panted. "You only waited, tricked me—"

He silenced her with a kiss. It was most difficult to remain coldly rigid with her lips closed when she was gasping for breath and flailing in the water. The hot interior of his mouth was electrifying as he opened it over hers. His tongue plunged in to twine with hers in a silent duel. Orlena pushed at his chest ineffectually as he propelled them effortlessly toward the bank where shade from an overhanging alder beckoned.

The sandy soil was gritty and full of rocks away from the water's edge, but an uneven carpet of tall grass grew out of the water and up the gently sloping bank. He carried her dripping from the water and tossed her on it. Before she could regain her breath and roll up, he seized her sagging, loose pant legs and yanked, straightening her legs and raising her buttocks off the ground. Unbottoned at the top, the trousers slid off with a whoosh, taking with them the ragged remains of her undergarments.

He looked down at her naked flesh, sun and wind burned, covered with scratches and bruises. Orlena shivered as the dry air quickly evaporated the cold water from her skin. She tried ineffectually to cover herself with her hands as she rolled to one side, unable to meet his piercing gaze. He reached down and scooped her into his arms again.

"Now, I am going to let you swim for a few moments while I get some medicine from my saddlebags. I do not think it wise to try to escape with no clothing. You are already burned enough!" With that he tossed her back into the icy embrace of the water and strolled off, heedless of his own nakedness.

Orlena fumed as she treaded water, watching him carry off the last remnants of her clothes. He was right. Where could she go in the mountain wilderness, naked and afoot? In only a moment he returned, leading the big black-and-white stallion. He took something from the buckskin pouch on what passed on an Apache mounts for a saddle and waded back into the shallows. "Spanish ladies seem to set great store by this," he said mockingly, holding up a piece of what looked to be soap—real soap! "It is not the jasmine scent you favor, but it is all I could find for our unplanned bathing." He held out the soap for her inspection. The unspoken command was in his eyes as he waited, waist-deep in the water, for her to come to him.

Orlena warred within herself. She could not outrun him and had nowhere to go, yet she hated to let him humble her by begging for the soap—not to mention having to expose her nakedness once again to his lascivious green eyes in order to reach the bribe. She treaded water, careful not to let her breasts bob above the surface.

"Toss it to me. I can catch quite well."

He smiled blackly. "Allow me to guess. Conal taught you. No, Doña Orlena, you must come to me—or stay in the lake until that lovely little body turns blue and freezes at nightfall." With that he sauntered toward the shallows, tossing the soap casually from hand to hand.

"Wait!" Orlena was growing cold already and the sun was beginning to arc toward its final descent beyond the mountain peaks to the west.

He turned with one arched black eyebrow raised and said, "I will meet you half way, but you must do as I command. I have already given my word not to take you against your will. Unlike your Spanish soldiers, the word of a Lipan is never broken."

That a savage could talk to her thus made bile rise in her throat, but she was trapped in the freezing water, hungry, naked, completely at his mercy. "I suppose I must trust your Apache honor," she replied through chattering teeth. Was it only the cold that made her shiver?

Very slowly she swam toward him. Very slowly he walked across the smooth lake bottom toward her. Orlena watched the sunlight filtering through the trees trace a shifting design on his bronzed skin. His arm and chest muscles rippled with every step he took. He had taken off the leather headband along with his other apparel and his wet black hair hung free, almost touching his shoulders. Without the band, he seemed less Apache, more white, but not less dangerous.

"Come," he whispered, watching her, knowing what this was costing her Spanish pride. Waiting for her, touching her without taking her, was exacting a price from him as well. He observed the swell of her breasts swaying as she moved through the clear water. Darkened almost bronze by soaking, her hair floated like a mantle, covering her as she touched bottom and rose from the water.

He reached out and drew her to him, unresisting at first, until he pushed back the wet heavy hair from one pale shoulder. "No," she gasped, but it was too late. He had one slim wrist imprisoned. Slowly he worked a rich, sensuous lather against her collarbone, moving lower, toward her breast. When his soap-slicked fingers made contact, she forgot to breathe. The tip of her breast puckered to a hard rosy point and the tingling that began there quickly spread downward. When he released her wrist, Orlena did not notice. His free hand lifted the wet hair from her shoulder and he spread the lather across to capture her other breast, gently massaging both of them in rhythm. She swayed unsteadily in the water. Although it was still cold, Orlena Valdiz had become hot. Night Wind cupped her shoulders and then worked the sensuous, slick suds down her arms.

She stood glassy-eyed and trembling in the waist-deep water, studying the rippling muscles beneath the light dusting of black hair on his chest. It narrowed in a pattern that vanished beneath the water. Just as her eyes began to trespass to that forbidden place, she felt a jolt as he reached that selfsame location on her! Quickly and delicately, he skirted the soft mound of curls and lathered over her hips, then around, cupping her buttocks.

"Raise your hair and turn," he commanded hoarsely, maneuvering her like a porcelain doll into shallow water. He could feel the quivering thrill that raced through her as he performed the intimate toilette. His own body responded, hard and aching, but he ignored his need and massaged the delicate vertebrae of her back, down past her tiny waist to the flair of hips and rounding of buttocks. "Now, kneel so I can wash your hair."

Like a sleepwalker she responded to his slight pressure on her shoulders and knelt with her back to him. He lathered the masses of hair, massaging her scalp with incredibly gentle fingers. Orlena imagined her maid back in Spain performing this familiar ritual, but this was not Maria and she was far from Madrid, alone in a foreign land, the prisoner of a savage!

His voice, low and warm, with its disquietingly educated accent, cut into her chaotic thoughts. "Lower your head and rinse away the soap."

Orlena did so, working all traces of the lather from her hair. Then she rose from the water, eyes tightly closed against the sting of the soap, and began to squeeze the excess water from her hair. Night Wind watched the way her breasts curved as she raised her arms above her head. Her waist was slim, her skin pale; she was so fragile and lovely that it made his heart stop.

He had used many white women over the years, but none had any more claim on him than to assuage his lust, more often to please his masculine pride. A despised Apache could seduce a fine white lady, haver her begging him to make love to her. Make love! Those other times had been more acts of war than love to Night Wind. Never had he played a waiting game, balancing gentleness with iron authority. Never before had he taken a white woman's virginity. And it was still far too soon, he knew, for that to occur unless he forced her. The feelings she evoked were dangerous and he did not like them. The anger betrayed itself in his voice.

"Now, I have bathed you. You will bathe me."

Orlena's eyes flew open and she blinked in amazement. "Surely you jest, but it does not amuse me!"

"So, I can play lady's maid to you," he said in a quiet deadly voice, "but you will not be body servant to a dirty savage."

She reddened guiltily, recalling her thoughts of Maria a moment earlier. He held out the soap in one open palm, waiting once more.

"No! I will not—I *cannot*." She hated the way her voice cracked.

"Yes, you will and you can—else the young deer Broken Leg is now roasting will not fill that lovely little belly tonight."

Ever since her first temper tantrum with the bowl of beans and the water gourd, she had learned the power of hunger and thirst over human pride. She had not been fed all the following day, only given water, until they camped last night. By then the mush of bean paste had actually been palatable. Now the fragrance of roasting meat wafted on the evening breeze. She salivated and her stomach rumbled. They had broken their morning fast at dawn with cold corn cakes and water, but she had eaten nothing since.

"I have clothes for you, in Warpaint's saddlebag," he motioned to the horse grazing untethered nearby. "Or, you can stay here all night, freezing and starving."

With a remarkable oath she had overhead a Spanish sailor use, Orlena stalked over to him and grabbed the soap.

Forcing her hands to remain steady was nearly

impossible as she flattened her lathered palms against his sleek dark skin and began to rub in small circles across his chest, then down the hard biceps on his arms. His chest was lightly furred with curly black hair. Trusting the steadiness of her voice only slightly more than that of her hands, she said curiously, "All the other men are smooth-skinned. Why do you—."

"You may think me a savage, but I am half white," was the stormy reply. Then he added in a lighter tone, "You have never seen any man's bared chest before, have you, Lioness?"

She stiffened at the intimacy of his voice, hating herself for her stupid words. "Of course not!"

"Then how did Conal teach you to swim—fully clothed?"

A small smile warmed her face as she recalled being a little girl with a toddler brother, cavorting in the pond at the villa in Aranjuez. "In fact, we all wore light undergarments. I was a child and never thought on it. But I do not remember him furred as are you."

He frowned. "Conal's hair is red. It would not show as easily as dark hair. Body hair is considered ugly among my people."

She looked up suddenly. "Then the Apache must think you uncomely indeed," she said with asperity.

"No. The Lipan accept me as one of their own," he replied with an arrogant grin, adding, "Woman, red or white, have never found me unattractive."

"Well now you have me the first one who does," she hissed.

"Liar," he whispered softly, watching as she lowered her eyes and busily applied herself to the disconcerting task he had set her.

Orlena felt the steady thud of his heart, angry at its evenness when her own pulse was racing.

Night Wind was having a far more difficult time looking calm than the furious, golden-haired woman before him could imagine. Lord, her small rounded breasts arched up enticingly as she raised her arms to lather him. Intent on winning this contest of wills with her, he clenched his fists beneath the water to keep from caressing the impudently pointed nipples. Smiling, he watched how she bit her lip in concentration as she was forced to touch his body. She kept her eyes fastened on her busy hands, not looking up into his face.

Orlena could feel him shrug and flex his muscles as he turned, allowing her such casual access to his body. She thought she knew it well from lying wrapped in his arms the past nights. She was wrong —how much different this was, with both of them naked, slicked by the cool water and warm sun.

"Turn so I may wash your back." She tried to emulate his command and was rewarded with a rich, low chuckle. When he did not move at once, she added, "You do not, for a surety, fear to turn your back on a mere female?"

"Not as long as my knife and any other weapons lay well beyond your reach," he replied with arched eyebrows. Then kneeling in front of her he added, "It will be far easier for you to wash my hair than me yours."

His thick, night-black hair was coarse and straight, shiny black as a raven's wing. She worked a rich lather into it, finding the massaging motion of her fingertips on his scalp soothing. Angry with herself, she shoved his head under the water abruptly, saying, "Rinse clean."

He came up coughing and splattering her with droplets. "You try a man's patience overmuch, Lioness." Then a slow smile transformed his face as he said with arrogant assurance, "Wash below the water, also, as I did to you."

She dropped the soap with a splash, but he quickly recovered it in the clear water. When he handed it to her silently, she moved around him and began with his back. Touching his tight, lean buttocks made her quiver with a strange seeping warmth in spite of the cold water. She finished quickly, forgetting to breathe as he turned around to face her again.

His eyes burned into her as he took her wrist and began to work her small, soapy palm in circles aorund his navel, then lower, beneath the water. When she touched that mysterious, frighteningly male part of him, she could feel its heat and hardness.

In spite of his best resolution, Night Wind let out a sharp gasp and his hips jerked reflexively when he closed her soap-filled little hand around his phallus. Orlena jumped back, jerking her hand free. At first she was uncertain what had happened, but then she realized what it was, and a small smirk curved her lips.

So, he is not as indifferent to me as he would pretend. On a few occasions when she escaped her *dueña*, she had seen animals mate in their stables. Always the male's staff had seemed an ugly, threatening thing to her. But those were merely horses and dogs. This was different . . . frightening, yes, but not ugly. . . .

She dragged her thoughts from their horrifying direction. Blessed Virgin, what was happening to her? She surely had not found the naked body of a man pleasing! And a savage at that! Like mares and bithces, women had to subject themselves to male lust in the marriage bed. But she knew well from her own mother's plight what the consequences were—a swollen belly and an agonizing childbirth. She backed away from him, clenching the soap unconsciously in her hands.

Night Wind struggled with his desire for her, but at last let her go, deciding the game had been played out long enough for now. Then he realized that she continued slowly backing away from him, all the spitting fury and innocent sexual awakening of moments ago evaporated. Her face was chalky, and she wrapped her arms protectively about her body as if warding off a blow.

"I did not intend to frighten you, Lioness," he said softly. "I gave my word not to force you, and I will keep it."

"I see evidence to the contrary," she spat, but refused to look at his lower body, clearly outlined beneath the water.

One long arm shot out and grabbed her wrist, prying the soap from her fingers. "We are both clean enough," he said gruffly, pulling the shivering woman behind him as he splashed to the bank.

Feeling her resistance, he released her in the shallows and said, "I have cloth to dry you and an ointment for your burns."

"And what of the small matter of clothing? You have destroyed the pitiful remnants of Santiago's shirt and trousers."

"I have more suitable garments—women's clothing with which to replace them," he replied reasonably, ignoring her as he pulled a long cloth from the piebald's saddlebag and tossed it at her.

Orlena dried herself carefully with the rough cotton towel, wincing at its abrasion on her tender skin. In a moment he returned from another foray into his pack with a small tin. "Pascal says this is a miracle cure for sun and wind burn. It will serve until the women of my band can tend you."

She eyed him suspiciously. His hair and chest were still wet but he had slipped on a pair of sleek buckskin pants and his moccasins. He held out the ointment like a peace offering. "Come here." A smile played about his lips. "After all, I need not repeat the rest of the sentence. You are already rid of your clothes."

"You promised me women's clothing," she replied with rising anger, but still she clutched the towel protectively in front of herself.

He waited until she approached, warily, then commanded, "Raise your hair first so I may treat your shoulders.

Still holding the towel draped around herself with one hand, she lifted her hair up with the other. Santiago's thin shirt had been ripped on the brushy shrubs and trees as they rode and her skin was both scratched and sunburned. His fingers were calloused, yet warm and soothing as he spread the salve on her skin with surprising gentleness. The sting evaporated magically, but she did not voice her appreciation, only turned to let him minister to her throat and arms, then her hands.

When he tipped up her chin to touch her windburned cheeks and nose, she was forced to meet his eyes. Again a sense of recognition niggled, then vanished as she observed his reaction to her.

"Ah, Lioness, you are too delicate for New Mexico. You should have stayed in Spain," he said with what almost sounded like regret in his voice.

She looked at him oddly, puzzled and afraid. Of him . . . or of herself? She honestly did not know.

Don't miss

NIGHT WIND'S WOMAN
by Shirl Henke

On Sale in April
At Booksellers Everywhere

THE QUEEN OF WESTERN ROMANCE

MADELINE BAKER

When Lacey Montana began her lonely trek across the plains behind her father's prison wagon, she had wanted no part of Matt Drago. Part Apache, part gambler, Matt frightened Lacey by the savage intensity in his dark eyes, but helpless and alone, she offered to tend Matt's wounds if he would help find her father. Stranded in the burning desert, their desperation turned to fierce passion as they struggled to stay alive. Matt longed to possess his beautiful savior body and soul, but if he wanted to win her heart, he'd have to do it Lacey's way.

__2918-9 $4.50

"A STUNNING GEM OF A BOOK THAT ESTABLISHES PATRICIA GAFFNEY AS A STAR!"– *Romantic Times*

THIEF of HEARTS

PATRICIA GAFFNEY

Beautiful young widow Anna Jourdaine feared her dead husband's twin brother, John Brodie. His manners were abominable, his language unbearably crude, and his heated glances made sheltered Anna burn with shame. But when Anna was forced to pretend to be Brodie's wife, she found herself weakening to his seductive appeal. In her brother-in-law's embrace, she knew that her future happiness depended on learning which brother was an immoral character and which was merely a thief of hearts.

__2973-1 $4.50